She Waits Where Shadows Gather

Michelle Tang

Cover design by Luísa Dias
Cover images © Joris Hoefnagel, National Gallery of Art/Public Domain, A.J.E. Terzi, Wellcome Collection/Public Domain, Étienne Denisse, Biodiversity Heritage Library/ Public Domain, Olga Vynnychenko/Getty Images, SteveCollender/Getty Images
Internal design by Laura Boren/Sourcebooks

Published by Poisoned Pen Press, an imprint of Sourcebooks
1935 Brookdale RD, Naperville, IL 60563-2773
(630) 961-3900
sourcebooks.com

Cataloging-in-Publication Data is on file with the Library of Congress.

Printed and bound in the United States of America.
KP 10 9 8 7 6 5 4 3

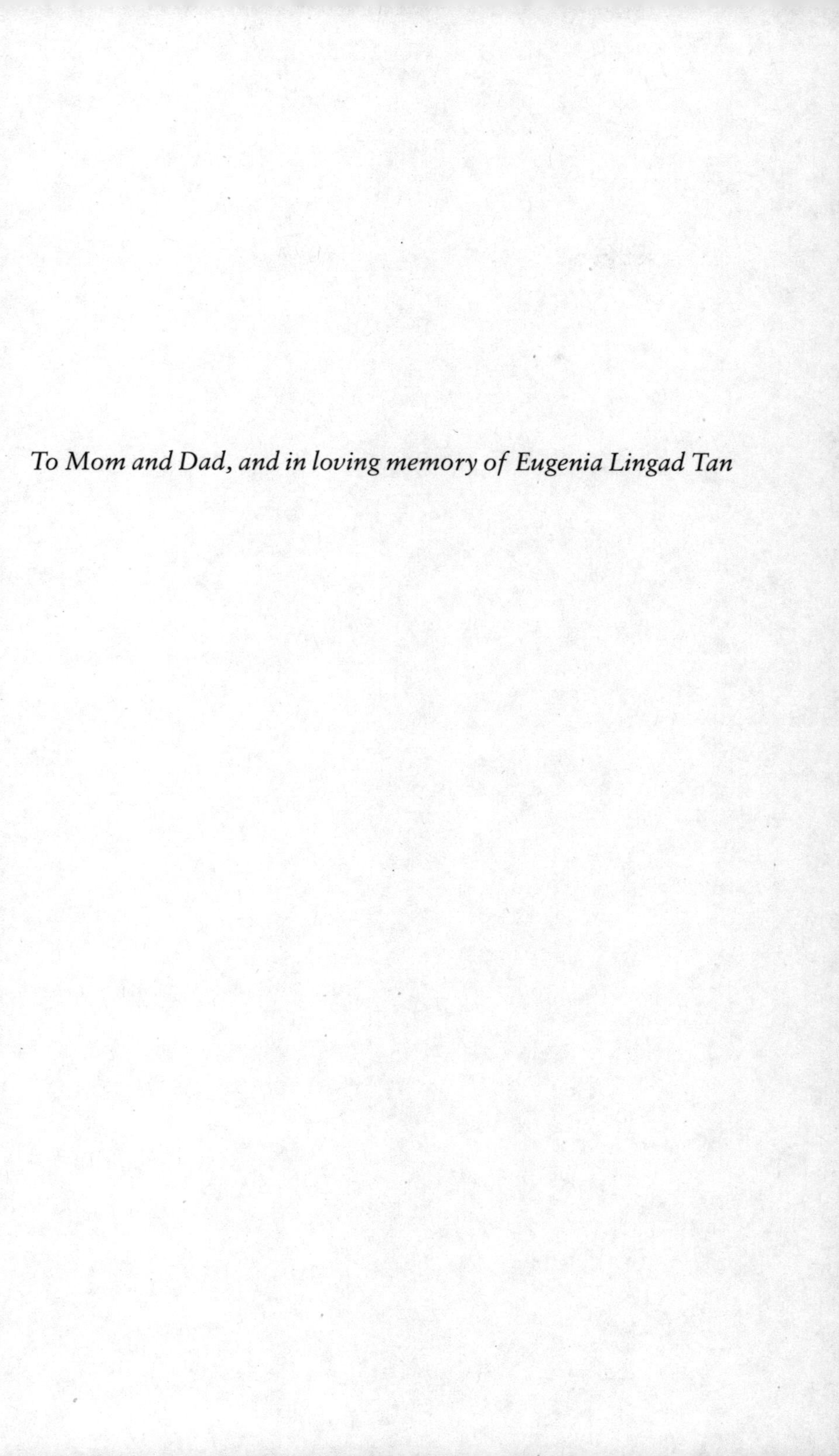

To Mom and Dad, and in loving memory of Eugenia Lingad Tan

CHAPTER ONE

Avery

Unease crawled beneath Avery's skin like a deep itch, hard to pinpoint and impossible to scratch. She resettled her shoulder bag, yanked at her shirt, and blew her hair from her face. Nothing helped. Avery grimaced and trained her eyes on the baggage carousel, where thick plastic strips hung from the opening like a filthy mustache, and a crowd waited for the mouth to vomit out their luggage.

The arrival terminal at Ninoy Aquino International Airport in Manila assaulted her with noise. Machines growled, baggage thumped, and people shrieked too loudly, too energetically, after such a long flight. The sounds grated on Avery's ears, making her wish once more for the deafening white noise of the plane engines.

Avery never traveled well. Fatigue was a gremlin waiting in every plane cabin, latching onto her as soon as she sat down and holding on for days. Until she shook the damn thing off, everything would feel distant and unsettled.

Her yoga teacher had once told her that humans weren't meant to move faster than they could run. "Vehicles leave the soul behind," he'd said, "and it can take time for the soul to catch up." She thought of his earnest face every time jet lag drained her.

"What about plane crashes?" she'd asked. "A bunch of people die over the Pacific Ocean, for example. Do their souls stay in the world, hovering over the wreckage like albatross?"

She could never remember his answer. Not that it mattered—nothing would make her believe in such nonsense, even if the memory was triggered every time she traveled.

Her tired eyes looked at the faces around her. Toronto was a multicultural city, but Avery couldn't remember another time in her life when everyone else in a crowd looked like her. It was strange: Most spoke in Filipino, which she didn't understand, and yet she didn't feel like she was in a foreign country she'd never visited before. Being around people who shared similar features made her feel a kinship with them, and as a result, she felt…safe.

"Purgatory must feel like waiting in an airport." Carlos slid an arm around Avery's waist.

"Is this segueing into another sales pitch about how Manila is heaven on earth?" Avery rolled her eyes, even as she leaned into him, inhaling his comforting scent. "I'm already here, with no return ticket." She frowned at the interlocking metal scales of the baggage carousel, at the unmoving plastic strips covering the square mouth. "And no luggage."

"It'll come. And then you'll be able to shower and take a two-day nap in our new home. You're going to love it here, I promise." The blades of the carousel began sliding past each other like sharpening knives, and her husband left her before she could respond.

It didn't matter if Avery loved it, not to her. Only that the things she wanted—needed—would come to pass.

Someone called Carlos's name as he and Avery wheeled a trolley loaded with their reclaimed suitcases and a box of Carlos's camera equipment away from the carousel.

Tessa, Carlos's sister. The short woman's stylish pompadour bounced as she hurried past the other passengers leaving the airport, a salmon swimming upstream. She threw her arms around Avery.

"Hi, Achi Tessa," Avery said, the honorific unfamiliar and awkward. "Thanks for picking us up."

"It's been too long!" Tessa squeezed her tight. As if they were actually family, instead of strangers who'd only met twice.

"Hey, Achi." Carlos grinned and held out his arms for his own hug.

"It's been too long," Tessa said again, and this time there were tears in her voice. "Welcome home, Shoti."

They followed her out of the airport to a waiting van and driver, who grabbed Avery's bag and slid it into the back. The evening air in Manila was warm and humid, like a bathroom after a long shower, and when she sat in the old van, the sickly sweet smell of dust and mildew puffed out of the upholstery.

The driver didn't bother to put on his seat belt as he pulled out of the airport onto the highway. Tessa turned back toward them from the front seat. "You must be starving. Mom and Dad are waiting for us at a Chinese restaurant. You want them to order anything special?"

Carlos's sister spoke to them in English, and Avery appreciated the effort to include her, even if Carlos answered in Hokkien. She wished they could forgo dinner and just go to the house—she needed to collapse into a peaceful oblivion before she'd care about anything like food.

"I'm okay with anything," Avery said instead, because she didn't know what Carlos had asked for.

"You should speak to her in Chinese, Achi." Carlos winked at Avery. "She's gotta learn."

"Plenty of time for immersion." Tessa turned back around to text on her phone. "Doesn't have to be right after an eighteen-hour flight."

Carlos reached out to take Avery's hand. "Thank you for moving here with me." His eyes twinkled like stars under the passing streetlights.

"'Til death." She squeezed his hand and tried to mean it. A few years ago, she would have, but now she looked out the window because she didn't trust her expression.

She was finally in Manila. Her parents were both from here, were married here, but immigrated to Canada shortly before Avery was born. They'd never come back to the Philippines; the memories were too painful for them. She had imagined drinking in the moment her feet first touched down on Filipino ground, but the gremlin gripping Avery's shoulders could not be shaken off. Nor could her sense of unease.

Palm trees and buildings broke the horizon, and tendrils of cloud obscured the sickle moon like reaching ghosts. Avery stared at a dated Coca-Cola ad with interest while Tessa caught up with Carlos. The images flooding Avery's eyes through the van's tinted window were both foreign and familiar—she'd seen pictures of this place, in family photo albums hidden away and covered with dust.

It was like Avery had traveled back in time, to a point before she'd been born, a place where her parents were happy and her sister Noelle was alive. It was comforting, and the uneasy itch that had plagued her since the airport receded. She was a babe in utero, safe in this in-between space. The hum of the engine and the cool air blowing from the van's dashboard made Avery's eyes drift closed. She was almost asleep when the van lurched to a sudden stop. The seat belt snapped tight against her body, rubbed hard against the left side of her neck.

"I see the traffic hasn't improved in the last twenty years," Carlos said.

Avery looked out the windshield. They'd left the relative emptiness of the highway to join a snarl of vehicles. Everyone was ignoring the lane markings on the road, but to her gritty eyes, there was a strange choreography to the mess. Motorbikes carrying too many people, packed together on the seat like sardines, sitting on handlebars, while holding small children, wove among trucks and brightly decorated jeepneys where people perched on interior benches. There was a cacophony of noise, from diesel engines rumbling to the different tones of multiple horns blaring to radios blasting music from various open windows.

She'd never seen anybody drive like this, and it was both shocking and exhilarating to come so close to colliding and yet emerge unscathed. It felt like a roller-coaster ride without any safety precautions. The driver hummed as he alternated between honking his own horn and shifting gears.

Eventually, they pulled into another parking lot. The restaurant was brightly lit from within and crowded, but as soon as they entered, a pale hand shot up from the sea of Asian faces. Tessa waved back and led them to a table in the back, where two people waited.

Carlos's mother, Evelyn, wore her hair in a short permed halo and dripped yellow gold jewelry. It was a wonder she could lift her arms with the heavy bracelets and rings, but she managed to make it look graceful. She stood to hug Carlos a long time and then patted the air near Avery's shoulder, her lipsticked smile almost reaching her dark-lined eyes. Carlos's father, Benji, had gained weight and lost hair since Avery had seen him at their wedding, four years ago. He shook her hand with both of his before embracing his son.

The food came quickly: steamed crab over vermicelli, deep-fried shrimp seasoned with chili peppers, mixed vegetables in an earthenware pot, white rice. Avery sipped her tea and forced herself to eat a little of everything. It was delicious, the crab especially, but her stomach was queasy from the time change and she fought to stay awake. When the meal was over, Avery stifled a yawn. The buzz of conversation stopped and everyone stared at her. "I'm sorry, did someone ask me something?"

"You still haven't learned Chinese, after all these years?" Evelyn said. "I learned it the first year I married Benji. Even our maids learn to speak it. No Tagalog, either?"

Avery forced her expression to remain pleasant. "It's hard to learn in Toronto, Mom. There aren't any Hokkien classes, and my parents only spoke English to us."

"Carlos should be teaching you. How will your children learn if you don't speak it at home?" As usual, the mention of children was a gut punch—not unexpected, but nevertheless painful.

Carlos cleared his throat. "A conversation for another time, Mom. We're tired and we want to go to the house."

"We've prepared a room at our place," Benji said.

"It's fine, Dad. We don't want to impose. I thought we were staying at Salcedo Drive."

Tessa shook her head, her short hair barely shifting with the movement. "Come stay with me then. I have twenty years of noogies to give you."

"It's no imposition, really—"

"It's not safe at Salcedo—"

They all spoke at once, talking over each other, but Evelyn's words were clear. Avery squinted at her mother-in-law. "Why isn't it safe? Like the floors are caving in? There's no furniture? Carlos said you'd started to renovate it years ago."

Evelyn pressed her lips together and exchanged a long look with Benji. "Only the bathroom, because it was broken. You know why we asked you to return home, Carlos."

He cast a glance in Avery's direction and nodded.

The conversation shifted back into Hokkien, and Avery wondered at the tension in her in-laws' faces. Wondered if Carlos had been honest about the reason he'd been asked to come.

Carlos kept dodging Avery's questions after Tessa had called him one summer night, had only said it was a "family matter that could take a while to resolve," and that his parents needed help selling their old house. When he'd received word that his production company was willing to fund a season of filming *Convince Carlos* overseas, it had seemed logical to just move—they'd only been renting their condo, and Avery had been looking for a reason to quit her administrative job. Here, she could focus on what was important to her. To them.

"We can talk about it on the drive to my place, Shoti. I have two guest rooms you can choose from, and I'm hardly ever home," Tessa urged.

Avery held her breath, but Carlos didn't budge. They'd talked about this on the long flight over, and he'd said that the last thing he wanted was to lose their privacy by moving back in with his family. "If the house is structurally sound, we're good to stay there. After all, you wanted me to get to the bottom of things, right? Living there is the best way to do that."

To get to the bottom of what? Avery frowned. Carlos made a living by investigating paranormal events for his viewers—was that why his family needed him, specifically, to come back? She dismissed the possibility. He wouldn't have moved them both across the world just for a ghost story.

"Let me put you in a hotel instead." Evelyn's perfectly shaped eyebrows drew together. "It would make me feel better."

"We're here for the next few months, at least. Maybe longer, if the show works out and Avery likes it. Salcedo Drive is sitting empty. It only makes sense that we stay there."

Avery yawned again, a jaw-cracking one she couldn't hide.

"Look, let them sleep there for the night. It's clean and we can leave them some of this food in case they get hungry," Benji suggested. "We'll take you for dim sum tomorrow morning, figure out long-term arrangements then."

"Deal. Can I borrow a car?" Carlos asked.

Tessa laughed. "When was the last time you drove in Manila?"

"Ahia William taught me before I left home. It's not like I don't drive in Canada."

Already he was calling Manila "home." Home was Toronto, where he'd lived for over half his life, where all their memories were. Where he promised they'd go back to, after a few months, two years tops.

Evelyn looked up from her phone, still typing. "Dolores will meet you there and stay with you."

"Mom, come on," Carlos said. "Dolores, of all people?"

"She insisted. You know how she is." Evelyn rolled her eyes and shoved her phone back into her Louis Vuitton purse with a curt gesture.

Avery had so many questions, but no one was paying attention to her.

"Are you sure you don't want a driver to take you home?" When Carlos shook his head, Benji sighed and slid his car keys to his son. "This is a new car. Please be gentle with it."

"A Benz? Nice." Carlos stood up and reached for Avery. Tessa pressed a bag of take-out food into Avery's other hand.

"Thanks for dinner," Avery said to Carlos's parents. "Toh sha."

And then they were out of the cold restaurant, back into the humid parking lot where drivers waited around cars and people stood outside chatting, unwilling to part even after the meal. The man who drove them here unloaded their luggage from the van and carried it to a dark SUV.

Carlos opened up the GPS on the car's bright screen and punched in an address. "Ready to start your new life, Mrs. Tam?"

The unease returned. She forced a smile and turned the AC vents away from her. "As long as it's with you."

Carlos drove carefully at first, slower than he would in Toronto. He picked up speed as he remembered how to work the stick shift. Manila seemed a blend of luxurious hotels and half-built buildings, of small storefronts and garishly lit bars. The people walking on the street were mainly Filipinos, thinner than her mother's siblings and her friends in Canada. There were many stray dogs, and young children that she shifted her eyes away from.

They turned into a street and pulled up to a tall metal fence.

A guard stood in a booth, with another nearby. Carlos leaned out the window and told them the house number. The uniformed men nodded and moved to pull open the gate. Her husband waved at them and drove on.

"How'd they know you were legit?" Avery asked.

"My mom must've called ahead. Or Dolores told them."

"She's a maid?" The narrow street was quiet past the guard booth. Houses loomed tall on both sides of them, with high walls of concrete and solid metal gates.

"Yeah. She's worked for our family forever. My grandfather hired her when she was a teenager and she's been with us pretty much ever since. My mom hates her for some reason." He turned left at the last house on the street and beeped his horn. A gate swung open a few moments later, and after Carlos pulled into the large paved driveway, an older man approached the SUV. "Welcome back, sir. Do you need anything before I go?"

Carlos shook his head. "Thanks, Bernie. Where's Dolores?"

"By the door there."

An old woman stood up from the front steps, graying hair pulled tight in a bun, wearing a simple dress wrapped around her thick frame. She and Bernie carried the suitcases from the SUV to the foyer before the maid returned with two plastic bags.

"If you don't need anything else, I'll go back to your parents'. I was just keeping her company until you arrived," Bernie said.

Avery looked out toward the dark, quiet street. "I didn't think it would be dangerous past all the gates."

"Not dangerous, ma'am. Dolores didn't want to wait in the house alone." Bernie moved toward a car parked farther inside the property.

"Salamat, Bernie." Dolores followed as the driver backed out of the yard, and then she pushed the metal gate shut and slid two dead bolts to lock it.

The house Carlos had grown up in was a tall, narrow structure with warped wooden shutters. In the darkness, Avery imagined the gaping gray slats were rib bones dangling from the sides of every window. *That's the gremlin talking. No more horror movies for you, drama queen.* She forced her eyes away, suppressing a shiver despite the warm humidity.

One of the bags Dolores carried turned out to be for them: bottled water and snacks and toiletries. She handed small bags of sugar, salt, and rice to Avery. "Tessa wanted you to carry this in the house before anything else. For good luck."

Once the door was opened, Carlos rushed her inside, slamming the screen door behind them so the mosquitoes wouldn't get in. This was their new home. A new beginning. The floors were made of polished narra wood, solid but ancient. Long trenches of darkness gaped between cracked planks, threatening to catch unwary toes. The walls were the same wood stain, and the light bulbs gave off a weak yellow illumination both here and in the rooms Avery could see from the foyer. She slid her feet into a pair of slippers set near the door before she took tentative steps down the hall. The furniture was old but well-maintained, with a dining room table that could seat ten and not a speck of dust.

"What do you think?" Carlos called to her.

Avery returned to him. "It's so much bigger than our place back home."

And darker, and bleaker.

The house felt strange, both abandoned and full of inhabitants, like Avery and Carlos were thieves breaking into a home only to find every person had suddenly disappeared. She wanted to whisper to avoid detection; she wanted to shout to break the heavy silence with some noise.

Dolores came in a moment later, carrying the bag of snacks to the kitchen, and a personal valise to a small room behind the kitchen.

"What's this?" Avery approached a large fabric-draped shape hanging from the wall. She reached her hand out to lift the thick material.

"It's a mirror. Don't touch it or everyone will freak." Carlos grunted as he carried their suitcases upstairs. Avery cast a look back at the dark shroud on the wall and followed him.

The hallway was pitch-black until, muttering to himself, he found a floor lamp in the corner and turned it on. Three doors were on their left, the stair railing ran down the right side, and a fourth door waited at the end of the hall. Carlos peeked into the first room. "I had a twin bed, and that hasn't changed, so I don't think we can stay in my old room."

He poked his head into the next room, skipped the third, and went to the door facing perpendicular to the others.

"Oh, this used to be my parents' room. They changed some of the furniture—I don't remember this bed or the TV." Avery stared at the door he hadn't touched: It was ajar, but there wasn't enough light to see. Was something shifting amid the shadows inside? Unbidden, the image of a strange man staring at her through the slit in the door came to her mind. Avery backed away.

Carlos returned to the hall to peek in the short corridor around the corner, between the third door and his parents' old bedroom. "The main bathroom was fixed up a few years ago. Let's stay here."

Avery cracked her neck and fought the urge to hurry through the hallway, forcing her feet to move slowly, calmly, toward Carlos. It was obvious that they were here for something more interesting than a house sale, and she intended to find out both what the problem was and why her husband was being so secretive.

She yawned. That was an investigation for tomorrow. Avery needed a good night's sleep, and she didn't care which bed she ended up in as long as Carlos was with her. The room he'd chosen was lovely, with French doors that opened to a small balcony, surrounded by gauzy, elegant curtains. Pictures of his family hung on the wood walls, begging to be examined more closely, but that would have to wait. The bed beckoned her, and right now she didn't care if it was new or as old as the rest of the house.

Though she shut the door behind her, which she never did at home, it didn't ease the sensation of being watched.

CHAPTER TWO

Carlos

The savory scents wafting from the dim sum carts that cruised between the white-clothed tables tempted Carlos's already full stomach. Chinese food in Toronto was excellent, but there was something special about the meals here. Maybe it was just the fact that he was back home after so many years away, with his parents and Achi to baby him.

His father reached for the teapot, refilling Carlos's cup before his own. Benji had aged in a way their weekly video chats hadn't captured, but the older man's hand was steady as he poured.

"Your mom and I talked about it last night, and we want you to stay with us. You could take the guest bedroom on the second floor, and you wouldn't even know we were there."

Carlos tapped his first two fingertips on the table in thanks before taking back his tea. *Here we go, just as I predicted.* Age hadn't changed his parents one bit. "We're fine at Salcedo Drive."

"Dolores doesn't want to be there. Not alone, anyway." Avery leaned closer to be heard. "She was waiting outside the house last night when we arrived, and this morning she left for the market and wanted to know when we were coming back."

"She shouldn't have insisted on living there then." Carlos

shrugged. They needed a spry, energetic maid instead of an old woman who refused to retire. Dolores reminded him too much of his grandfather. She creeped him out.

"Insensitive jerk," Tessa coughed into her fist.

"Fine. Take her back then. Can you lend us someone else?"

Avery's eyebrows rose in disbelief. "You're talking about people, not property. What about what they want?"

Benji shook his head. "Dolores feels very strongly that if any of us stay at Salcedo Drive, she should be there too."

"She can't stay out in the hot sun all day if we leave the house," Avery said, "That's ridiculous. What is she even afraid of?"

The clatter of empty dishes and chatter of other tables grew loud in the sudden silence.

Carlos's family turned accusing eyes toward him. "You made her move here and you didn't even tell her why?" Tessa hissed. In English, unfortunately, so Avery could understand. "You are *such* an asshole."

"Tessa," their mother snapped. "Don't be crude."

"I'm forty-four, Mom. I can say 'asshole.' And even you have to admit that's an asshole move." Tessa turned to Avery. "What did Carlos tell you about why we called him back home?"

Avery looked at him, her eyes wary. Carlos tensed. He'd told her that they'd asked him to come home because they didn't feel capable of handling the move, and Avery certainly wouldn't react tactfully if she found out the real reason. *For the love of God,* he thought, but he wasn't sure what he wanted her to say to get him through unscathed.

"He told me he had to help get the house ready to sell," Avery answered slowly.

Attagirl. He squeezed her hand beneath the table, as impressed as ever at their connection, which barely needed words, before he changed the subject. "We'll hire a second maid. Give Dolores some company so she's not left alone in the house. It's a lot of work for one person, anyway, especially an old woman."

"A second maid, just because Dolores is scared?" Evelyn frowned.

Carlos smiled at his mom, the smile that got paranormal fans streaming every episode of *Convince Carlos*. "We'll pay her salary. It's the least we can do. You're going to need a trained maid when Dolores finally retires, anyway."

When their mother didn't protest again, Tessa jumped in. "I can ask around and get you a list of people who might be interested. Give me a couple of days. But if anything happens...if you change your mind for any reason, you're always welcome to stay at my place." She looked at Carlos and spoke again in English, the snitch. "In the meantime, Shoti, be honest with your wife."

They didn't speak much on the drive home. Avery stared out the window at the city while Carlos stifled one yawn after another, cursing his lack of sleep.

He'd been eager to return to this damn place that had started everything. Maybe, if he could see everything with mature eyes, the nightmares would stop. The house's energy was still heavy as hell, though. Like a predator in the shadows, waiting for him to drop his guard. He'd just managed to fall asleep last night when Avery had shaken him awake.

"Carlos. Do you hear that?" she asked.

He waited. Nothing. "Nope."

She shook him again. "There's someone walking outside the bedroom."

"Old wood creaks, babe. You'll get used to it." Sleep was an insistent undertow tugging him under.

Avery's elbow stabbed into his ribs. "Listen! The footsteps."

Once the slow thumps came to his ears, he couldn't unhear them. The sounds were incessant: too irregular to be mechanical, too frequent to be ignored. His body tensed in the silence between each sound, anticipating. Dreading. Slumber slipped away from him like an ebbing tide, leaving behind sharp fragments of familiar fear. *You're not a dumb kid anymore, Carlos. The old man and his ghost stories are long gone. It's just an old building.*

"I don't hear anything. Probably the house settling," he murmured.

"You don't hear someone pacing back and forth in the hallway at one in the morning?" Avery slipped her feet out of the blanket. "It's probably Dolores. I'm going to ask her to stop."

Carlos swallowed past the lump in his throat as Avery strode across the room and yanked the door open. She froze when the hallway presented no elderly maid. Total darkness greeted her instead. She shut the door tightly and returned to him, her brow furrowed.

"I told you. Old houses make weird noises. You'll get used to it." He held out an arm and she snuggled against his side. Avery's breath eventually steadied and deepened. She didn't stir even when the sounds started again. Carlos stared with gritty eyes at the bedroom door handle each time the footsteps drew close.

You're smarter than this. You've outgrown this childish crap, he told himself. He'd made a career disproving such bullshit, as if that could reach through the years to comfort the young, terrified child he'd been. With his grandfather long gone, the house was nothing but old wood and cracked tile. It was safe, just noisy. Carlos forced his eyes shut, ignored his heart hammering in his throat, and waited for exhaustion to suck him into oblivion again. Sleep had eluded him for hours.

Carlos yawned again and squinted against the sunlight as he turned into their driveway. Dolores stood waiting and opened the gate for their car to pull in. The maid bent to pick up her grocery bags where she'd left them in the shade. Avery hurried out of the car to help the old woman carry things inside. Carlos smiled; his wife was too good for this world. The smile faded as his eyes focused on the narrow, dark house, looming over them like a malevolent villain.

Avery pulled him into the sitting room as he walked through the door and shivered at the sudden drop in temperature. "Why is she so afraid of being alone here, Carlos?"

Don't talk about it in the house. "It's not a big deal or anything that'll affect you, I promise. Just silly family tales that older generations cling to." He should have told her at the restaurant, or on the plane, but he was worried about what Avery would say about his backward family, worried about how he'd feel about her if she mocked them. His wife was kind, but she didn't tolerate fools.

She tilted her head at him. "Why does Dolores insist on staying here if she's frightened?"

Don't talk about it here. "I'll tell you everything. Just…give me some time."

Avery narrowed her eyes, but she nodded. "I asked Dolores to buy some brighter bulbs for the house. That should help the gloom."

"Carlos?" The voice was distant, just at the periphery of his hearing. He sat on his childhood bed, lower and smaller than he remembered. His fingers clenched against his old Superman blanket as he stared at the closet door. And at the attic hatch, set in the ceiling above it, which still haunted his nightmares. Carlos was a child again, exhausted eyes straining against the darkness, praying nothing moved, that the attic door stayed shut.

A hand touched his shoulder. He jumped to his feet, fists ready and a curse on his lips.

"I didn't mean to startle you, Carlos." Dolores smiled at him, her features both familiar and transformed by time. It was as if her face was sculpted with wax and had melted downward over two decades. "I've been calling you for some time." Her English was just as good as it always was—she'd gone to the same school as his mother and her siblings, another sign of his grandfather's, his lolo's, favor.

"Lost in my childhood, I guess." He forced a chuckle, wiped a drop of sweat from his temple. "What did you need?"

"The maids are here." Dolores headed back downstairs, her footsteps heavy and slow on the steps. He waited until he caught his breath, ran a clammy hand through his hair, and followed her.

The first applicant entered the dining room with hunched shoulders and darting eyes, like a nervous bride. There were much fewer women than he'd expected; of the dozen names Tessa had given him, only two had scheduled an interview. The other woman waited in the kitchen for her turn.

Sunlight shone through the windows and seemed to place the applicant under a spotlight. Forehead glistening with sweat, the woman blinked rapidly at Carlos and Avery, who sat across the large dining room table. Though she was nowhere in sight, Carlos was sure Dolores was within earshot, listening to her potential partners as if she had a choice in the matter.

Avery leaned forward to address the young woman perched on the chair. "Fatima, what is your experience with children?"

Carlos fought to keep his annoyance off his face.

"Oh, I love children." The young woman's eyes lit up. "How many do you have?"

Avery recoiled. She placed a protective hand against her stomach and hunched over, as if to hide its flatness. Carlos turned away from Avery's rapid blinking; he fought the overwhelming urge to comfort her, while self-hatred coiled its barbed wire grip tighter around his guts. What the hell did she expect, asking a question like that? It happened so often you'd think she would have learned her lesson by now. And yet, she wouldn't shy away from her own pain, wouldn't stop poking at bruises, hoping they'd eventually stop hurting. That was the way she was—a porcelain juggernaut.

Fatima, perhaps sensing the job opportunity was in danger, tried to fill the awkward silence. "I raised my eight brothers and sisters. And this home would be so lovely for a young family—there's so much room, and most of the ghosts here have a nurturing energy."

Fear slithered through Carlos's body like tainted blood, prickling the skin between his shoulder blades. He pushed away from the table and leaned back against his chair. *Don't talk about ghosts in here.*

Avery raised her eyebrows. "What did you say?"

Fatima made a vague gesture that seemed to encompass the entire house. "The spirits? Mga multo?" Her brow furrowed.

"We know what you mean." Carlos forced a smile to reassure her. "But where did you hear such rumors?" Their staff would have died before admitting that anything more than humans and mice resided in the house. Had his parents hired someone new and indiscreet?

Fatima's eyes widened. She glanced at the door to the kitchen as if considering escape. "It's gossip lang. An old house like this… of course people talk."

"What have you heard?" Avery asked. Carlos suppressed a sigh.

The maid's throat worked as she swallowed. "They say things move on their own here. Doors slam closed, and there is screaming late at night. I'm so sorry, I thought someone would have told you."

Fatima thought they didn't know. Carlos shook his head at Avery, whose face had sharpened with interest. Avery didn't believe in ghosts—or in anything that wasn't backed up by evidence, really—but she loved to hear stories, tried to explain phenomena away with science. It was part of what made them so compatible, even after ten years: She loved hearing about his show, and he loved her attention. They were two cynics among the gullible, especially in their own culture.

Avery gave him a careful look and took over the rest of the interview. They worked like a well-oiled machine at this point, the most wonderful partner he'd ever had.

Most of the time.

The sensation crawling over his skin like a colony of sharp-limbed ants faded. No wonder so few people from his sister's list of candidates had shown. They'd probably stayed home when they realized which house was looking for help.

The last woman was old, nearly as thick and stout as Dolores.

"You've heard the rumors of this house, Iris?" Avery asked.

"I don't believe in ghosts," old Iris said. "But I'll work with them if I have to."

Carlos stole Avery's next question. "We do not yet have children, but this may change. How are you with kids?"

His wife slipped her hand into his, beneath the table, and squeezed. Rarely, it was his privilege to be a juggernaut's protector.

Iris grinned. She had a big gap between her front teeth—that and the mischievous twinkle stripped years from her lined face. "I'll work with them if I have to, too."

At the end of their interview, when the sun was setting and the mosquitoes began to land on their windows, Carlos stood to walk Iris out. He took her out the front door, wanting to test her reaction to the dark, narrow spaces, to the shrouded mirror. There was something comforting about her: He could already picture her in the large house, silent as the shadows, unobtrusive until that glimmer of humor flashed. She would help steady Dolores—he certainly wouldn't choose another person who believed in the ghost stories; they'd just rile each other up.

The older woman's eyes lingered on the large mirror hung on the wall, its surface covered with a dark shroud. Carlos waited, but Iris moved on without asking. *Excellent*.

"It's rare to find a person here who doesn't believe in ghosts," he said.

"I tell you this as an older woman, sir. I have had many friends and relatives die before me, and I've seen no sign of their spirits. The world is hard enough for the living. Why would anyone choose to return?" Iris shrugged and slipped through the doors, the humid dusk swirling around her.

He strolled past the wood floors, the dark-stained planks smoothed by thousands of steps over time. He remembered every jagged hole in the floor through which darkness peeked, had skipped over them as a child, in fear of something thin and long reaching out to grab him. Young Carlos had truly believed something lived in the floors, and in between the walls: They'd whispered to his young ears and threatened to catch him when he wouldn't come closer.

They'd been here three days now, long, exhausting stretches of jet lag and visitors, of bickering and pillow talk. The house was much smaller than he remembered, which didn't help the stifling sensation that surrounded him as soon as he'd returned. He pulled at the collar of his polo shirt. Nothing had happened beyond the strange, familiar noises. The weight of the house, pressing on him without pause. No wonder he wasn't at ease here. The whole house felt wrong. He tilted his head, stretching out the tension that knotted his shoulders.

Part of him regretted not asking more questions of Fatima. What else had she heard? Probably that the famous paranormal debunker, the star of *Convince Carlos*, was in search of a maid, and she thought this would improve her chances of being paid Canadian dollars.

Avery, still stunning beneath the unflattering light of the chandelier above her, was staring at her careful notes. God, he'd loved her once. Loved her still, in a way that both pained him and gave him hope, depending on his mood. They'd moved here for their own reasons: For Avery, it was a last-ditch attempt to conceive, while Carlos wanted her to return to the devoted woman he'd fallen in love with. Both of them were searching for happiness in their marriage once more and had moved to the Philippines in a desperate attempt to find it.

"If we have two maids, that helps support two families while we're here, right?" Avery asked.

"Right." He slid his hands over her hips and pulled her closer to him. "You could have sinigang every night."

She smiled, pressing against him, and there was a challenge in her eyes. "I liked Fatima."

"You didn't find her a little…flaky?" He inhaled the green apple scent of her hair.

"She's *bubbly*. She'd be great around—" Avery's smile grew strained. "She'll be great."

"I liked Iris. We need someone who will help Dolores, not make things worse."

Avery pulled away from his reach. "Well, it's your house, your money, I guess. But Iris must be in her fifties. I thought the younger woman might help Dolores more." She smirked at him. "Was that what you didn't want to tell me? That you think this house is haunted?"

Don't talk about it here! "You're right, as usual. Fatima it is. Why don't you go give Dolores the night off? She can come back whenever Fatima starts. Let's you and I go for a drive. We'll talk in the car."

She stared at him for a moment and went to find the maid.

Ten minutes later they were driving through their neighborhood. Carlos loved his father's Mercedes, and he focused on the unfamiliar streets so he wouldn't have to see Avery's inevitable reaction. He felt better being out of the house—it was like taking the first breath after coming out from beneath a blanket. His mood lifted. Salcedo

Drive had always affected everyone that way, like the misery within seeped from the walls like lead paint.

Carlos sighed. "As a culture, Chinese Filipinos are very superstitious. You know this—think of your parents. My family is no different. They believe in a lot of nonsense, always have. It's part of the reason I'm so passionate about disproving this stuff on *Convince Carlos*." He hesitated. "Dolores says she saw my grandfather in the house."

"Doesn't your grandfather own the house? Why did Tessa call you back just because someone saw him?"

He squeezed the leather steering wheel tight. "Well, because my grandfather died ten years ago, just before you and I met." Carlos had refused to come back for the funeral, couldn't justify the money and time spent to say goodbye when his grandfather had terrified him most of his young life. Carlos had arranged a huge bouquet of flowers to be sent to the funeral parlor and called home to give his condolences. It took months before his mother and Tessa would speak to him again, but they eventually got over it.

"So they saw…his ghost?"

"Dolores did. She's worked with our family forever, like I said, and that was the first time she'd ever claimed to see his spirit. My family thinks there's a reason he's come back."

"So the ghost that the rumors are about is your grandfather, with what, an important message from the grave?" God, he could hear the smile in her voice. She was *laughing* at him. He clenched the steering wheel tighter.

"Tessa suggested I come down here, do my *Convince Carlos* spiel, and figure out what Dolores actually saw. Then everyone will be comfortable selling the house."

"And you didn't think twice before moving me into a haunted house, I guess?" Avery asked in the fake-calm voice she used when she was trying not to yell. Her glare burned into the right side of his face. "Or warning me about your crazy family?"

"Gee, I wonder why someone might be reluctant to tell you anything." Carlos fought to keep the bite out of his voice. "You don't believe in ghosts. I knew you wouldn't care about anyone thinking the house was haunted. And my family has been nothing but nice to you. Don't make fun of them."

They were quiet for a long moment, long enough that driving the luxury car lost its appeal. Sighing, he turned the car around and headed back to Salcedo Drive.

"You're right." Avery's voice was cool, and she wouldn't look at him. "I'm sorry I called your family crazy. But you should have told me the real reason we were coming, whether or not you figured I'd care. That wasn't your decision to make, and I might not have come if I knew we were doing all this for some ghost crap."

She'd reacted just like he expected, how she always reacted when he came home with stories from his show, and Carlos knew being honest would only fan the flames of her ridicule. Lolo had taught them all not to give attention or speak of the spirits, or the activity would worsen, but he'd be damned if he said anything that woo-woo to Avery.

"It's not a big deal, the house. I just don't like talking about ghosts and stuff inside it. Other than that, it's just a place to sleep while you learn about our culture," he told her instead, as he rubbed her thigh with his right hand. "While we focus on us."

They pulled into the driveway, and Carlos had to get out of

the car to open the gate. Avery stared at the building, expression unreadable, until he turned off the engine.

She followed him into the house, back into the dining room, and sat down at the spot she'd left her interview notes. The silence stretched between them, layers upon layers, until it seemed impossible to tear through. Maybe he should have told her before they'd left Canada, but it was too late now.

Carlos cleared his throat to get her distant gaze to focus on him. "I'm going to arrange a house blessing. It'll be a nice way to show everyone the house at once, socialize a little." He didn't want to admit it to Avery, but he'd feel better having a priest come into each room, knowing people who cared about him had burned candles and prayed.

Avery's eyes widened. "You said your family was worried, not you. Surely you don't believe that this place carries some, what, some old dead ghost?" He flinched, but she ignored it. "I thought you came back to prove your family wrong."

"When other people outside the house have heard, though..."

"Carlos, Fatima was just repeating gossip."

"I agree. The rumors she reported were vague. Or maybe she thought we'd hire her for more information." Carlos slipped his hands into his pant pockets and jingled the loose change, the once-familiar coins made foreign by too many years away. "House blessings are just for good luck."

"Your sister made us carry in bags of sugar and rice before we brought in the luggage. I think we're set on good luck."

"We didn't have a priest go around."

She snorted. "What's a priest going to do if the house is haunted? Sprinkle holy water like a scene out of *The Exorcist*?"

He kept his voice calm. Reasonable. "People expect a housewarming here. It's traditional."

Her laugh was a brittle, sharp thing, glass cracking under strain. She'd been so moody lately, so quick to anger. "Since when do you give a damn about tradition? People *traditionally* have children, Carlos. They *traditionally* see doctors if there's a problem. Why do I have to go along with whatever you want when you won't even show up to a couple of appointments?"

"It's an afternoon of small talk and eating, Avery. It's not eighteen fucking years of neediness and soccer practice and bad attitude. You can't handle three hours of compliments and small talk?"

"*You* get small talk. *I* get questions. Invasive, embarrassing questions that make me feel like I... See? The fact that I have to explain it to you again just shows how little you—" She shook her head, her mouth pulling downward as she swallowed some emotion too big to voice. "No housewarming, unless you want to host it yourself. I've moved across the damn world for you, left my whole life behind, and you couldn't even be honest with me. So until you're ready to compromise on things *I* want, then you'll have to do without."

Carlos forced himself to breathe slowly. His heartbeat thudded at his temples. Avery had been under a lot of stress and medication. Her hormones were probably still raging, and he wasn't convinced that she wouldn't get on the first flight back to Canada if he yelled back. But God, the words were begging to come out of him, little bullets of hate that would puncture deep holes in her puffed-up fury. As if she hadn't come here for the promise of a life of ease, living off his family's money and searching for Asian fertility solutions while he worked his ass off.

He forced his hands, still in his pockets, to unclench. The house's atmosphere wasn't helping. "I think we both need to cool off. We can discuss the house blessing like adults when we're less exhausted." He strode out of the room, back toward the study, but hesitated at the yawning darkness beyond the doorway. In there sat his desk and chair, and the light of his closed laptop winked with a demon's red eye. If Carlos had been in their old place, he'd slam the door closed and sulk inside until Avery was ready to make up.

The front door beckoned instead. Grabbing his car keys from the table near the door, Carlos escaped the hot anger emanating from the dining room, where Avery still fumed, and the cold chill of dread that had twisted his guts ever since he'd returned to the house where he'd grown up.

CHAPTER THREE

Avery

The front door clicked shut. Icy fingers of disbelief crawled between her shoulder blades and gripped her head. There was no way Carlos had actually left her alone in *his* family's house, not after all that nonsense about ghosts.

She peeked into the empty hallway. The new bulbs didn't brighten the dark space; they merely cast more shadows along the walls. Avery stared at each one carefully, her heart thudding loud—from anger, not fear—as she searched for Carlos's form.

"It isn't funny," she said.

Silence.

"I know you're still there," she tried to sound confident, in case he could hear her. "Stop trying to scare me."

A voice whispered near the stairs, coming from the dark void of his office. Relief soothed her ire like a warm blanket, and she went toward Carlos's hiding place expecting him to jump out at her with every step she took.

He could be such a brat. Avery always teased him that it was obvious he was the baby of the family from the way he acted, and in retaliation he would chase her onto the bed and swaddle her in their blanket like a newborn while she shrieked with laughter.

She waited at the side of the office doorway to take a deep breath and remember which wall the light switch was on.

"Boo!" She lunged into the room and flicked the old brown switch.

The light flickered and was slow to brighten, but Carlos didn't grab her, or jump at her, or run.

Hurt filled her as she realized the room was empty.

The bastard actually left.

But then who had whispered?

"Dolores?" Avery called out, annoyed at how small and tremulous her voice sounded.

It took another beat of silence before she remembered they'd sent the maid home, and the realization that she was utterly alone in the old house hit Avery's solar plexus like a blow.

The hall light flickered.

Electricity was often unstable here, Avery told herself as she hurried up the stairs. She would spend the night in their room, cozy in bed, and give Carlos hell when he got home.

The hallway waited for her to cross, the doors opening wide into dark rooms that could contain anything. She forced herself to walk past the first two rooms, refusing to turn her head and look at what waited inside.

It's normal to feel scared right now, she told herself. The gooseflesh, sweat, increased heart rate—all of this was a result of her hindbrain, honed through centuries of evolution to be wary of possible threats, and not because there was anything in the house that could actually hurt her. Not only that, she was also jet-lagged, and the fatigue gremlin that had attached to her on the plane could be playing tricks on her senses.

She stopped before the third door, unable to force herself to continue. Unlike the others, the door was only cracked open a few inches, revealing a strip of dark bedroom; despite her logic, Avery was suddenly certain that something was inside, waiting for her to pass by.

Dry-mouthed, tight-throated, she leapt for the doorknob and yanked it toward her, pulling until the latch clicked into the strike plate of the doorframe.

It was hard to breathe normally with her heart racing. She fought the urge to pant, open-mouthed, as she walked, her sweaty back straight, into the master bedroom and closed the door firmly.

She was changing into her nightgown when she heard a click down the hall, followed by the slightest creak of old hinges. Avery refused to look into the hall and check. There wasn't any point: Only one other door was closed on this floor.

There was sure to be an explanation, but somehow, in an utterly empty house, the door to the third bedroom—the room closest to hers—had reopened.

"Which bath fragrance would you like, ma'am?" Fatima's voice echoed from the large bathroom, through the hall, out to the small balcony in the master bedroom. The young maid had been eager to start work immediately, and Dolores was happy to return to the house now that she had company in the maids' room by the kitchen. The older maid had been training the younger all morning, filling the house with rapid-fire Tagalog and "Opo" in staccato counterpoint.

Avery spoke as little Tagalog as she did Hokkien, but she understood from Dolores's gestures that the mirror in the hallway, the large shrouded one, must always be kept covered. What was the point in hanging it up then? Why not just leave it collecting dust in some closet somewhere?

"Ma'am?" Fatima poked her head into the bedroom.

Avery blinked. "The lavender oil, please." Lavender was for relaxation. Despite the jet lag finally fading, she still couldn't sleep well at night. The house made noises that kept waking her up: The old wood creaked like footsteps down the hallway and over their heads, and the air conditioner—"aircons," as the Tams called them—hissed like angry whispers. She thought at first it was Dolores, but the sounds continued all night, even when Dolores was sent to her family's home on her days off. Anyway, why would the old woman be pacing above them when her bedroom was on the main floor, and who would she be whispering to?

The bedroom closest to hers throbbed with presence, even when Carlos was beside her, even in the daylight. She couldn't come up with a rationale for it and refused to ask anyone else if they felt it too. Avery forced herself to look in the room every day, at the dated, dingy bedspread and the ancient furniture. There was nothing menacing about it, but the sense of being watched wouldn't leave her. She also hadn't tried to close the door again, seeing no point: It was an old house, and no doubt the door kept opening because the wall or doorframe was tilted.

Avery took another sip of green tea and gazed out into the distance, where palm tree fronds swayed in the warm wind like kelp in a cerulean sea. This was one of the only views from the house she enjoyed. Even here, she had to keep her gaze above that red adobe roof to the right, below which the reality of poverty became all too apparent. Paradise was a fragile, impermanent thing.

The thought was enough to break the spell. Her eyes lowered to street level, lingered on the corrugated metal and moisture-damaged wood that served as roofs, these scavenged materials propped atop crumbling cement walls, shelter for God knew how many people. How many children.

Not the time, Avery. She shook her head to clear it. The next twenty-four hours were important: Her ovulation test, brought all the way from Canada despite the limited luggage space, had turned positive this morning. Technically, she had a seventy-two hour window in which she could be fertile, but already her left ovary was spasming, a sharp cramp like a knitting needle piercing her lower abdomen. Once the egg left the ovary, they only had a day to fertilize it before it became nonviable.

She'd left her reproductive endocrinologist in Toronto. Her last medically monitored attempt at conceiving had stopped in July; she resented these wasted weeks spent moving across the world. There hadn't even been anyone to ask about a specialist: Everyone here, regardless of status, had too many children to understand the loss she endured each and every month.

In desperation, she returned to researching solutions online. There must be things she could do to prime her body for fertilization. Avery was no fool; she looked for legitimate websites and checked the references and citations listed to make sure it wasn't some mumbo jumbo. So many charlatans had come up in her hours of searching for resources. Amid the healthy diets and the visualization meditations, there were websites selling fertility tonics and moon spells and sacred stones. If she'd had the time, and if she for one second believed it would make a difference, she would sic Carlos at these con artists. *Convince Carlos* could do a couple of episodes on these scams. They were predators, these businesses, luring in desperate women and giving nothing in return but debts and regrets. But they were like Hydra—cut off one head and two more would crop up.

Avery smiled her thanks at Fatima as she passed by the young maid. The bathwater was the perfect temperature, and despite the sunlight streaming in through the frosted glass windows, every candle Avery had placed around the bathroom was lit.

Slender flames danced on the wicks, reflected in a mirror that spanned one entire wall, bobbed distorted and scattered in the ripples of water as Avery sank lower, the tub so deep she could submerge her whole body. It was large enough to fit another person, even. She was grateful that this bathroom, at least, had been one of the rooms Carlos's family had seen fit to renovate, the rest kept polished and ancient like a multilevel shrine to their ancestors.

Never in her life did she imagine such luxury in her own home, however dated. She had been reluctant to come at first, but Carlos's suggestion that Eastern medicine might work where Western failed clung to her—she was out of money, and hence out of treatment options, if they stayed where they were. In the concrete bustle of Toronto, where their small condo had only a narrow shower and the echo of ringing phones followed her even into dreams, Avery could never find herself at peace. Here, she could meditate, lower the stress hormones in her body, and visualize herself pregnant and healthy. Studies had been done to prove these methods were effective: Olympic athletes practiced visualization, after all, and MRI scans showed the same brain centers activated as when they actually won. Mind over matter.

Anyway, it wasn't harmful. It didn't cost money, and what if it helped? Avery inhaled to a count of four, tried to fight the cynical voice that mocked her attempts to visualize her womb brighten with health, that undermined her efforts, until she found that her jaw was clenched in her struggle to *force* relaxation into her body, like one might blow air into a stiff balloon.

She yawned. After their fight several days ago, Carlos had come home around midnight, crawled into their bed, and kissed her perfunctorily before he went to sleep. Being in his childhood home was affecting him. Anyone could see it. He smiled less, glared more, was quicker to anger. When she tossed and turned all night, tensing each time footsteps seemed to pause at their door or thumped above them, Avery swore that Carlos's eyes were also open. She could see them gleam in the moonlight streaming in through the window. What was he watching for?

The house was creepy, no doubt about it. The rooms were always gloomy, the atmosphere like a mausoleum, as if noise was unwelcome even as the space echoed with voices and floorboards creaked, unbidden. There were daily brownouts, and the smell of melted candle wax, sulfur, and smoky incense mingled in the air. The aircons were noisy boxes that sat inside window frames and dripped condensation outside. But the furniture was solid and well-cared for, and everything was clean. Inside the gated community, things were quiet and safe.

Except for the weird thing that had happened last night.

Three hard, distinct knocks on their front door had woken them up at 3:00 a.m.

"Carlos? Did you hear that?" she asked.

"Ignore it," he answered shortly. He was always short with her lately, his patience with her fading the longer they stayed at Salcedo Drive.

"What if it's Dolores trying to come in, or someone who needs our help?"

"Dolores has a key, and there's a gate around the property to keep strangers out. Whoever's at the door shouldn't be there." Carlos turned his back to her, signaling the end of their conversation.

She crept downstairs without slippers, the wood varnish tacky beneath her bare feet, grumbling under her breath. This was *his* damn house, so why did she have to check the door? So much for chivalry.

Avery peeked through the peephole—from the exterior light, three shadowy figures waited, their faces partially obscured by large hoods. She squinted; the short one looked like a young woman, and the two taller figures elderly men.

"Can I help you?" She called through the door.

No answer. No movement at all from the three strangers.

Maybe the wood was too thick to hear their response. Avery knew the screen door was locked. She'd seen Carlos check it before bed. And yet, what good would come from opening the door to strangers at this time of night? Strangers who'd somehow passed through the thick walls and metal gate?

That's irrational fear talking, Avery chided herself. Taking a deep breath, she opened the door. The porch lamp flared bright against her night vision, and when Avery squinted past the light, the front step was empty.

She locked the door and returned to bed, shaken and annoyed. Carlos hadn't asked last night, nor mentioned it this morning, and she wasn't going to give him the satisfaction of telling him she'd been tricked. If he wanted to know, he should have come down with her. Avery wasn't sure if it was a weird distortion of light through the peephole, or if the locals were playing some prank on the new neighbors.

Maybe they should try staying at Carlos's parents', or at Tessa's. But Avery couldn't stand the idea of being someone's permanent guest, forever making small talk at the table until familiarity made them stop caring about pleasantries.

Anyway, Carlos was adamant there was nothing to be frightened of in the house, and except for last night's visitors—or lack thereof—nothing overtly spooky had happened since their arrival. It was disappointing, in a way. After Carlos had finally confessed why they'd moved here, she hoped to see something unusual that would explain the Tams' fears. It had been almost a week now and there was no sign of Carlos's lolo, nor anything strange at all, aside from being woken up by actual roosters crowing at dawn, and all the house rules she was supposed to follow. Her own parents were particular about things like respecting one's elders, but nothing like this.

The Tams had too many strange habits, most of them nonsensical. Covered mirrors were to always stay covered. When she slept, she had to keep the closet doors closed and make sure she couldn't see her own reflection or that her feet weren't in line with the door. Otherwise she might lose her soul, or attract bad luck, or all her mangoes would be sour, or something. She was supposed to kill any insects on sight, which she'd do anyway. Dolores, and now Fatima, trailed close behind her as she moved through her day, leaving things exactly as the Tam family wished. As if they were worried about the consequences should any rules be broken. No, not worried. As if they were *afraid*.

It was too quiet in the bathroom. She should have turned on music, something to drown out the sloshing of the water and the sound of her own breathing, which was suddenly too fast. The flickering candles reflected in the mirror were no longer peaceful, and it suddenly occurred to her that this giant mirror wasn't covered like the one in the hall. An episode of *Convince Carlos* came unbidden to her mind—the one about a medium. What was his name? Like it mattered; it was probably a pseudonym. He'd start his séances by lighting a candle in front of a large mirror in the room. He said that mirrors were doorways, and the candle called spirits forth.

He had stained yellow teeth, and he wouldn't stop smiling at her with them. "You seen those houses with the candles in their window, a sign of welcome? It's the same with the dead, who after all, were human once. The window, the mirror, both entry points for the hungry."

The chill across her breasts and back pulled her back to the present. She'd sat up out of the bathwater, perhaps an unconscious move to blow out the candle nearest her, and goose bumps had popped up on her wet skin.

Her phone, left near the wide edge of the tub within arm's reach, buzzed loud against the marble. "Shit!" Avery jumped, her heart thudding hard. She swiped to answer the call with a wet finger.

"You sound out of breath, darling." Carlos was with other people. She could tell by his voice, how vivaciously he spoke.

Avery placed a hand against her chest. "I was trying to relax. You know"—she lowered her voice—"to get ready for tonight."

"Speaking of tonight, a few people from work are coming over. We'll be there in about an hour. My family might get there earlier, depending on traffic."

"You're giving me less than an hour's notice to prepare the house for guests?"

"The house doesn't need preparing. It's clean. Just send someone for takeout, and we're set." The good cheer in his voice strained.

She nodded to herself. He'd be in a good mood after everyone left. She wouldn't have time to relax, but they could still try to conceive. Today, and maybe tomorrow morning. "How many?"

"Maybe two dozen? Twenty-five including Father Michael."

Suddenly there wasn't enough air in the room. Avery stood up with a loud splash of lavender-scented bathwater. "A priest?" Her naked reflection glared back at her, stringy haired, fiery eyed, sopping wet. "You son of a bitch, you're blessing this house without my consent."

A long pause before he spoke again, and it was his real voice, the one without the joviality. He must have stepped away from listeners. "It's *my* house; why would I need your consent? It would make the maids feel better, and what's the harm?"

"The maids?" Avery cackled. "You did this for the maids? Don't make me laugh. You only do things for yourself." She made her voice mocking and childlike. "Was wittle Carlos afwaid of the scawy ghosts?"

"It's not just for the ghosts." He snapped. "You want a baby, right? Did you ever think that asking for a priest to bless our house, to bless *us*, might make your wish come true?"

"Well, in that case, I should have written to Santa the last two years; maybe I'd have found our baby in a stocking on Christmas."

"Avery, you know what your problem is?" She could picture his face, just by the anger in his voice. His nostrils would be flaring, his eyes narrowed. "You need to have faith in something greater than yourself."

"And you need to think about someone other than yourself,

you selfish asshole." She ended the call, fought the urge to whip the phone at the mirror, and screamed wordlessly in frustration.

She was still staring at her wide-eyed, panting reflection a few moments later when a timid knock came through the door. Fatima's voice, muffled but concerned. "Ma'am? Are you all right?"

Avery pulled at the drain plug and watched the water level drop. "I'm fine, thank you." Always fine, even if she was spiraling into an abyss of despair she didn't know how to come back from. "Fatima, Carlos is coming home with two dozen people in an hour. A house-blessing party and then dinner. Can you and Dolores make sure the house is ready, please?"

"Opo, ma'am."

Avery pressed her palms hard against her eyelids and fought back tears. She couldn't cry now, not when people would be sure to notice her swollen eyes and red nose. Damn this selfish man, and damn her foolish heart for forgiving him every time he chose his desires over her own. But she'd given him ten years of her life, and she'd never loved anyone as much as she did him. It felt too late to back out now, to start over with someone who would never compare to Carlos. She wanted *his* children, little products of their love with her hair and his twinkling eyes. But at times like these, she wondered what she was still doing in this marriage—why would she want to have a child with a man who was himself a child?

Worse than the anger, though, was the sense of powerlessness. He would be in no mood to make love after their fight, and the twinge in her left ovary that was their potential child would be lost once more. So much for trying to relax for this ovulation window, but she needed his participation more than she needed to meditate.

Weariness made her limbs heavy as she dried off and dressed.

She would make sure the housewarming went smoothly. Nothing would move the smile from her face—not invasive questions from strangers, and not Carlos's simmering anger. Tonight, perhaps resentment would prove a more fertile incubator than love. God knew she'd tried everything else.

Avery applied her makeup carefully. She wanted no cracks in her facade, wanted to convince Carlos's new coworkers and the family members she had not met that he had chosen well for his wife. That they were as in love as they appeared.

When she was finished, she stared at the candles, still flickering happily. They reminded her of the life she'd wished for as a child, standing before her birthday cakes with her eyes clenched tight. Now, as she extinguished each flame, darkening the room in increments, it seemed she was bidding goodbye to the hopes she'd nurtured for decades.

The smoke lingered for a moment, a sign that something bright and hot had burned here. Then it, too, disappeared.

CHAPTER FOUR

Carlos

Dolores opened the door for them, and Carlos was pleased to see she was neatly dressed and unsurprised at the guests he brought with him. He'd half-worried that he'd find confused maids and Avery's closet empty.

Instead, dark wood gleamed with polish, fresh flowers adorned tables, and every light was on like it was an open house. So many people present chased the pervasive gloom back into the walls like a fresh breeze. His colleagues' admiration at the sparkling floors and richly decorated rooms were a salve to his simmering anger, and the vinegar and umami scents coming from the dining room were further balm.

Avery came down the stairs to greet him, hand sliding lightly down the banister, and it was as if he himself were seeing her for the first time with the rest of his colleagues. She wore a modest blue dress that even a priest could not fault. Her black hair gleamed, and her smooth tan skin glowed with good health. She'd taken the trouble to put on makeup, and at this sign of her support, desire, startling in its intensity, filled him.

Carlos stepped toward her, sliding his hand through her silken hair to grip the back of her head. He let his kiss linger, let the press of his lips convey the apology his mouth could not. He would reward her for her good behavior tonight, he promised himself, and for the weeks that followed. He owed her that much.

She stared lovingly into his eyes after his kiss, as if they'd never fought, as if they were the couple they'd been four years ago, before she'd decided to strain their marriage with her obsession over children.

"Welcome to our home," Avery smiled at the others. "You must be starving after a long day on set. Please, come have some refreshments."

"We haven't started filming yet," one of his writers said. "Just planning out the season." The crowd began to follow her toward the kitchen, when the doorbell rang again.

Carlos opened it to find his parents and sister. Achi Tessa nudged him hard with her shoulder. "Such late notice, Carlos. I could have had a hot date."

"Somehow, I knew you were free." He grinned and dodged her punch. She held a square white box tied with yellow ribbon in her other hand: a housewarming present, no doubt, even though it was Tessa's house as much as his.

"Stop it, both of you. How can you be so old and yet so childish?" His mother scowled, her eyes darting toward the black-garbed priest beside her.

Carlos shook the man's hand. "You must be Father Michael. Thank you for coming on such short notice." The priest was taller than Carlos, his shoulders wider, his features sharp and attractive. The cameras would love him; maybe he would be willing to be filmed for the show. "I always picture priests as stooped old men, for some reason."

Father Michael grinned easily. "God willing, you will be right, eventually."

Evelyn and Tessa passed out candles to the others, lit them, and followed Father Michael into each room. Carlos's grandparents' old room was just as he remembered, as if Lolo or Lola would come wandering in any second. Carlos eyed the old rocking chair, half expecting to see an old man sitting in it, glaring into the covered mirror as if he could see through the dark, thick material.

The priest sprinkled holy water and said the prayer he had for each bedroom. "Protect us, Lord, as we stay awake; watch over us as we sleep, that awake we may keep watch with Christ, and asleep, we may rest in His peace. Grant this through Christ our Lord."

Avery's face was frozen in a polite expression, pleasant and respectful, but when everyone murmured "Amen" in response to Father Michael's prayer, her lips remained still. Carlos could imagine what her thoughts were, as sure as if she whispered mockingly in his ear: "Is it God pacing around the house at all hours? When does the 'rest' part of 'rest in His peace' come in?" Once he might have smiled at that joke, but this was not the right place for such irreverent humor. He frowned at her to discourage her from thinking such thoughts.

Someone nudged him, and he started. The priest had finished and the crowd was waiting to leave, but Carlos stood in the doorway. He walked into the hallway and pointed to the last door. "Our bedroom is just there, Father."

The guests moved on, and Carlos chanced one more look back at his grandparents' room, trying to see if the blessing had changed the energy, or the gloom. The room still seethed with malice, even a decade after Lolo's death. The old man's disapproving glare, stern face, and strange mutterings passed through Carlos's memory like an errant ghost, and just as he did as a child, Carlos felt the urge to flee from his grandfather's presence. He shivered and pulled the door shut behind him as he left. It unlatched and creaked open a couple of inches, as it always did.

When the prayers were over and the candles blown out, they ate. Half of the party sat in the dining room, and when there were no more chairs, the others ate standing around the kitchen island. His aunts on his father's side crowded around him like hens, clucking at him in Chinese.

"Oh, Carlos, how handsome you've become. Hien yen tao!"

"You look more like your grandfather every day. And Avery is so sui. You look like a celebrity couple."

He let their praise wash over him as he savored the juicy crunch of the lechon in his mouth—everything tasted different here, spiced with the authentic Manila climate and garnished with the taste of ease.

Father Michael's attention was monopolized by Carlos's mother, devout Christian that she was, and Tessa, who seemed to know him as well. But Carlos was surprised to find Avery speaking quietly with the man. She had fled the general conversation once people began speaking of children. He didn't blame her—pointed questions always followed—but what could she have in common with a priest? She held open the small flat box, twelve inches square, that Tessa had brought, its yellow ribbon untied and trailing. As Father Michael spewed some nonsense and pointed to the box's contents, a circle made of woven palm fronds bright with red and gold paint, Avery nodded, rapt with attention as if the priest were some sort of god. Actually, now that Carlos thought about it, the priest's nose was too pointed for the camera, his eyes too beady. He'd definitely bore the viewers with his awkward manner.

Someone called his name. His uncle Philip, already ruddy-cheeked and bleary-eyed, held up an empty beer bottle. Carlos gritted his teeth and acted as the man's waiter, bringing him a fresh one.

His uncle took the drink and patted Carlos's cheek. "Your lolo would be proud to see the man you've become."

The food in Carlos's stomach churned. He'd spent his life trying to forget his grandfather's last words to him, as if fate was an arrow he could dodge.

"Excuse me, Tito. I have to see to the other guests." Carlos moved away before the man could reminisce any further.

At some point, Tessa's voice rang out over the buzzing conversation. "That's Kumakatok!"

The people around her fell quiet.

Avery shushed her, glancing around at the others, flinching her eyes away from Carlos's. Father Michael, the devil, was lurking around his wife, of course. Tito Philip approached the trio, and Carlos turned away, unwilling to hear more about his grandfather.

Unbidden, Lolo's childhood lessons came to Carlos's mind. Kumakatok: Three shrouded figures that knocked on the door in the middle of the night signified an impending death in the family. He thought of last night's knock at the door and cursed himself for not bothering to ask Avery who it was, and then he cursed Avery for blabbing to his overly superstitious sister. Avery couldn't have seen Kumakatok at their door. There was no such thing, another lie spouted by Lolo to scare children, and surely she would have told him if three shrouded figures faded away right in front of her. Carlos scowled at Avery, angry that she'd confided in Tessa instead of him. Before they'd moved into the house, she'd told him everything.

Afterward, when the food had been eaten and his parents had taken Father Michael home, the house continued to feel lighter. Surely no spirit could withstand the power of a blessing. Maybe there'd be no reason to search for Lolo's ghost after all. He turned to his staff. "I feel like celebrating. Take me to the best bar on Thursday nights."

A writer glanced at his watch. "No can do, Boss. I'm late getting home as it is, and my wife works the night shift. I've got to—"

"Aside from Joe, who clearly doesn't care about being part of the team, who's with me?" Carlos grinned at the others, waiting until all of them returned weak smiles of their own.

"Carlos, you're going out?" Avery asked. "I thought that you might want to rest after your long day."

He knew what that meant, could read the pleading in her dark eyes even if she hadn't said a word. Disgust at her need, at his reluctance, burned a hole in his guts, a hole he desperately needed to fill with alcohol. "We won't be out late. Just a couple of drinks to celebrate, get to know each other better. I'll be back before you go to bed."

Carlos gathered his team and ushered them out the door. He nodded at the lone man who opted out of the fun, and made a mental note to find a replacement. He wanted his team devoted to the job, and to him. That was the problem with Avery—she couldn't understand that he had to show the same dedication. People would never follow a hypocrite.

The bar they took him to was dimly lit and bustled with noise. A live band performed on stage, but they sat far enough away that they could still converse. Carlos basked in his colleagues' admiration as he asked them flattering questions about their experience. Without him, there'd be no show, at least six months of paid work, so they owed him respect.

They traded stories and funny experiences on their various sets, and nodded raptly while Carlos explained how things were done in Canada and how the attitudes toward the supernatural differed.

They told him about the White Lady of Balete Drive, and of the manananggal, the vampire that separated its torso from the rest of its body to hunt for victims at night.

"So if you're in a forest and you come to a pair of legs just standing there, what do you do?"

Carlos laughed. "You stake it in the nuts?"

The cameraman pointed to his pocket. "No, Boss. You sprinkle some salt or uncooked rice over the exposed waist. The manananggal comes back down before dawn, can't fit exactly back onto its body because of whatever you sprinkled on it, the sun rises, and you've just killed a vampire."

"I never saw that before, and I've seen every season of *Supernatural*." Carlos typed out *waist-splitting vampire* on his notes app, beneath his notes about a Filipino witch called a mangkukulam. There was a ton of folklore he could tap into while he was here, stuff other shows wouldn't think to do. He wondered if he should bring his crew in to investigate his own house, but dismissed the idea. That would only spread the rumors further, and his mother would die of the scandal.

One of the writers leaned toward him, her face flushed pink

with alcohol and her glasses smudged. “In your other seasons of the show, have you ever seen anything that you couldn’t disprove? A psychic, a telekinetic, a haunting?”

He shrugged. “When you can reproduce the phenomena outside of the house, that’s no problem. How a medium might shake the table, create knocking sounds on the walls—you find the wires and the speakers. That stuff is easy. It’s harder for things that are based on personal accounts alone. But as for any people who have made me believe there is more beyond our realm than our God? Not yet.”

Faces came unbidden to his mind, those he’d failed to convince, despite sound explanations, those the show had left behind after “solving” their ghost problems. Carlos squashed those faces down where they belonged and slapped his empty glass on the table. “Now, tell me, what can we do differently here, in the Philippines? How will we make this season of *Convince Carlos* stand out?”

He was driving too fast. Too fast sober, and much too fast after the drinks he’d downed at the bar. They hadn’t hired a driver yet, and anyway, he liked driving, especially a car like this. He had promised Avery he wouldn’t stay out too late; he wanted to get home and take his wife while the buzz untethered him from the unease he felt inside the house. It would be different now, of course, after the house blessing, but he wanted this extra insurance.

Carlos considered slowing down. If he were in Canada, with cameras everywhere and speed traps, he would. Here, things were different. He remembered sitting beside his older cousin one day, before Carlos had left for the University of Toronto. Ben was speeding, and a police officer gestured at him to stop. Ben cracked his window and threw money out onto the street, barely slowing. The moment, short as it was, filled Carlos with a sense of power he couldn't help but pursue the rest of his life. Why should base standards and responsibilities apply to him? And so far, this attitude had served him well. He was rich, famous, had married a beautiful woman, and his new team adored him, fought over each other to fulfill his simplest requests.

Part of his speed was due to fear. It was a miscalculation to ask his new production crew for ghost stories before his dark drive home. The tales ran through his mind, the googled images flickering in his memory as fast as the streetlights flashed by his windshield. The show's cameraman, Manny, told them that he once saw himself inside an elevator before he'd even stepped in. The sight made him back up, out of the elevator, shaking his head at the inquisitive glances of the others inside. Then a fire started in the elevator shaft, a common enough occurrence here, but once the stalled elevator doors were pried open, the firemen found the small space full of smoke, and not a person alive. Manny swore he'd seen his own ghost, coming back from the future to warn him and prevent his demise.

That was a new one—time-traveling ghosts, though maybe too similar to the theory of shadow figures being entities from another dimension. The show had never covered herbalism or feng shui before, either. They could talk about the myths and practices, and ask for concoctions that could be analyzed and disproven. Carlos smirked; he should start with his sister. His whole family was superstitious, but Tessa was the worst. Always with her jade bracelet to protect her and her Bagua jewelry to ward off bad energy, always looking for feng shui's poison arrows and moving furniture around to improve energy flows.

He could mine Father Michael for stories as well. He might have witnessed strange things during a house blessing, or seen something eerie when performing last rites or overseeing a funeral. Hell, maybe he'd performed an exorcism. Avery might have stories from him. After all, she'd spent so much time with the priest during the very housewarming that she swore she didn't want.

His phone beeped. As if his thought had summoned her, Avery's message popped up over his GPS. As he strained to read it in the alternating illumination of streetlight and shadow, he hit something. A pothole, a curb, it didn't matter. What mattered was that the tires jerked to the right, and at the speed he was going and the alcohol slowing his reflexes, he lost control of the car.

The world whipped upside down and righted, coins flying from the cup holders to snap against the windows and his face. Metal shrieked, and broken tempered glass cracked and popped. His world was inverted, the rosary hanging from the rearview mirror pooling against the glass-strewn roof—the car must have landed upside down. Carlos stared at Avery's name on his phone, at the car symbol flashing in place on the GPS highway, and tried to catch his breath.

A slender man stood at the side of the road, staring at the upended car.

"Help!" Carlos called out. "Help me out."

The stranger walked toward him, and Carlos tried to move.

Pain came to greet him then, an unwelcome lover that sliced beneath his skin, invaded muscle and bone. His nerves sang, a never-ending crescendo until all he could hear was the chorus of agony, and slices of his life flashed through his mind, all the way back to his childhood. And then he cursed Manny and his ghost story, because before Carlos died, he swore that the man who approached the car wore Carlos's own face.

CHAPTER FIVE

Avery

The hospital was nothing like Avery had imagined, ignorant North American that she was. From her mom's old stories and photos of when Avery's older sister was born, she pictured rows of sick patients, and harried nurses dressed in crisp white dresses and matching nurses' caps. The beds would be old and metal, the floors and walls grimy, like she'd seen in a horror movie once.

Santo Domingo Hospital was bright and clean, tastefully decorated, and filled with technology that looked modern, as far as she could tell. In the ICU, every patient had their own room filled with futuristic-looking screens and sensors and wires. Unfortunately, the sole visitor chair was more reminiscent of an ancient torture device. Avery tried to find a comfortable position in the unyielding plastic chair she'd dragged closer to the bed. She stared at the bruised and swollen face of her husband, his mouth levered open by a plastic tube. It didn't even look like him, and she had to ask the nurse to make sure of the patient's name. Perhaps they'd made a mistake and called the wrong person? But no, the name and birth date were confirmed, taken from his Ontario license, and as she stared, some of his features began to look familiar.

The doctor had warned her that Carlos was gravely injured:

a concussion, fractured jaw, broken clavicle and ribs, and internal hemorrhaging that had required eight units of blood before they could stabilize him. Even knowing this, Avery was shocked when she saw her husband. Tubes invaded his body, thick and thin, draining and infusing. At the head of his bed, a monitor traced his heart rhythms, beeping steadily, while a plastic bag at the foot of his bed collected blood-tinged urine from his bladder. The artificial rasp of a respirator forcing his lungs to inflate at regular intervals made her think of the time they went scuba diving off Grand Cayman, and he'd taken photos of her feeding frozen peas to the fish. Did she have any pictures of him? She should have taken more. A wave of self-loathing filled her, as bitter and hot as the burnt coffee cooling in the Styrofoam cup nearby. All their memories, and so few pictures to show for it, except for her own goddamn face smiling in every one. She must have some photos of them as a couple; she remembered approaching strangers to take them, half nervous they'd say no and half nervous they'd take off with her phone. She worried that he'd need a funeral, and the few pictures she had of Carlos were stored back home, an ocean away.

Carlos's parents were praying the rosary outside in the waiting room, because the ICU only allowed one visitor at a time. When they'd first arrived, after Avery had called them, Carlos's mother had cast a baleful eye at Avery and said, loud enough for the entire waiting room to hear, "He was perfectly fine when *we* left him." But her voice had cracked, and Avery, no stranger to covering deep emotions beneath a thick veneer of hostility, let it be.

Had he been fine? Carlos never liked to be limited by rules, but he'd never been careless with people's lives. She was grateful, no matter what happened, that he hadn't hurt anyone in his drunken collision with a lamppost. This was the question that kept bobbing to the surface of the ocean of grief and fear that she was treading water in. Did he do this intentionally? Had he been trying to end his life for some reason? No. Avery knew that Carlos would never give up anything he owned, not easily, unless he was done with it. This was an accident, a foolish, regrettable accident.

The machine started beeping faster, and Carlos began to choke. He spasmed beneath the thin beige blanket that covered him, and a nurse came from a nearby computer and injected something into his IV line.

"A sedative, to keep him from pulling out his breathing tube," she explained to Avery.

"Could he be in pain? Is that…? I just want to make sure he's comfortable."

"We're giving him morphine around the clock." The nurse wore running shoes and scrubs, just like in television shows, and had an air of weary competence about her. She pulled up a stool beside Avery's chair. "This is always a difficult discussion, and the doctors are optimistic that Mr. Tam will wake up, but have you two ever talked about how long he would want to stay in this condition?"

"Never. It didn't seem possible. He never even caught colds." Avery wiped her eyes, her careful makeup from a few hours ago a distant memory. "But I know him. He'd want us to do everything we could to save him, as long as there was a…a chance."

The nurse nodded. "He has been saved once already. God willing, he will fully recover."

The mention of religion offended Avery. Hadn't God put Carlos in this very situation, stopping his heart for four minutes? Why then would she pray for the same god to save him? Still, they weren't in Canada anymore.

Perhaps this brought comfort to most of the people here. Even if it seemed at odds that someone who made their living based on modern medicine would believe in something as intangible as a god. All in all, the nurse's intentions had been kind, and frankly, Avery didn't have it in her to make a fuss. "Thank you," she said quietly.

She stared at her husband's face and wished she were foolish enough to have faith in religion or talismans, something that could provide her comfort in this awful time. And yet there was nothing anyone could do or say—not her family's messages, nor the hot drinks Tessa kept bringing her—that would thaw the frozen spike of fear inside her. Maybe that's why people believed in things outside of themselves...to find hope and comfort in a power that might load the dice in their favor.

Two days later, Avery left the hospital to shower and change. She had not yet braved the jeepneys, those communal vehicles people boarded and hopped off of in the middle of the street. She wasn't sure how money changed hands or how to tell where they would stop. Instead, Tessa had sent Avery home with her driver, while she took over the watch, and promised to message Avery if anything changed.

Carlos's superstitious sister had tried to hang bright red knotted tassels to improve his health, and Bagua mirrors that she swore would ward off bad spirits. The ICU staff had told her to keep them away, possibly because she had hung these items on his IV poles and around all his machines. Tessa compromised by taping one of the octagonal mirrors above his doorframe, facing outward, to prevent negative energy from entering his room, and a red knotted tassel dangled from the window blinds to attract health and good luck.

"He's vulnerable in this state," she told Avery, forehead puckered with worry, as she pushed a bracelet of carved wooden beads onto his wrist. A solid jade bracelet hung from the other. "I'm his older sister. I'm supposed to take care of him, and instead..." Tessa lifted her head and set her jaw, but her eyes were wet. "The doctors and nurses will help his physical body recover, and until he is strong enough, I will protect his spirit."

Avery thought she'd fall asleep in the car, but she found herself staring out the window at Manila and its people, her eyes ravenous for sprawling landscape and constant movement, so different from the small hospital room and Carlos's still form.

Dolores opened the door for her. The older woman didn't question her about Carlos, which filled her with gratitude. She merely murmured in consolation and asked what Avery needed. Avery requested some food to eat and some more to take to the hospital, things that she could nibble on during the long, uncomfortable nights.

The house still felt *wrong*. She was exhausted and faced with impossible choices, and yet there was a strangeness that set her teeth to clenching once she entered her home. It was as if the days away had reset her senses, like a bite of sorbet to cleanse the palate, and now the presence of the house hit her anew. Despite her desperate need for a shower, for sleep, Avery balked at the base of the stairs. The second floor always felt worse, and right now she was a raw nerve.

Instead, she wandered into Carlos's office. He hadn't been in here much, hadn't even bothered to unpack the paranormal equipment he'd taken pains to bring from Canada. She wondered what the devices would show if she checked the house for temperature drops or electromagnetic fields.

Dolores found her sitting at Carlos's desk. The maid slid a bowl of noodle soup toward her, and Avery's mouth watered at the smell. She took a bite and nodded appreciatively, releasing her chopsticks to wipe her mouth. "This is delicious, Dolores."

The maid frowned. "We don't stick chopsticks into food, in this house. It's bad luck."

"Oh." Avery felt chastised, embarrassed, angry. Who gave a damn about her chopsticks when her husband was near death? "I'm sorry. I didn't know."

Dolores left her to eat in peace. As she chewed her noodles, Avery flipped open Carlos's laptop and checked his recent search history. She wasn't sure what she was looking for—what he'd been looking at the night before the crash, perhaps—to prove to herself that he hadn't brought her here only to try to leave her.

Avery's eyes scanned the search terms, the food in her mouth turning into tasteless mush the further she read.

Houses that feel hostile. Natural causes for footsteps on wood. Whispering in old houses. Cursed mirrors. Filipino ghosts. House blessings and spirits.

Avery shut the laptop and pushed away from the desk. He'd denied hearing or feeling anything she'd experienced, and yet he'd been researching explanations. To reassure her? Or himself?

Avery used the sudden anger at Carlos's deception to do what she'd long wanted: She pushed away from his desk and paused at the doorway of the study, looking for the maids. No one was around. Before anyone could stop her, she strode directly to the covered mirror in the hallway and lifted the shroud.

Nothing. Just a normal mirror, showing Avery looking haggard and foolish. The glass was distorted in some areas, so that at first glance, it seemed someone with long dark hair stood behind Avery, but she shifted to the side and the blurred effect disappeared. Of course this family would believe a cheap mirror meant it was cursed.

"Guess I'm cursed then," she said to her reflection before releasing the cover.

Avery's scorn powered her up the stairs. She paused in the middle of the hallway, her mood darkening until it was as heavy as the atmosphere. If she closed her eyes, she felt surrounded by people, could practically feel them brushing by her. An insect buzzed, or a person whispered. Someone stared at her from the dark gaps between the wall planks.

Avery shook her head. Irrational nonsense, no doubt reinforced by Carlos's laptop. Hadn't she just seen how full of shit this family was? She went to her walk-in closet and pulled out her suitcase. It reassured her to see it within reach, a life preserver on a ship.

She could have another bath, to soothe her temper and nerves, but Avery needed movement, even if it was only water sluicing the hospital grime and worry from her body. She turned on the shower, as hot as she could stand it. The noise of water splashing against tile erased the incessant rasp of Carlos's ventilator, and she lost herself in the routine of shampoo and conditioner and body wash. She let the hot water drum against her scalp and shoulders. After she was clean, she would…what?

Avery pretended it was just water streaming down her face, even if her skin was stretched tight with grief. The doctors said Carlos's chance to make a full recovery was highest in the first two years after the accident. After that, his progress would nearly plateau. She was thirty-six. Two years could cost her a lifetime.

Words were ineffective at moments like these, sieves that failed to carry the emotional weight, the burden, of her thoughts. Without Carlos healthy, she had just lost her chance of having children.

Maybe artificial insemination? A sperm donor? Avery pressed her forehead against the cool tile. How would she care for Carlos and a baby?

The simmering resentment inside her spiked into a skin-numbing rage. She should have left the selfish asshole months ago, before they moved to a new country and he'd driven himself to death.

The traitorous thought slithered into her mind. Why shouldn't she leave? He had family here, money, while she had nothing, had sacrificed everything for his family's ridiculous request. She could return to Canada, reclaim her old job as an administrative assistant and cocoon herself in her old life until nothing here could touch her. Maybe she'd meet someone there, or maybe she'd save enough for artificial insemination, and have the children she always wanted. It was possible. That future glowed with possibility, full of freedom and her own choices. So many miles away, she could pretend the move had never happened, could imagine they'd parted ways as they should have two years ago, when she begged him to have children, to meet with the reproductive doctors, and he had refused.

Her parents would love more grandchildren. They'd always told her siblings that they were ready and willing to babysit. Never Avery though. Her parents had hired a BaZi expert—a fortune teller—when each child was born, and gave the "expert" the baby's full name, English and Chinese, as well as their birth date. Her siblings had bland, pleasant futures, according to the fortune teller's enigmatic calculations. Avery's, however, was both confusing and grim; it loomed over her head like a cage, stifling her growth, until she moved out of her parents' house.

Avery was doomed to fall in love with a dead man: The tragic fortune was a ghost from her future, haunting every day of her present.

Her mother had wanted her to go to a convent. "Better to love the body of Christ—at least he rose from the dead, and your seat in heaven will be assured." There were no offers to babysit, just discouragement, to protect future children from losing their father.

She'd been nervous to tell Carlos when they were dating, in case it changed his mind about her. After all, he was from the Philippines too, and he'd complained his own family was superstitious. The sunlight had streamed through her apartment window onto the pillows where they lay intertwined, and they'd closed their eyes against the summer brightness. Here, blinded from each other, she could pretend they were confessor and priest.

Carlos had laughed and, rather than drawing away, tightened his arms around her. "Every one of us will love the dead, at some point or another. Just no touchy-touchy. There are laws against that." His voice had roughened. "Prophecies and predictions are nonsense. People can change, and their fates with them."

Was that the moment she'd fallen in love? Where had that feeling gone? Was it dashed away when he saw her pain and chose not to alleviate it, or was it chiseled away over the years with his casual selfishness, until all that remained was the rock-hard stiletto that carved away at her heart?

A dark figure walked across the bathroom, obscured by the steam against the glass shower stall. For a moment she thought it was Carlos, before she remembered.

Avery froze. "Dolores?" She called out. "Fatima?"

There was no answer. She cracked open the door and peeked out. No one.

Despite the hot water, Avery shivered. She shrugged away the thought that she'd just seen Carlos's lolo. She was exhausted, and distracted, and nothing more. Avery washed the dried mascara from her eyes to prevent further illusions. She rinsed the soap from her body and turned the water off. Her face reflected in the mirror was pale and drawn, but from the determined set of her jaw she knew that she'd already come to a decision.

However bad her marriage with Carlos was, she was going to sacrifice everything to care for him, to help him recover. She could never face his family if she let them take their grown son home, not when she was his wife. She'd never be able to face herself, no matter how far away she flew. They'd said the vows, hadn't they? In sickness and in health?

'Til death would they part. Only, hadn't Carlos already died once? What did her future hold now that her cursed fortune had been fulfilled?

CHAPTER SIX

Avery

Despite the bright light streaming in through the window and the heat lines wavering above the concrete of Salcedo Drive, Avery shivered in her damp robe. She never felt warm enough inside the house for some reason, whether the dark-stained wood wouldn't relinquish the cool air or the sunlight failed to warm it. She headed into the closet for a light sweater, and the housewarming gift Tessa had given her at the party caught her eye.

"Don't show my parents," Tessa had whispered as she handed the white box tied with yellow ribbon to Avery. "They think this stuff is all witchcraft. But Father Michael knows about the power of symbols." Tessa winked at Michael, who grinned.

"I still remember Tessa shocking the nuns at church." He peeked into the box as Avery unwrapped it. "Ah. A handwoven decoration, not the dark object I feared."

Tessa had woven palm fronds into a round mat about the diameter of both of her hands. Chinese characters were carefully painted on each exposed square in red and gold.

"It's for protection. Hang it above your bedroom door, okay?"

Tessa instructed. "It should keep any entities from entering the room. If it works and you want more, let me know."

"Thank you. Did you make it yourself?" Avery asked. She kept her voice polite. Was this the life Carlos had escaped when he left for Canada, zealous religion and secret occult rebellion?

Tessa beamed. If she'd had suspenders, she'd have snapped them. "I did. I whispered a prayer of protection with each row I braided and with each character I painted."

The box, trailing yellow ribbon, interested Father Michael, and he told her stories of the folk magic and superstitions many of his congregation believed in. "The children are told to look away from hearses, and everyone turns their head when a coffin is lowered into the ground."

"Why? What are they afraid will happen?" Avery leaned closer. This was far more interesting than talking about other people's pregnancies.

"They're worried that their souls will be sucked into the hearse, or buried with the coffin. And after leaving the cemetery, they can't go straight to their house, in case they take a spirit home with them."

"People are so fixated on the paranormal here." She shook her head. "Souls being sucked from bodies, spirits following people home, charms to prevent spirits from entering rooms. It's just entertainment back home."

Tessa snorted. "You probably don't even recognize when things involve spirits. Ever experienced déjà vu, or knew something was going to happen before it did?"

"Of course, but that has nothing to do with—"

"That's your own soul, remembering a future event. That's why it seems so familiar."

"Tessa, surely you don't expect me to believe that. It's just your brain misfiring, making you think something is familiar when it isn't."

"What about psychics then?" Tessa didn't sound mad. She'd adopted a patient tone as if she were educating a stubborn child, but she had a determined look on her face. "How do they get their premonitions? How do people know what omens mean?"

"They make it up. Anything can be an omen. Like the idiots who knocked on our door in the middle of the night. I could say it meant I was going to win the lottery, when the real explanation was that three bored jokers played a prank—"

Tessa's eyes went wide, but it was Michael who asked. "What happened?"

"Nothing. Just some people trying to scare us." She tossed her head impatiently. "What were you going to say about psychics?"

"Three people knocked on your door in the middle of the night?" Tessa repeated. "Did you open it? Was it one young woman and two old men?"

"Well, yeah. How did you…?" Avery stopped herself from saying anything further. It would make sense that the pranksters took advantage of well-known superstitions to scare their targets.

Tessa shouted, "That's Kumakatok!"

Avery shushed her sister-in-law, glancing around at those who might have overheard and avoiding Carlos's intense gaze in the process, but an old man had looked in their direction and hobbled near.

"Avery, you remember Tito Philip," Tessa reintroduced them. "My mom's younger brother."

His breath reeked of beer, his nose and cheeks freckled with broken blood vessels that spoke of heavy drinking. "You have to be careful here," Philip warned. "Bad things can happen when you open the door to strangers."

"She saw the three knockers, Tito," Tessa tattled. "That's bad, tell her."

The old man widened his red-rimmed eyes. "There's worse things than omens. When I was a kid, someone knocked on the front door." He gestured vaguely toward the foyer. "That door right there. And my little sister, Estelle…she—"

"Philip!" Evelyn had snapped, suddenly appearing beside them.

Philip's prominent Adam's apple bobbled as he took a long swallow of beer. "Anyway. Be careful in this house."

"Wait, I want to know what happened," Avery protested. She nudged Tessa, who had lost her smile. "Do you know?"

Tessa nodded. "But not the whole story. Everyone's always been really hush-hush about it, because of what happened after. Look, if you really want to know, wait till everyone leaves, and then ask Dolores. She was hired just before it happened."

Avery hadn't found the chance to ask after the party. People had lingered to chat with each other, and she'd helped the maids clean up. And then the call from the hospital had come, changing the trajectory of her life. Well, she had time to hear the story now. She opened the bedroom door. "Dolores? Could you come up here, please?" This was a pointless distraction, but Avery needed something to take her mind off the worry and grief that clung to her like the scent of shampoo after her shower.

The old woman's footsteps were slow, slower as she climbed the stairs, and Avery chastised herself for not going down to find her instead. She compromised by meeting Dolores on the stairs, but the maid waved her back to her room.

"I'm slow but steady," the old woman said as she entered Avery's bedroom, not even out of breath.

"I wanted to ask you about something that happened when you first came to work for the Tams." Avery gestured to one of the armchairs near the balcony, inexplicably nervous. "Please, sit down."

Dolores perched in the chair and waited, an expectant expression on her lined face. They'd had small conversations since Carlos and Avery had moved in, but the older woman was quiet, and Avery didn't want to overstep some unknown line by asking too many personal questions. By contrast, Fatima was talkative and open, and Avery soon felt as comfortable in her presence as if the maid were a younger cousin.

"I was talking to Tessa about someone knocking on our door in the middle of the night, and then Uncle…Tito Philip started to tell us about Estelle?"

The old woman stood up, more quickly than Avery expected. "Not in here. This is not really my story to tell."

"What's the harm? It sounded like something that happened decades ago," Avery urged. It would just be superstitious nonsense, but she would do anything for a distraction from her life right now. She moved toward her closet. "I'm sorry for calling you up here. I didn't mean to make you uncomfortable. Tito Philip told me to be careful in this house, and I was just curious." Avery stared at her clothing, trying to decide which outfits would be most comfortable as she coiled in the visitor chair beside Carlos's hospital bed.

As Avery slid by the suitcase she'd pulled out, she eyed Tessa's gift again, shoved into the very back of the walk-in closet. Maybe she should hang it above the door, like her sister-in-law had suggested. Why shouldn't she?

It didn't go with the decor, for one, and Avery didn't believe in knickknacks and spirits, nor that one could control the other.

And yet, the bedroom was definitely cooler than it should be. The sense of being watched was still there. If she closed her eyes, she might imagine that there was someone in the room, near the corner where the shadows gathered deepest at night.

There's enough horror in your life these days that you don't need to go imagining more.

When she turned around, a pair of shirts in hand, Dolores stood by the French doors of the balcony. "Out here," the maid said. The alcove felt uncomfortably small with the two of them out there, but the sun blazed down against Avery's still-damp hair and goosefleshed skin, warming her immediately. Dolores shut the door, as if afraid of them being overheard from inside.

"It happened a few weeks after I was hired," Dolores whispered. Her breath smelled of garlic, and her eyes, blue-limned with cataracts, bored into Avery's. "Carlos's mother took an early dislike to me, but I got along well with her brother and sister. I was playing with Estelle when someone knocked on the door. Estelle beat me to it. She was only nine, and she loved visitors."

Dolores broke eye contact and looked far outward, toward the hills, as if her gaze escaped where her body could not. "Estelle spoke to the person at the door for a minute. I couldn't see more than a silhouette, because of the sun behind them. I waited, to see what the stranger wanted and to keep an eye on Estelle. I had just done her hair in two long ponytails, and they swayed back and forth as she shook her head no. She wore a simple yellow dress with white flowers embroidered on it. Eventually, Estelle turned around and went upstairs."

"Did the stranger leave?" Avery's voice also dropped to a whisper.

"No. I moved closer to see. The stranger was a Filipina, and she stood waiting outside the screen door. Mumbling to herself. She was dressed in dark colors, her hair long and loose. I followed Estelle upstairs to ask what the lady wanted. But something was wrong. Estelle was just...*standing* outside her parents' room. At first, I thought she forgot what she'd gone upstairs for. She forgot things sometimes. But then I saw Estelle's face." Dolores grimaced at the memory.

Avery gripped the twisted railing around the balcony and let the hot metal ground her. It was all too easy to picture a small girl in the narrow, dark hallway, standing immobile. Had Estelle stood in the same place Avery had, just before her shower?

"Estelle was having some sort of fit. She was grunting and grimacing, jerking and sweating. It frightened me, and I called out to her, but she didn't answer. I shook her arm, and only then did she look up at me, broken out of whatever spell was laid upon her."

Avery waited, but Dolores remained silent. "Then what?"

"I will never forget that little girl's words. Estelle said, 'She wants Ma Ma.' Then I knew something was really wrong. That wasn't something a little girl would say, not with such fear on her face. Estelle's father was out, but her mother was home. I told Estelle to stay put and ran to get her mother. Ate was having coffee outside, in the back. By the time I brought her into the house, Estelle was already returning to the front door. She wasn't moving right, like her body had forgotten how to move. I reached the front door to watch her pass something small to the Filipina, and then the strange woman left." Dolores chewed on her lower lip, shaking her head.

"What was it? Did you see what was in Estelle's hand?"

"I wasn't sure at the time. It seemed crazy. I expected money, or jewelry. But it looked like a handful of hair, like when you pull it from a hairbrush."

"Hair?" Avery repeated. It was a letdown, like a movie that didn't live up to its hype. After the way Evelyn had snapped at Philip to be quiet, and the hush-hush way everyone spoke of the event, Avery assumed something valuable had been lost, instead of a lifeless part of the body. Hair was a worthless, but strangely intimate, gift for a stranger, and the idea of giving away a handful of hair made Avery uncomfortable for reasons she didn't understand.

Avery took a deep breath, preparing to thank the maid and head back inside, when she caught the expression on Dolores's face. The old woman looked haunted, as if the memory reached through the decades to possess her. Tension filled Avery's body in empathy. She wanted to smirk, to joke, the way she would have if Carlos had told her this ridiculous tale, but there was no room for levity in Dolores's story, or in her countenance. It would be like painting crude pictures with holy oil during someone's last rites.

Dolores kept talking, like a wagon rolling downhill, unable to stop. "Estelle's father came home and became frantic when he heard what happened. He tried to get Estelle and me to describe her, but she just looked like a normal woman to us. He warned us all that he had powerful enemies, and forbade any of us to open the door to strangers again. Then he left the house. When he came back that night, I saw him tying a red string necklace around his wife's throat. But it didn't stop what happened after."

Someone rapped on the balcony door. Avery jumped and squawked at the sudden noise before she recognized the face on the other side of the glass. She gestured, and Fatima opened the door, looking at both maid and mistress curiously as she spoke.

"Ate Tessa called—Kuya Carlos is awake."

CHAPTER SEVEN

Carlos

His body was pain and his breath was pain and his life was pain, and his blood crooned a crescendo of agony until his back arched, until his skin wept, until his mouth whimpered, until his mind gave him the mercy of oblivion.

The next time Carlos regained consciousness, real, solid consciousness, instead of the weaving in and out of awareness he'd done in the hospital, they'd already moved him back into the house.

He thought he'd been dreaming again, the same dream he'd had since the accident, where he stared down a long, unfamiliar hallway at a bright sunlit door, but when he blinked his eyes open, it was just afternoon light glowing behind the white lace curtains and dated wood-paneled walls. His parents' old bedroom—the one he and Avery had chosen as their own. The faded pictures were a comfort, though he cast an uneasy eye at the uncovered vanity mirror. He remembered asking his parents as a young child why some mirrors had to wear "clothes" and being told that the shrouded ones were dangerous. And that all mirrors could steal your soul if you fell asleep while able to see your own reflection. Who knew how many antiquated stories had been corrupted over decades until they became superstitions his grandparents demanded everyone follow, like religious rituals?

As if the thought of the old couple compelled him, Carlos looked out of the open doorway. His grandparents' room loomed across the hall, always dark despite the blazing sun, just the way Carlos remembered it. The room was a pulsing presence in the house, an incessant heartbeat, as if Lolo was still inside, staring out through the crack in the door with his rheumy eyes.

I'm becoming more and more like the old man every day. He felt a sharp needle of fear at the thought, trailing a tangled thread of memory. *No, I'm not. I'm nothing like him, will never be like him.*

His grandfather hadn't always scared him. Carlos could remember sitting on Lolo's bony knees in the rocking chair, holding his hand during walks, sharing the old man's desserts.

As he matured, something made Carlos realize that Lolo always alternated between sadness and anger. He grew frightened of his grandfather's stern face, even if it warmed into a smile at the sight of family. At night, a whispered voice in his room warned Carlos to be wary of the old man, said that Lolo was dangerous and hid horrible secrets inside Salcedo Drive. The warnings were easy to believe; even as a child, he felt there were too many things kept from him, too many conversations that hushed into quiet whenever anyone approached. Just like in the hospital, when people spoke over him and about him as if he were just a trauma case rather than a person.

Carlos tried to turn his head away from the doorway. All he could move was his gaze. He was a balloon, tethered to his body by string, apt to blow away in the slightest breeze. After the crash, in a deep state of shock, Carlos had felt as if he were looking down on his body as the paramedics worked to pump life back into him, a feeling that recurred occasionally as he recovered in the hospital. In light of the injuries he'd endured, maybe this sense of distance was a mercy. He wondered if he had somehow damaged his spinal cord, if this numbness was a sign of paralysis. Oh God, what would he do if—

Avery swept into the room and closed the door. She sat at the foot of the bed, near him but not touching. As if she were afraid to touch him. Or she had no desire to.

"Oh, Carlos." Her voice broke, anger and sadness intermingled, and she buried her face in her hands.

He wanted to reach out to her, to say her name, but he was as powerless over his body as she was. A discomfort shuddered through him, one that morphine couldn't touch. He was responsible for this—for her helpless posture, her defeated and tear-stained face. In ten years of knowing the woman, he'd never seen her like this. She'd always been so strong. He didn't know she loved him to this depth. "I'm sorry, Avery." He couldn't hear his own voice, weak as it was. During a moment of consciousness at the hospital, he'd overheard the doctors say that the emergency intubation damaged his larynx. Maybe she could read his lips?

If only she'd look at him. If only she'd stop crying.

"Avery?" Tessa's voice, muffled through the door.

"One second." Avery cursed softly and hurried to the closet. She emerged with the box trailing the yellow ribbon Carlos had seen her holding at the housewarming. God, that day felt like a lifetime ago.

She pulled out the woven ornament and hung it on the clothing hook behind their bedroom door before throwing the box back into the closet.

With unbelievable effort, Carlos whispered Avery's name. Pain dragged jagged nails from the inside of his throat up to his damaged jaw, and back down again to his fractured clavicle. She sniffled loudly at the same time, swiping at her eyes, and opened the door to hug his sister tightly.

"He's pretty doped up on pain medication, so the doctor says he shouldn't be suffering. I can ask Dolores to sit with him so he's not alone." Avery looked back at the bed, her gaze just grazing Carlos's, and gestured to the hallway. "Let me get you a coffee or something. You must be exhausted."

"With lots of cream, thank you. But don't rush. I'm just happy to be out of the hospital." Tessa looked inside their bedroom. "Even if he looks like death warmed over." She seemed to age as she studied the framed picture of Carlos and Avery on their wedding day that sat on the night table.

"You don't think your mom's too mad at me, do you?" Avery asked. "I know Carlos would prefer to stay in this house, instead of with your parents. We talked about it before he got hurt, that night at dinner."

Tessa shrugged. "She'll get over it. It's actually better for her to keep some distance from him, because of what happened to her sister. That's probably why Dad took your side."

"Her sister?" Avery repeated, but Tessa peeked behind the door and found the ornament Avery had hastily hung on the hook.

"Oh, wonderful! You're using my charm! Ideally it should be nailed above the doorway, but this works just as well, I'm sure."

Avery smiled politely, but it was obvious to Carlos that she was humoring his sister.

The two women left him then, leaving the door ajar, but almost as soon as their voices faded down the hall, the slow tread of Dolores's footsteps grew louder. He remembered that sound as well, another beat to his childhood, though the tempo had slowed over time. The old maid appeared, solid and strong, but she didn't come into the bedroom, like Carlos expected. Like Avery had asked her. She merely poked her head through the doorway and stared at Carlos with sad eyes.

"Kawawa naman," she murmured to him with pity. And then she was gone, slipping inside his grandparents' room, shutting the door behind her. A moment later, it creaked ajar once more. Dolores had always done that, treated her boss's room like it was her own. His mother had always muttered to her siblings that Dolores spent more time with Lolo than any of his actual children, but that was another thing he wasn't supposed to overhear.

Before he could ruminate on Dolores's behavior, another voice caught his attention, whispered from the door.

"Suitcase. Her suitcase."

His eyes moved to their closet, which stood open. Had her luggage always been visible? No, she'd pulled it out. She was obviously planning on abandoning him, fleeing back to Canada when he most needed her.

Carlos gritted his teeth, welcoming the pain that came with it. He had been feeling so numb that even the sharp ache of bones under strain was an improvement. What kind of woman would leave her husband at a time like this? When she was the reason he had crashed in the first place? If she hadn't been nagging him to come home early, hadn't stared at him with her sad eyes as if blaming him for her empty womb, hadn't distracted him with her text, then he wouldn't have crashed.

And yet, he couldn't forget how broken she'd looked a moment ago.

He was foggy, slower than usual. It was the brain injury; the doctors and nurses had warned him about cognitive dysfunction. Or they'd warned Avery and his family; they hadn't spoken directly to him unless they were assessing him with their overloud voices. The nurses especially he couldn't stand, their loud, bossy cheer abrading away at his self-control like a cheese grater. He wished Avery had allowed his family to hire a private nurse, one that focused only on him and wasn't constantly leaving the room to deal with other patients. He had died for four minutes, for Christ's sake. What other patients needed more attention than him?

His brain wasn't working as it should, not quite. He knew that. And yet the wrongness of the situation itched beneath his skin, distracting him until he couldn't ignore it anymore.

Who was whispering to him by the doorway?

"Who's that?" He rasped. Still nothing. His ravaged throat from the ventilator tube and his weakened lungs, his recently wired jaws all conspired to silence him, to steal away his words before they could reach his lips.

Somehow, the voice just outside the room heard. "I am always here."

"Is that you, Achi?"

"No." A laugh, a quiet titter that made Carlos shiver. It was a woman's laugh, one that tickled at the edge of his memory. Could it be Dolores, from Lolo's room...or the new maid, whatever her name was? Fatima, that was it. At least part of his brain still worked.

"She's going to leave you. Or hurt you while you're at her mercy."

"Avery wouldn't hurt me. Why would you say that? Who are you?" Carlos tried to turn his head from the pillow, tried to see beyond the doorway, but his body betrayed him again. He lay back, exhausted from his efforts, and stared up at the white ceiling. Wondered if—not if, *when*—he would return to his former strength.

The strange, quiet laugh again. "It's what I would do."

At her words, childhood memories flooded into his mind. The long nights where he lay in the dark, waiting for sunrise, afraid to move, to show any sign he was awake. Avoiding looking into the dark corners, double-checking the closet door was shut. Staring above the closet door, where the attic hatch waited for him to fall asleep. Pretending the whispers were from his sheets rubbing together or just the aircon hissing...hissing from beneath his bed.

An image accompanied the others, one he thought long forgotten: young Carlos staring at gray powder spilled by his bare feet, hurrying to shove the mess into the cracks between the wooden floorboards and under the bed so no one would know what he'd taken from his grandparents' room.

Chasing that vivid memory was another, one that he'd avoided for years. Lolo sitting on that creaky old rocking chair in his perennially dark room, staring at the shrouded vanity mirror as if he could see through the black fabric. He bid Carlos to sit on the floor before him. Carlos was leaving the next morning for the University of Toronto and had expected some words of wisdom, maybe some money, and so kneeled on the cool hardwood while he waited for his grandfather to talk.

The old man stared at something in the corner of the room for a long moment before he nodded.

"You're going to end up like me, Caloy," Lolo had said, using his nickname for Carlos, and his filmy eyes seemed like they looked beyond Carlos's features to his very destiny. "We share the same fate and will make the same mistakes. For me, it was too late for anything but regret. I pray you will have a brighter end."

The message rang with import—a prophecy foretold. His grandfather's voice clanged inside him, resonating like a bell. Carlos knew these words would come true, and regretted that he'd heard them. Regretted what he would become.

He didn't want to be the creepy man who could talk to the dead. Even if many seemed to revere his grandfather, the old man had always talked about enemies as well, those who feared his abilities or hated how he helped others with curses or possessions.

Lolo's behavior unsettled Carlos as soon as he was old enough to know better, and his grandfather mumbled and talked to people who weren't really there. Carlos wanted to be successful and well-liked and, well, *normal*, and that wasn't going to happen if he ended up hiding in a dark room of his own, glued onto a creaky rocking chair.

Carlos had escaped with some excuse, but it was too late—dread had taken root inside him. Over the years, he'd expected the fear to wither away as he refused to feed it. Instead, fear of the future threaded through him, intertwining with dendrites until it invaded his dreams and affected every decision he made.

Now, twenty years later, it seemed Lolo's curse had caught up to him. Hadn't so many of the people he'd hosted on *Convince Carlos* professed paranormal abilities after they'd had a close encounter with death? They'd covered stories from people who reported their spirits leaving their bodies, watching the doctors fighting to save their lives as if floating above them. Some claimed they'd seen the future, and carried back dark, terrible warnings. Several became mediums afterward, to pass on messages from the departed. When clients complained of seeing spirits, Carlos suggested schizophrenia or drug use to account for the visual hallucinations. Now that it was happening to him, he was having a hard time calming the jackrabbit beat of his heart, or stopping the cold sweat that dampened his body and soaked into the bedsheets.

Was a ghost lingering by his doorway now, or was it brain trauma? Opioids could cause hallucinations. He didn't know. All he knew was that he needed to get better—to see if the voice stopped, to get back to working on his show.

And for Avery's sake. He didn't think he could stand to see that posture of utter defeat anymore, not when he was the reason. They had their problems, but his love for her was undying.

Fatigue swept over him, pulling him into the sea of unconsciousness. The unseen woman's prediction, the girlish titter, scraped at his thoughts. Would he be safe alone and helpless here, with that ghost whispering threats? He blinked at the door. Tessa's artifact hung there. She believed in it, and belief held power. No spirit could pass through that door.

Carlos wondered what his own skepticism might do to the artifact, and he tried desperately to keep his eyes open for the whispering woman.

Sleep pulled at him, a tide carrying him out to sea. He fought against it: If he was unconscious, he was vulnerable. *What are you afraid of?* Carlos asked himself. *What more can you lose?* His body was already ravaged, his mind unstable from concussion and medication.

It was the house's effect. He'd always hated to sleep under this roof, regardless of which room he lay in. Slumber meant he couldn't run if he needed to, although he couldn't remember what there was to run from—was it Lolo or the ghosts he'd purported to see, or was it the whispering woman who somehow felt as familiar as this building, as if she were a part of it?

Carlos tried to move his aching body and failed. It didn't matter if he slept or not, or what dangers lurked in wait. He wouldn't be able to run from anything in his current state.

He was as helpless as he was as a child, and just as trapped.

CHAPTER EIGHT

Avery

Avery grew to hate the house. It was old and dark, with too many stairs and shadows. Despite the size of the rooms, the walls always seemed to close in on her, and even the new lightbulbs Dolores bought couldn't make the damn place cheery. For one, the bulbs kept burning out, no doubt a voltage or electricity issue. The few lights that remained were not enough to overwhelm the creeping gloom.

The house transformed light. Whether it was the hue of the paint or the type of old glass in the windows, even the tropical sunlight beaming full blast into a room was diluted into a wan yellow. It was the color of sickness, of urine-soaked sheets or jaundiced skin, and she could understand why the gullible might believe this place was haunted.

The walls were dark wood where they weren't plastered with faded wallpaper, and the floors were the same dark stain. Coupled with the mingling scents of chalky must and cloying mildew, Avery had started to imagine she was in a coffin, slowly running out of air.

She tied her hair back, avoiding her reflection in the bathroom mirror, and lifted the basin of water from the sink. Her husband blinked open his eyes when she came in, the rest of his body unmoving.

"Rise and shine, Carlos." She set the basin on the night table and opened the blinds before gently washing a moist cloth over his face. The covered vanity mirror pulled at her eye like a mysterious figure, always in her periphery. "Did you sleep well?"

Her husband stared at her, cheekbones and jawline more pronounced after the doctor removed the wires. They weren't sure how much he understood—occasionally he nodded or shook his head, but mostly he seemed not to hear her. Still, his warm brown eyes followed her every movement.

Avery found it hard to look at him. Even aside from the facial injuries, the wounds where the windshield glass had cut him, and the cruel purple bruise that lashed diagonally across his chest from the seat belt, he was different. He'd lost the bulk of good-living he'd developed, so that only skin and thin muscle remained, the muscle fading over the four weeks since he'd been bedbound. Gone was his obsession with his phone, the often contemptuous expression on his face. Without his forehead creased in stress or temper, his face seemed younger, like the accident broke the barrier not only between life and death, but also between past and present. He looked like a lost love to her, like meeting an ex-boyfriend unexpectedly on the street. She felt strangely nervous in his presence in a way she couldn't explain, as if they were on a first date instead of trapped in a miserable situation.

Mostly she had trouble meeting his eyes. They weren't Carlos's. Oh, they were his exact shade, the dark brown irises that glowed caramel at the right angle, but the way he looked at her was different. Like he watched her with admiration instead of ownership, perhaps. It was unfamiliar and made her feel too much, like she might burst into tears if she stared into them too long. Not that she was ever far from crying, these days.

She gave him a bed bath the way the nurses in the hospital had shown her, brushed his teeth, and emptied his urine bag before she checked that the condom catheter was still secure on his penis. So far, she'd managed to take care of these intimate tasks herself. It made her feel better, daily punishments for her traitorous thoughts. She'd stowed the suitcase away when she realized how often she glanced at it.

Downstairs, Fatima sang, her voice high and sweet, as she cooked breakfast. The sound echoed and distorted before it reached Avery's ears, until it seemed the maid's voice was joined by others.

"Can you hear her? I always wanted a house full of singing and laughter," Avery said, before she had to bite her lip and wipe at her eyes. Her emotions were contradictory and confusing, intense and near the surface. She wasn't sure which would overwhelm her at any given moment, but they all ended in tears.

Fatima only sang when she was downstairs. Despite her professed comfort with ghosts, and having steady Dolores for company, the younger woman had to visibly steel herself before ascending the stairs. The maid told anyone who'd listen that since Carlos's accident, the energy had become more negative, especially upstairs. Now that Dolores was never in the house alone, the older maid didn't seem to care where she worked, so it was mostly her heavy footsteps that plodded along the hallways outside the rooms.

Tessa, with the luxury of no longer living at Salcedo Drive, and made brave by the fact it no longer stood empty, became fascinated by the upper floor. She, perhaps after chatting with Fatima, agreed that the "energy felt different," and wondered aloud if it was a problem that burning incense and opening windows would solve, or if the spirits didn't like Avery and Carlos staying here. Avery expected her over again today, with more books and a compass and a trunk full of plants and mirrors to redirect chi. Avery had to walk carefully, especially at night, because there were always new plants or moved furniture after Tessa's visits.

"At least you'll hear more voices than mine today. Tessa is coming over soon." Avery smiled at Carlos, waiting for a sign of acknowledgment that didn't come. Did he not know his sister's name anymore? She slipped an unopened bottle of meal replacement shake into his limp grasp, just to see if he'd hold it, but it toppled over onto the bed.

As she spoon-fed the thick fluid into his mouth, Avery showed him a photograph of them together, taken at Pearson Airport before their flight. "Do you remember this? Right before we came? We were so excited to be moving somewhere warm." His eyes studied the phone screen, and she searched for a spark of understanding, of recognition. He stared too long at his own face, as if he was studying his own features, and then his hand slid clumsily across the bedsheet to touch hers.

Human cells conduct electricity, and the movement of electrons creates magnetic fields. Avery knew this from her research into precious stone magnets that guaranteed conception for the low, low price of two thousand dollars. She could have saved herself the hours of basic physics research and simply allowed Carlos to touch her. Her entire world, past and present, narrowed until only his fingertips trembling on the back of her hand existed: He sent her a love song of soft warmth, comforting vibration, and a magnetic current that rendered her unable to pull away even if she wanted to. But why would she ever want to? It was like when they first kissed, the slide of their lips against each others' saying more, bonding them closer, than mere words or flirtations ever could.

The doorbell rang. Tessa's voice greeted whoever had opened the door. And then—another voice, a deep rumble that she seemed to feel in her bones.

Avery flushed at the warm look she saw in Carlos's eyes as his hand dropped away from her. She pulled a light blanket over his vulnerable body, rubbed Vaseline over his lips so they'd stay moist, and went downstairs.

Her sister-in-law had brought Father Michael. Avery stopped at the base of the stairs and touched her hair, self-conscious of her appearance in front of a stranger. *As if anyone would care if I forgot to put on mascara.* Avery suppressed the self-disgust her vanity sparked inside her. She'd just had a beautiful moment with her husband, even if it might all be in her head. After all, who knew how he really felt, after all that had happened? Four weeks since the accident, and already she was worried about her appearance. What would happen in four years? Oh God, would he still be bedridden? She squashed the fears that bubbled with every thought of the future.

"Avery?" Tessa's face loomed close to her, eyebrows raised in concern. "Avery, you okay?"

Avery blinked and took a firmer grasp on the banister, gently waving away Tessa's hand on her other arm. "I'm a little tired. I must have zoned out while you were talking to me, I'm sorry." She looked up at Father Michael, focused on the white square at his collar instead of his features. "Thank you for making the time to visit, Father. Can I get you something to drink?"

"Dolores is bringing coffee to the dining room. I'll be down in a little while." Tessa made her way up the stairs to visit her brother. Carlos's parents came twice a week, with a trauma specialist they paid to assess his progress. They'd hired a physiotherapist as well, who came every second day to work his muscles and to prevent contractures. They offered Avery money and food, but she sensed no warmth from her mother-in-law, only blame. Avery dreaded the judgment in their eyes, as if she had been the one to pour alcohol down his throat or had flipped the Mercedes at breakneck speeds.

Tessa was different. She took work calls on her phone, or sent texts, but otherwise seemed to have put her own business on hold to help her brother. She came often, acted as invasively familiar as Avery's own siblings, and spent more time talking to Avery than sitting vigil by her brother. "Carlos would want me to make sure his wife was okay," she always said, right before she bullied Avery into eating more. She was wrong—Carlos only ever cared that he was prioritized—but Avery appreciated the gesture all the same.

Avery perched on the edge of a high-backed chair and smiled at Father Michael, who sat with his hands folded over the table. Silence filled the space between them like the dust motes in the air—she was too drained to be social, too consumed with dark thoughts to ask about the mundane. An annoying buzzing tickled at her ear. She'd heard it intermittently today but only now realized it must be a fly or some other insect. It was louder down here.

"It's kind of you to come," she said finally.

"It's my genuine pleasure. I've known Tessa since I was a child." He grinned at the memory, his eyes crinkling. "She used to teach Sunday school, and made up half the answers. I didn't realize until

I went to seminary school that the prayers she taught all the kids weren't real."

"They were real to me, Father." Tessa clumped down the stairs and plopped beside Michael. "Maybe you can bless my brother before we leave today? Any little bit helps."

"Of course."

Dolores appeared at the doorway. "Ma'am, may I bring breakfast out?"

"Please."

She and Fatima brought out Vienna sausages and corned beef, lightly toasted pandesal and garlic fried rice.

The old woman turned to Avery as they set out the food. "You didn't use the stove this morning, did you?"

Avery gave her a polite smile and shook her head. Was this a hint that the maids shouldn't be cooking every meal? "No, but I don't mind cooking."

Dolores turned to give Tessa a meaningful look. "This is the third time Fatima or I have found every element on the stove turned on."

"It sounds like we need to replace it," Avery suggested firmly.

Avery added milk to her coffee and forced herself to eat after Dolores left the room. Tessa's forehead was creased with worry as she chewed. For a while the sounds of water running and the two maids chatting in the kitchen took over the room. The muted buzzing Avery couldn't escape tickled at her ears, but neither guest seemed to notice it.

"How do you think he's doing?" Tessa asked. "He doesn't seem himself."

Avery chewed longer than she needed to and swallowed carefully, her mind racing. Tessa was right, of course, but he'd been through so much. No one would be the same after an ordeal like that, and it was probably expected that she felt like she was caring for a stranger instead of her husband.

“Give him time,” Avery said, in lieu of everything else she wanted to say, but not in front of a priest. A man of God wouldn’t understand the split second of hope she felt every morning, before she opened her eyes, that her husband had died during the long hours of the night, freeing her from marital duty. Or that sometimes, she almost preferred this weak, concussed Carlos to the sarcastic man who would abandon her for days while he filmed his show and laughed at her bone-deep need to be a mother. They were sinful thoughts, quickly suppressed, evidence that she wasn’t quite herself either: Carlos’s accident, the aftermath, and living in this dark, creepy house were changing her.

“I worry it’s the house,” Tessa said, as if she’d plucked the thought from Avery’s mind. “The ghosts in it, you know. When people are weak, they may be more susceptible to such things. Their bodies might be taken over by stronger spirits.” Tessa turned to Michael, who nodded soberly.

“And then what?” Avery asked.

“What do you mean?”

Avery smirked. “Say Carlos’s body is taken over by another spirit. What happens to his? Does he have to kick the squatter out, like a bad tenant? Or does he have to hang around the house and wait for another, weaker person he can kick out of their body like musical chairs?”

Tessa tsk-tsked at her. “It’s beyond my knowledge to know these things.”

Tessa was just like her yogi friend, Avery thought, talking

nonsense about souls separating from bodies but having no answers to any follow-up questions.

Her sister-in-law took a sip of coffee. "Have you experienced anything strange?"

"Strange? What's normal?" Avery forced a laugh. "I'm in a new country, in a new house, with a bedridden husband. If something abnormal was happening, I'd probably sleep through it." Not that she ever slept well at night, but they didn't need to hear that.

"Fatima tells me there are angry spirits in the house. And something in the walls," Michael suggested.

"Have you seen my grandfather?" Tessa asked. "Or anything else?"

"I don't believe in ghosts," Avery said flatly.

"You would if you grew up here. The house has a long history of hauntings." Tessa scooped more corned beef onto her plate. "Growing up we heard noises and things would move, but only my lolo had the Sight. He would sit in his room and tell us the stories of the spirits who lived among us. He always told us that there was a reason for ghosts, a reason why the dead didn't rest."

Avery was too tired to school her expression, and her sister-in-law tsk-tsked again. "Typical North American skepticism. Carlos was the same way after he moved to Canada. He started his show because he wanted to disprove all paranormal phenomena. And yet, skeptic that he proclaims to be, he's been too scared to come home."

After the meal, Tessa wandered around the house, mumbling to the small compass she held in her hand. Avery took Michael upstairs, to see Carlos, and looked away from the pained expression that passed the priest's face when he saw the figure in the bed.

Michael took hold of her elbow and stepped out of the room, into the hallway. The skin he touched still pulsed with warmth moments after he let go, as if her nerve endings missed his compassion. "I'm so sorry. I can't imagine what you must be going through, Avery."

She tried to shrug it away, like she did with everyone else's platitudes, but under Michael's unrelenting gaze, her lips trembled until she clamped them together, and she gazed down at her slippers. "It is what it is."

"It must be very lonely for you here, and I understand the difficulty in confiding in Tessa, or the women you employ. Tessa actually asked me to come visit today, not just for Carlos, but to see if I can help you with your burden."

Another shrug. She longed for Carlos to moan, as he sometimes did, or for Tessa to call upstairs. Anything to break the spell of intimacy that was tightening around them. And yet she did not want to step away, to break this moment of connection. It felt like this moment was hers, hers alone, and not merely a facet of Carlos's influence. He was the closest thing she'd felt to a friend since their plane had landed here.

"If things get overwhelming, and you need an ear, or a prayer, please don't hesitate to call me. Or, if you're more comfortable with another woman, I can ask one of the nuns I know to reach out." He handed her a business card, and she took it to make the moment of claustrophobic sympathy end.

Something startled the breath from Avery, and her head whipped toward the nearby door. As her heart hammered in her throat, she realized Michael was staring in the same direction, his eyes wide. They'd both noticed it, then: A sound below their ability to hear it, or maybe they sensed movement. But as they waited, the band of fear squeezing Avery's rib cage loosening, whatever it was did not repeat. The air grew heavy with tension, but they were alone in the hallway. Was it Father Michael's disapproval she sensed, so strong it forced her to step farther away from him?

"Thank you, Father."

"Have faith, Avery. God will see you through this." Michael turned back toward the bedroom, his face somber.

Avery flinched. *Faith? Might as well believe in ghosts—at least people reported signs that they existed.*

She wandered downstairs; listening to the priest speak to her husband felt like an intrusion. The buzzing came again. Avery followed the sound to the large shrouded mirror in the hallway.

Something made her hesitate before she lifted the heavy black cloth. It wasn't the thought of bugs—she'd grown up camping in Ontario forests every summer and couldn't care less about them, even ones as large as horseflies. Perhaps it was the combination of remembered horror movies and the close way the house pressed in on her that weakened her nerve.

Ridiculous. She was turning as bad as her in-laws. Avery grabbed a newspaper from the kitchen—Dolores read it every morning—and rolled it into a weapon. The shiver of apprehension squatting behind her sternum irritated her, and she chastised herself before grabbing the bottom of the mirror's cover. She lifted it up slowly, intending to smack the fly before it grew startled enough to take flight.

Avery screamed.

She dropped the cloth and backed away, gasping, the rolled newspaper growing soggy in her moist hand. That was no housefly. Never in her life had she seen insects that large, their grotesque brown carapaces glossy and thick.

Tessa ran downstairs. "What's wrong?"

She felt foolish. God, did she ever feel foolish, but she pointed a trembling finger at the mirror because she didn't trust herself to not scream again.

Her sister-in-law raised her eyebrows and turned toward the mirror. Slowly, she lifted the cover, just as Avery had. She burst out laughing. "Welcome to the Philippines, girl. We grow them big here!"

Tessa took the newspaper cudgel from Avery's limp grip and made short work of the two cockroaches. The crunch of their shells breaking on impact and the short squirt of green-yellow guts across the glass made the corned beef Avery had eaten seep upward from her throat, and she swallowed hard to avoid vomiting. Swallowed again.

She watched as Tessa flattened the rolled-up newspaper to scoop up the insect corpses from the ground. "I'll throw these out by Wilma. Dolores is not a fan of these things either," Tessa said, and raised her voice to call out. "Fatima! Halika dito!"

The young woman came as she was bid. When Tessa asked her to clean the insect gore from the mirror, Fatima's eyes grew wide, but all she answered was "Opo, Ate."

Avery followed Tessa out to the paved yard. The heavy heat hit her, like diving into an overly warm bath, but it chased the shiver from her bones.

"Who's Wilma?" she asked her sister-in-law.

"I'll introduce you two." Tessa winked over her shoulder.

"I've never seen anything beyond mosquitoes and flies here," Avery said, her cheeks burning hotter than the rest of her body. "I'm sorry if I scared you."

"No problem. These filthy things are everywhere. And lizards too. But you won't see them so often here. Dolores was trained *very* well by my lolo." Tessa tossed the bugs onto the dirt. "This is Wilma, a mango tree Carlos planted as a child." The ripe mangoes hanging above them lightened the air with subtle sweetness.

Oh. It pleased her to think of her husband as a child, planting a small seedling that would grow to bear fruit. "Your grandfather didn't like bugs?" Avery asked.

Tessa chuckled again. "That's an understatement. One time, when we were kids, Carlos and I found this dead mouse. It was filled with maggots, and flies, and just...blech. I can't believe we weren't grossed out, but we were like, poking it with a stick, and then Lolo found us." Tessa lost her smile and shook her head, as if in disbelief. "You know, my whole life, that was the only time I've ever seen my grandfather angry. It was the scariest thing I've ever seen. He freaked. Started yelling and *set fire* to the poor dead mouse. And then he burst into tears." She rubbed her butt cheeks. "I still remember when my mom found out what we'd done. Couldn't sit down for a week."

"That seems like an overreaction," Avery said, ignoring her own screams a moment ago.

Tessa shook her head. "No, it was totally our fault. We knew about the drama that went down before we were born. We knew how he and Lola felt about bugs, even though we didn't think of it at the time."

"What happened before you were born?" *Had clouds passed over the sun, or did it just seem darker and colder suddenly?*

Father Michael appeared in the doorway. "I've blessed your brother, Tessa. Can you take me back to the church? I have another appointment."

"Of course, Father." Tessa gave Avery a perfunctory hug and ran to grab her things.

Avery stood in the driveway and waved goodbye to them until Fatima closed the gate. When they were gone, and her nose had grown so accustomed to the scent of mangoes that she could no longer smell their sweetness, she left Wilma and returned inside.

The mirror hung there as if nothing had happened. She peeked beneath the cover. *The sight of the clean mirror would soothe the grotesque experience*, Avery thought.

And it did, but Fatima had left a smudge. No, not a smudge—fingerprints on the lower right edge. Avery breathed on the area and used her shirt to wipe it away.

The fingerprints remained. She peered closer and rubbed again. Pressed one of her own fingertips against the mirror by comparison.

Frowning, Avery let the shroud drop into place.

Somehow, the fingerprints had been made on the other side of the glass.

CHAPTER NINE
Carlos

His boredom was the second worst part of the accident. Avery was out of the room most of the day, unless she needed to get something, and when she came in, her face was so miserable it felt like further punishment. Fatima never came upstairs. Dolores plodded outside the hallways on this task or another, but his voice was no louder than a rasp, and if she could hear him call for her, she ignored him, only visiting him for a few minutes each time, always with that infuriating look of pity on her old face.

Carlos was so sick of the room, he wanted to throw the framed pictures onto the floor and smash the damn mirror. *Once I can move*, he promised himself.

He was getting stronger, day by day. He was sure of it. With enough concentration and effort, he could move his bruised limbs, though they felt impossibly heavy and not quite his own. His progress was the only thing keeping him sane. Alone in the room, he focused on stretching, slowly sliding his hand to reach for nearby objects, moving each leg inch by inch, ignoring the pain in his broken ribs as he moved.

Avery entered the room without warning, or maybe he'd been so focused he didn't hear her approach. Carlos abandoned the folded newspaper he'd been trying to pull toward him and lay flat. He wanted to surprise her with his progress, give her something to smile about. He watched her at night, while she tossed and turned on the bed as if moving to the beat of the footsteps outside their room. When she finally lay still, tears slipped from her closed eyes to soak into her pillows.

Every morning she sat at the edge of the bed, facing away from him, and sighed before standing up. It killed him, that exhalation, like all the joy in her had died. He vowed every morning to do right by her, to make her smile. And yet, every time he tried to reach her, with words or touch, she shut him out. Surely, she wasn't still angry over his accident, not when he was the one bedridden and suffering. Even now she hurried through her tasks, barely looking at him, and when she spoke, it was a quiet murmur he could barely hear. No one ever knew what was in a woman's mind, but she made him feel invisible.

"Avery," he said. His jaws didn't move much, still too stiff from being fractured, and his voice box wasn't healing quite right.

She paused. Waited, while refusing to look at him. Instead, she gazed at the newspaper beside him, and slid it back to its original place, erasing the distance he'd painstakingly moved it.

"I'm sorry, Avery." Damn it, when would he get his voice back? All he could manage was a hoarse whisper through clenched teeth.

Carlos waited for Avery's reaction, searched for a softening of her features to show her anger had cooled, but she turned away from him and hurried from the room without a word. She still blamed him. So much for working on their marriage in Manila.

As quickly as a car flipping over, his desire to please her turned into rage. *Bitch. Ungrateful bitch.* As if she were the one who had been injured, as if it were her life that was ruined. She was living in his house for free, with maids to wait on her, when all she could have afforded back home was a roommate, and she dared turn her back on *him*? The sunlight turned blinding, igniting miniature fireworks inside his skull. The concussion had left him with photosensitivity, and of course Avery had put him in the brightest room in the house.

Dolores came in while he fumed. She, at least, wasn't angry at him. She was on his side. While she tidied the room, she spoke to him about news and family, and though she didn't give him much chance to answer, the interaction comforted him.

"Your sister is a fool. Do you know what I caught her bringing into this house the other day? A Ouija board. In *this* house, as if it were some American horror movie. I made her leave it outside." Dolores shook her head. "As I get older, I worry more and more about you children." She gave a sad chuckle. "I know you're adults now, but you'll always be kids to me."

She sat at the foot of the bed and looked directly at him. It was more kindness than he'd received all day, and his eyes blurred. He would ask his parents for a private nurse. He needed stimulation and attention; otherwise, he would never recover with Avery doing the bare minimum for him and then fucking off to do whatever else she wanted. Resentment bubbled inside him, a poisonous broth that energized his body as it drained his spirit. And worse, he couldn't express how he was feeling. Hell, half the time he didn't know *what* he was feeling, wobbling between wanting Avery to talk to him and cursing her beautiful, self-pitying face.

"Be at peace, Carlos. You need to rest," Dolores said. She sang him a lullaby, something she'd sung to him as a child. Slowly, he was lulled to unconsciousness.

The voices in the hall pulled him back to awareness. That was another thing: He kept losing time. It was something he meant to mention to the doctors, whether these blackouts were true losses of consciousness or just him falling asleep throughout the day because of the pain medication or healing process. He was only aware of it by the way the light from the balcony and windows had traveled across the room when he opened his eyes.

He peeked through the door to see Avery talking to a man outside of Lolo's room. They were standing too close, too intimately, for strangers. His wife's shoulders were hunched, tense, as if expecting to be hurt. If rage could lend Carlos strength, he would have torn the room apart. He thumped his fist futilely against the bed.

The pair stopped talking and looked in Carlos's direction as if he'd called them. It was Father Michael, the handsome bastard who'd monopolized Avery during their housewarming.

Carlos closed his eyes and feigned sleep. He'd be damned before he made small talk with the lecherous priest.

More lost time. He became nothing and only found his way into his body again when the woman in the walls whispered to him. "You want to hurt them?"

He tried to ignore her, to suppress the fury that built inside him until he wanted to explode. Finally, because he needed an outlet, he answered. "Yes."

She tittered. He'd been afraid of her when she'd first spoken to him in the doorway, but even if she was just a hallucination, she was the only friend he had. She seemed to voice his darkest thoughts so he didn't have to. Well, whispered. The fact that he had lost his voice and this woman only spoke in whispers was not lost on him, and he was sure a psychiatrist would find that meaningful.

"So hurt them. Make them suffer." She made her esses sharp, like a hiss. A childhood memory niggled at his mind, but his recall had always been poor, worse since the accident.

"I can't." He paused. "Not yet."

"Do you want me to? Hurt them?"

Carlos snickered. "If I'm stuck in here, so are you."

"I can go anywhere in this house."

"You are an auditory hallucination created by a brain contusion."

"I have always been here. Don't you remember me, little boy?"

He shivered. The memory niggled again. "Prove it then. Come in here." He held his breath, regretting the words. Was it only vampires that needed invitations?

A long silence. "I can't. Not this room."

Carlos looked at Tessa's gift, still hung haphazardly on the door hook.

"Remove it, and I will come in," the woman said.

"I…don't think I will." He whispered through his stiff jaws. "Go knock down something of mine so Avery can see." If the voice could do that, far away from him, it would prove she was real. And it would remind his disloyal wife that she was married.

A young woman passed by the open door. The sunlight from the other rooms spilled into the hallway, rectangles of illumination before the shadows swallowed her once more. Her dress was old-fashioned, and so translucent he'd once thought the material threadbare until he realized he could see through her back, too. She grew more wispy as she walked away from him until the last door of light, when she never reemerged from the shadows.

This. This was the worst thing that had come from the accident.

The whispering he heard was bad enough, but the people he saw... Carlos told himself every time that these were his childhood nightmares brought to life by his concussed brain, that his lolo had suffered from senility or delusions and the family had just played along. But a larger part of him was wondering if something had really happened when he'd died, some change that allowed him to see beyond the veil.

If what he was seeing was real, then Lolo had been right all along, and the house was full of ghosts. Some, like this young woman, seemed to be residual hauntings, ghosts doomed to repeat the same scene regardless of what happened. There was a little girl he sometimes saw who he'd caught staring at him, and who disappeared when he turned to look at her. The knowledge gave the footsteps creaking in the attic above him, or in the hallway when everyone should be asleep, even more weight. Carlos, trapped as he was, vacillated between waking Avery up and staring at the door handle to make sure it wasn't turning of its own accord. He always opted to let her keep what little sleep she claimed. Anyway, it was obvious she heard them too by the way her eyes tracked across the ceiling as if tracing someone's path.

The sense of helplessness reminded him of being a child again. He remembered the long flights of stairs, each step so high for his small legs, and the black cat that coiled bonelessly between the banister spindles, startling him every time. The long hallway where he'd dash from lit doorway to lit doorway, afraid of the ghosts his family always alluded to and shushed each other to silence about. All of them were frightened, but they stayed in the house because Lolo refused to move. His grandfather seemed impossibly old to Carlos, even back then, and while Lola had been round-cheeked and soft, the patriarch had seemed stiff and aloof. Carlos had peeked in on his grandfather's room each time he passed, curious about the man who rarely spoke. Lolo listened—to the chatter of his family, the maids, the black-and-white television that was always on a low, mumbling volume. And when he spoke, it was treated like Moses coming down from the mountain with the commandments.

The last time Carlos had seen Lolo had been the night before he'd left for the University of Toronto. He would never forget his grandfather's last words to him—they'd chased him across oceans and decades into his nightmares, and now he was back in this godforsaken house full of memories that haunted as much as the ghosts. How had Lolo known what was going to happen, so many years before it came to pass?

The young woman floated down the hallway, always disappearing before she reached the end. She did that every day around this time, five slow trips before dissipating. Bored as he was, he didn't dare ask her why she never reached the last door. He was afraid, with his new abilities, that it would snap her out of the eternal loop and she would scratch at his door the way the whispering woman did.

Carlos reviewed what he knew of spirits, what he recited so often for the benefit of viewers of his show. There were different types of hauntings. This one, who didn't interact with the environment and repeated the same actions every time, was considered a residual haunting. It was said that they could be created by an event so joyous or traumatic that the energy imprinted itself in the room. This was similar to the Chinese superstition not to buy used furniture or clothing unless the buyer knew the previous seller, because the object might carry with it negative energy or luck. No one had ever been able to prove residual hauntings existed, not on his show, at least. And yet here he was, staring at the proof as it disappeared right before his eyes.

The whispering woman was probably an intelligent haunting, someone with ties to this realm that wouldn't let her move on. Either she didn't know she was dead, had unfinished business, or had a strong emotional link to someone who had lived or would live in this house.

Then, if Dolores was to be believed, what kind of entity had his grandfather become?

Lolo's voice came to his mind then, shrinking Carlos back to a naive boy sitting at the foot of the old man's rocking chair. "Ghosts are not like you and me, Caloy. We have three dimensions and must obey scientific rules, but souls are not of this world. Time and distance and gravity mean nothing to them. Spirits of the elderly can look like children again when they return to haunt their family homes. Sometimes they come from the future to warn someone of danger. And rarely, they can cross the world in an instant, at the time of their death, to wish a loved one goodbye."

Carlos pulled his mind away from the memory before he remembered Lolo's warnings about demons and shadow figures. He still had nightmares of them.

He prayed that Tessa's handmade craft continued to work, that its protective effects didn't dissipate over time like the scent of incense did. Or if they did wear off, that he'd be well enough to get up, pack a bag, and escape to his parents' house. And then Avery could see how it felt to be abandoned. Until then, while he was at her dubious mercy, Carlos had to play nice. He was an actor, so it wouldn't be hard to keep her sympathetic to him. To pretend he didn't despise her. That he still loved her, even.

He just needed to get stronger. Carlos took a deep breath and reached toward the newspaper again, using the impotent rage he held for his wife to fuel him.

CHAPTER TEN

Avery

How are things?" Claudia asked.

Avery shrugged, even if her sister couldn't see it over the phone. "Awful?"

"Are you sleeping any better?"

She threw her legs up on the worn couch in the sitting room. "Let's not talk about me. Let's talk about anything else but me, or Carlos, or the house. Please. How's Mom and Dad? Henry?"

As Claudia obediently began to fill her in on their family's lives, Avery clenched her eyes shut and tried to concentrate on the familiar voice in her ear. She pretended that she was back in her tiny apartment, chatting with her sister, while Carlos was out late filming. Back in Canada, the noises and footsteps that clattered around her were just loud neighbors. Avery had never yearned to return to the past before, not even to her fondest childhood memories. Now, her entire body ached to go back. Everything was hard here, distanced by culture and language and her ignorance. She clung to Claudia's voice like it was a life preserver in a turbulent storm, though it was her own emotions that threatened to drown her.

She swiped at the wetness on her cheeks. "That's awesome. I'm sorry I missed the big dinner."

"Mom's been praying every day that Carlos will get better. You just need to hold on until he does."

Avery shook her head. "A priest was here the other day to bless him, for all the good that did. Didn't Mom learn anything since Noelle?"

"If it helps her, what's the harm? A lot of people find comfort in religion, and having faith gives people strength to keep going." Claudia was using her social worker voice on her, and instead of keeping Avery calm, it made her angrier. She couldn't say what she was really feeling when everyone was so damn positive and...fake.

"Oh, that's what I'm missing then. Not sleep or rest or a healthy husband, just faith," Avery snapped.

Claudia clucked in sympathy. "Come back home, Avery. Even just for a break. Four weeks is a long time to take care of someone, and you said he has family there. Let me buy you a ticket for your birthday."

Avery flinched as if her younger sister had slapped her, and faced with the prospect of actual escape, her anger drained out of her. Leaving felt like giving up—on Carlos, on their marriage, on herself. She couldn't just leave, not after she'd spent so many years building the life she wanted with the man she loved. Not when he stared at her with those trusting, loving eyes. "No thanks. I've... I've got to go. Tell everyone I said hi, and I miss them. I love you."

"Avery. Talk to me. I can tell you're not okay."

Avery tried. She really did. Her mouth opened and closed but couldn't find the words that could unravel the tangled knot of emotions choking her. That if she went home for a short break, she could never force herself to come back. That Carlos was the love of her life, and it was killing her to see him shrinking before her eyes. That her period had come and she didn't even know how to go to the store herself and had to ask Fatima to buy everything. That her desperate need for a baby—babies—was beyond rationality, as if the ghosts of her future children haunted her. That this house seemed to suck all joy from her until all she had left were the darkest of thoughts.

She felt so guilty, wanting something so selfish and small when there was suffering all around her, but Carlos's accident had shown her that life was short and precious and she needed to wring from it every drop of happiness that she could—before it was too late, and it may already be too late. It was too much to say. Broken down like this, they sounded like petty complaints compared to what Carlos must be going through, and when she tried to explain this to Claudia, Avery found she couldn't breathe.

"I can't." Avery hung up and began to pace across the sitting room, rubbing her arms. Past the gauzy curtains, Dolores swept the cement free of debris. There was nothing like grass around the house, just dirt and Wilma the mango tree. The lack of vegetation and the high gray walls around the property made it feel like Avery was serving a life sentence for some unknown crime.

But that wasn't right. She knew exactly what she had done wrong, every step of the way. Being swayed by Carlos's good looks at a mutual friend's barbecue. Getting too excited that she'd found another Chinese Filipino in the wild, even if she spoke none of the Hokkien or Tagalog that he was fluent in. Not asking how he felt about children before they moved in together, before they got married. Coming all the way here with him. Agreeing to stay on this highway when she didn't like the destination, and continuing to ignore the off-ramps as she drove farther and farther from where she wanted to be.

Wood scratched against wood in the empty hallway. Avery slowed her steps, looking this way and that for a sign of movement. Nothing. She suppressed a shiver, forced herself to turn her back on the doorway, and resumed her pacing.

Tomorrow she turned thirty-seven. As a child, she'd wanted to be a veterinarian, a writer, a fireman. After cancer had claimed her older sister, Avery wished she could be a Vulcan, so she could render herself immune to the grief that followed.

Avery had no job, had not even had time to exchange any money into pesos. She was dependent on the mercies of her husband's family while she was in the Philippines, and her husband might or might not recover. She hadn't even been sure if she wanted to stay with him before they'd come here, and now she couldn't make herself leave. Guilt proved a stronger tie than marital vows.

Two years past thirty-five, that age where the risk of birth complications increased. Her eggs were aging, and she regretted not freezing them two years ago. She'd had no idea that things would take so long, that they'd have such trouble, that Carlos would refuse to provide semen for the procedures or allow her to use a donor. "Can't we just do it naturally?" he'd say, and could not be budged.

God hadn't intervened. Not with Noelle's leukemia, not with her infertility, and not now, when Carlos lay silent and staring in the bed, while time ticked on and hours were wasted in futile prayer. He was improving though, wasn't he? Just so painfully slow that she couldn't see the progress each day, like watching a plant grow. The thought of Carlos made her smile, despite her dark mood.

When she cared for him every morning, when his eyes focused intently on her face, she could feel the love emanating from him. Today she shaved his face. She'd tried a couple of weeks ago, when he was asleep, and had accidentally cut him. Until the scab had healed, Avery hadn't dared try again. Her hand shook as she spread the shaving cream into a foamy lather, Carlos's facial hair making her fingertips tingle as it slid against her skin. He turned his face toward hers, and there was no sense of the wary judgment she expected, especially after she'd hurt him last time.

"Hold still," she warned, bringing the razor close. Before the accident, he might have said something about her being more careful this time, but now he didn't speak. There was only trust in his eyes, and some emotion she couldn't read.

Before the blade could touch his skin, he flinched. She yelped and recoiled, an apology tumbling out of her before she noticed his lips had quirked into a small smile.

"You—you're teasing me," she gasped, and smacked him. He gave her a slow, obvious wink, setting her heart leaping and her lower abdomen tightening, before he turned his face toward the razor again.

Something new was growing between them, a fragile, tender understanding like a blooming flower—silent, but no less beautiful. Life was hard now, because she couldn't stand to see her husband in this state, because the house filled her with dread and stole her sleep, because the future she dreamed of was looking less and less tangible, but there were moments of wonder in it too. She had to focus on the good, or she'd never survive. But here, in Salcedo Drive, there was so little good.

Something scratched against wood again. Avery waited for it to repeat, standing still, eyes searching for movement.

Had that picture on the far wall always been crooked? She approached the collection of small framed photos, eyes squinted.

All were straight, except the lopsided one. As she watched, the picture swung to the other side like a pendulum, its wooden frame sliding against the wood panel with the same sound she'd heard. She peered closely at it, looking for the cause of its movement.

It sprang from its nail and crashed to the ground at her feet.

"Jesus!" Avery shouted, leaping back. She'd seen the damn thing move—the top edge of the frame had lurched up and toward her in one motion, as if someone's hand had shoved it from below.

"Ma'am?" Fatima came in. "Susmaryosep!" She backed into the hallway, crossing herself, her eyes scanning the room wildly.

Avery looked around the room, heart racing, but didn't see anything that might have caused the maid's reaction.

"Fatima?" she called gently to the terrified young woman. "Can you get Dolores, or a broom, please?"

"A...broom?" Fatima knew what a broom was. Her English was excellent. But the maid's hand trembled against her thin chest, and her large brown eyes showed too much white.

"A"—Avery wracked her limited vocabulary—"walis, please?"

The maid nodded. "Opo! Right away, Ate." She disappeared and returned with both broom and Dolores, clutching the old woman's arm and whispering rapidly to her.

Dolores's cloudy eyes tracked *something* as it moved across the room, finishing on a section of the far wall, near the floor. She patted Fatima, handed the young maid a paper towel trailing dark threads in her hands, and shooed the young maid out of the room. "I'll take care of it."

Ignoring Dolores's "Careful, ma'am!" Avery bent to pick up the picture frame. The glass had broken upon impact, and she shook the shards onto the floor. The photograph was faded brown and sepia with age, instead of black and white. Carlos stood stiff and unsmiling beside a boy, a hand on the child's shoulder. No, not Carlos. She peered closer, trying to find details lost to the years. This man resembled her husband but was older and thinner. Carlos didn't own a Barong, the formal high-collared shirt worn here. His lolo, maybe? And this must be young Carlos—she recognized his features now, obscured by youth and a ridiculous haircut.

Lolo's ghost appeared in the house; that's why Carlos had agreed to come. And now a picture of the man leapt from the wall. Was it Lolo who had dropped the photo where she couldn't help but see? Preposterous, yet Avery had witnessed it with her own eyes.

The aircon clattered on noisily, making her jump, and she realized Dolores was still standing in the doorway, still holding the broom, still staring at the wall.

"Oh, I'm so sorry. Let me get out of your way." Avery stepped carefully around the glass, her cloth slippers offering little protection, and moved farther from the aircon's breeze. She shivered. Sweat had bloomed over her skin, and both to warm herself and to get the nervous energy out of her legs, she began to pace again.

"Do you believe in ghosts, Dolores?" Avery spoke over the tinkling glass and swishing broom bristles. "Is that what made the picture fall?"

Now why would she ask *this* woman about ghosts? It was Dolores's sighting of Lolo's spirit that had started this whole ordeal.

The older woman, sweeping the mess into a dustpan, took a moment to answer. "Old houses have a history. Over the years and many families, they can take on an energy that lingers, the way cooking smells stick to clothes. Floors might creak; some say it's mysterious footsteps. Others might say it's the house remembering."

"I watched this picture jump from the wall without anyone near it. Why would that happen?" Avery's hand shook as she gestured to the picture frame she still gripped. Her frantic mind recalled the clump of dark thread Dolores had given to Fatima, but Avery knew it wasn't really thread. "What was that you were holding when you came in? In the napkin?"

Dolores grunted as she stood up and met Avery's eyes. "It was your hair. Gathered from your hairbrush, the floor, the shower."

Then she walked out of the room, and the sound of glass falling into the plastic garbage can rang from the kitchen.

Avery put the photograph down on a side table and interlaced her fingers together to keep them still. There had to be an explanation for all this. The hair was probably the family's superstition, given what had happened to Estelle. And the nail was probably loose and her pacing had vibrated the walls.

She moved closer to the wall of photographs and touched the single exposed nailhead. It didn't move. The wood around it was darker where the picture had hung, protected from the sun's bleaching rays.

The skin on the back of her neck prickled. She was being watched. Dolores's gaze had tracked across the room to focus on a large gap in the wall, about knee height. Avery crouched down to press her eye into the crevice.

The wooden boards were sticky against her cheek. Light from the room reached into the black void like long, skeletal fingers, and the space between one wall and the next was narrow and claustrophobic. Here, out of the maids' reach, dust and cobwebs thrived. She stared into the dark slit for a long time, straining her eyes for movement.

You're cracking up, girl. Avery pictured what she must look like to an observer, crouching on the floor and staring into shadows. She sat down on the hardwood and laughed, the adrenaline from the scare fueling her amusement until tears leaked from her eyes. Carlos needed her to stay skeptical, to make evidence-based decisions for him. Not to buy into the bullshit the rest of his family espoused. But she *saw* that picture move by itself. And the entire house felt different, somehow. Angrier, since they'd brought Carlos home from the hospital. And damn it, she *knew*, without being able to put her finger on it, that Carlos was different. It was like closing her eyes and knowing that the person who walked into the room was a stranger. Half the time, she resented him for trapping her in a foreign place, where every day she waited for him to get better or to get worse, because either of those might set her free from this never-ending limbo. But then when she was with him, afraid to make eye contact with his familiar-unfamiliar eyes, or when she dreamed of him at night, her body flared with attraction. Desire. A level she hadn't felt for him in years, not since they'd first fallen in love.

To hell with this self-pity. Carlos encountered this kind of crap fifteen shows per season, and she knew her next steps. First, to disprove supernatural phenomena, she had to gather information. And for that, she needed to interview prior inhabitants to learn about what had been witnessed in this house. She reached for her phone and called Tessa.

"Hey, Avery, kamusta?"

She wanted to ask her sister-in-law about the house and their childhood, but she didn't know where to start. *Hey, I think this house is haunted. Plus, your brother is weird and unfamiliar now, and I might like him better this way?*

"...Avery?" Tessa repeated.

"Sorry, Achi. Do you want to get together on Thursday?"

"Sure! You want anything in particular?"

How about a ride to the airport? Avery sighed. "Anywhere is fine. It's my birthday tomorrow, and...and it's my treat, okay?" She'd just charge it, to hell with the exchange fees or the amount left in her bank account.

"Your birthday!" Tessa's voice lost its ebullience. "Oh, Avery. I'm so sorry you're spending it like this."

"Yeah, me too. I've gotta go, Achi." Avery swallowed hard, trying to shove down the sob climbing out of her throat.

"I'll text you the details after I make some calls."

Avery fought back tears and recited song lyrics until her breathing steadied. She couldn't go out in public like this, not when she was always so quick to cry. She hated how soppy and weak she felt. This wasn't who she was. This was what Carlos's accident, what the house, was turning her into.

Claudia was right. She had to talk to someone. Her thoughts were nonsensical and chaotic. She didn't even recognize half of them. She missed her friends back home, but she didn't want to admit to them that the big life change she'd been so excited for had turned to shit.

Maybe a psychologist? Avery considered asking Evelyn or Benji for money for therapy, and chuckled mirthlessly to herself. Might as well ask them for a plane ticket. She closed her eyes, imagined what it would feel like to be on a plane ride home, with only the travel gremlin for company. The guilt would never stop following her if she left. Guilt and her soul could carpool all the way back to her body.

She'd help Carlos with his family problem first. If Avery could accomplish what Carlos had come here to do, and figure out what Dolores had mistaken for Carlos's grandfather, the Tams could sell Salcedo Drive and she could return home with a clear conscience.

Over Carlos's dead body.

Avery stiffened. Was that her own thought, or a whisper into her brain? The phrase took on a sinister cast when she considered her husband's frailty. She glanced at the gaps in the wall, grinning at her like missing teeth, and shivered.

CHAPTER ELEVEN

Carlos

Carlos, do you hear that?" Avery mumbled.

He stopped what he was doing, letting go of the lamp he'd been sliding across the night table. The heavy glass had been scratching against the wood, but he'd thought her too deeply asleep to hear. "Hear what?"

Dolores came in then. "Good morning."

"Good morning. Dr. Chen is coming at ten today." Avery yawned and sat up. She pushed herself upright in the bed.

Dolores, who was putting away clean laundry, overheard. "I can make coffee."

Carlos nodded as well. He had a few concerns he wanted to bring up to the doctor, and he'd slept through the last visit. He blinked away the remnants of his dream, the long hallway lined with pictures and the sunlit door at the exit fading as he focused on the women in the room.

"Do you want me to wash Carlos before the doctor gets here?" Dolores asked.

Avery hesitated at the offer. She looked exhausted. She moved sluggishly, and her clothes hung looser on her. He wondered if Avery would agree, if she would accept help to give herself a break.

At least she had stopped crying in her sleep, though she tossed and turned just as much.

"No, thank you." Avery picked up her hairbrush. "I'll take care of it." She peered closer at her brush bristles and cried out in disgust. "Ugh, there are tiny *bugs* all over this."

She flung it onto the vanity and examined her hands and arms. Dolores rushed to get a garbage bag and tied the infested brush inside, muttering prayers Carlos could just barely hear.

When the maid left, he waited for Avery to bring a basin, but she heaved that long sigh he both expected and dreaded, and went to the bathroom in the hallway. She didn't return.

That was fine with him. His parents would come with the specialist, and they'd see how neglectful his wife was. The fact that they weren't here, sitting at his bedside every day, really showed how little he mattered to them. He'd never be their main priority. There were always other people to worry about, and he'd always been so *capable*.

His yaya had been kind, but distracted with an ill mother. He'd had Achi Tessa, who was nurturing and patient, even as a child, and she babied him endlessly. He basked in her attention until he turned eleven, and then their parents had given her permission to get a dog. The moment Sho Pao came into Tessa's life, Carlos was discarded again, a playmate when the puppy was taking a nap, someone to read only two books to instead of a dozen.

When he'd left for school, he'd gravitated toward drama, where he could pretend the audience and their adoration were for him alone, at least until the curtain fell. A few of his girlfriends had become infatuated with him, but he couldn't make himself reciprocate the same intensity.

And then he'd met Avery. She was as stunning then as she was now, and he couldn't take his eyes off her. She was dressed in raggedy jean shorts and an old football jersey, and she drew every eye at the barbecue. Even the way she ate her hamburger was elegant, graceful, alluring. He'd worked up his nerve and approached her with a plastic cup full of wine. Falling in love had never been easier. As smoothly as the sun set, as natural as the grass beneath their feet.

The best day of his life was every day he spent with her. Finally, his hunger for love was sated, equal only to the love he felt for her. They were soulmates, the perfect complement. Carlos had never told her this, of course, because he understood she had no faith in anyone or anything, and refused to believe in anything that couldn't be proven or reproduced in a similar setting.

And then they got married, and she started talking about children. It was like Achi Tessa and Sho Pao again, but worse, because he couldn't imagine losing Avery's love. He lived to make her happy, but he couldn't share her with anyone else. It was too much to ask of him—she might as well have asked for his life. Even that would be easier, because he wouldn't be around to suffer the loss of her.

His mother's voice drifted up the stairs. Carlos tried to clear his throat, to pry his stiff jaws open. He'd tell the doctor about the blackouts, how he wasn't improving as fast as he should be, and they'd take him back to the hospital where he'd actually be cared for. Then he remembered how he'd had to share the nurses with other patients, and seethed with frustration. How could anyone expect to recover from a near-fatal—hell, it *had* been fatal—injury when the help he was getting was so irregular and…impersonal? Frustration and rage choked him. The light streaming through the balcony doors flashed into his eyes, and directly into his brain like incandescent arrows.

Carlos had lost time again. He awoke, frantic, and tried to check the position of the sun. It was raining. He could hear it on the windowpane, but he didn't think he'd been out too long. He saw the doctor in the hallway, standing just outside of his grandparents' room. Had he done his assessment already, and not been alarmed that his patient was unconscious?

"Doctor!" he called, as loud as he could. It was a scratch of nails over bedsheets, a scuff of boots over cement. Practically noiseless. Carlos struck at the lamp on the table beside him with all his strength. It was a feeble blow, but it was enough to topple the light. It smashed loudly on the floor, and the murmur of conversation nearby stopped.

His mother appeared in the doorway then and cried out at the sight of the broken glass. "Sayang, that was brand-new. This house is cursed, Benji. My poor boy." She wept, her careful eyeliner running down her powdered cheeks.

Carlos was speechless. Had he ever seen his mother cry like that for him? Even when he'd left home for Canada, he'd searched for a sign she would miss him, but she was bright-eyed and blowing kisses as he carried his suitcase to baggage check.

"Doctor, please. Can we do anything more? More physiotherapy sessions, or change his diet, or send him back to the hospital?" his dad asked, handing Evelyn a handkerchief and rubbing her back.

Dr. Chen was a middle-aged Chinese man with a straggly beard who spoke English with a Hong Kong accent. "Sure, we could try readmitting him to do some more tests and some more aggressive physiotherapy. I'll call you when I receive his blood test results, but I don't expect anything too abnormal. He's urinating well, his wife says his stool is normal, and I don't notice any signs of organ dysfunction. I really can't explain his lack of progress." The man hesitated and scratched at his chin. "My mentor, who is more old-fashioned, might suggest that the problem is spiritual."

"Spiritual? What does that mean? We've had a priest come already." Evelyn gestured around the room as if house blessings were visible like suspended crepe paper decorations.

"My mentor would say that maybe there are angry spirits around him, keeping him from recovering. Stealing his energy."

"So we should bring him to the hospital for sure, then. Separate him from any spirits, Doctor?" His mother pressed her lips together.

"But you said before…that if he stays in the hospital, he has a higher chance of infection, right?" Benji asked. "Is that more dangerous than him staying here?"

The doctor checked his watch. "There's always an increased risk of infection in hospitals, and in his weakened state, this could be deadly. But there is benefit to being at the hospital too. Namely, it would ease some of the strain on his caregivers."

His mother and father exchanged a long look. "We'll talk about it with his sister and Avery," Benji said finally. "We'll let you know tonight." Dolores came upstairs to clean up the broken lamp, nodding respectfully at the doctor as she passed.

What about him? Carlos raged. What about asking the fucking patient what he needed? He opened his mouth to say exactly that when the doctor's next words stopped him.

"I should remind you that with trauma cases, especially with neurological injuries, time is of the essence. A patient will do the most recovering within the first year of the event, and after that, progression is much slower. If Carlos doesn't improve more swiftly, he may never get back to his baseline."

"We should move him." His mother's voice trembled.

"But an infection could set him back further," Dad argued. "And what if there are spirits in the hospital too?"

"I can't make any guarantees that he'll improve if he's an inpatient, and unfortunately, I can't make the decision for you. Both staying here and readmitting him has benefits and risks." The doctor nodded at them both. "I've got to go to another appointment, but I'll be in touch once the blood tests come through." The doctor walked down the hallway alone, glancing into Lolo's bedroom as he passed.

They'd taken his blood? He hadn't even felt it. Surely if he was asleep, a needlestick would have woken him. His losses of time were deeper than mere slumber, then.

The doctor's words struck him. His recovery was too slow. "I'm scared, Mom. Dad." Carlos rasped. "I don't want to be like this forever."

Dolores gave him a sympathetic look. "We will continue to pray," she murmured comfortingly.

"Aside from prayers, what else can we do? What if we moved him to our house?" his dad replied.

"What if the move makes things worse?" Evelyn wrung her hands together. "He'd be much farther from the hospital if anything were to go wrong. Our new house might have spirits too."

The knot of resentment twisting his bowels seemed to loosen, or maybe that was a child's response to being near his parents and knowing that they cared. His mother had *cried* for him. She never showed deep emotion. Hadn't been able to, after losing her sister.

His parents left as Dolores swept up the shards of lamp. After, the old woman settled herself on one of the armchairs near the balcony. "Your mother brought some lugaw. She made it herself."

"Surprised she had time," Carlos muttered.

Dolores tilted her gray-streaked head at him. "Heh? It's hard to hear you. Speak louder."

"She doesn't come to visit enough." It hurt his throat to shout that way, like steel wool scouring over blistered flesh, but Dolores nodded and sat back.

"It's difficult for Evelyn to see her son this way," Dolores said. "Especially after Estelle."

"That was decades ago."

The old maid sighed. "Seeing you on the bed, half dead, is hard for *me* to see, and she wasn't my sister. Can you imagine what it must be like for your family? It's too much for your mother to relive, Carlos. She shouldn't have had to live through it once."

He shook his head. Old history shouldn't supersede present suffering. "I feel like I've been sidelined by Auntie Estelle's death my whole life." He'd never be able to confide in his family this way, but Dolores was safe as an outsider. "I never even met her, but everyone expects me to understand why my family is the way it is. I've tried to be understanding, but I've never needed my family more, and they're still putting Estelle before me."

Dolores was quiet for a moment. "When you've lost someone so precious as a parent, a sister, it makes you afraid to love again.

Some might hold their love back. Others might get lost in other, darker, emotions. Would you love as freely if you lost Avery?"

The very thought chilled him. He could never love anyone with the same intensity as he loved his wife, no matter how much time had passed. Was that why he was feeling so much resentment toward her? Afraid she would leave him while he lay vulnerable, thus killing him a second time?

"I meant to ask the doctor about my blackouts," he said, instead of sharing the hollow ache of fear in his chest. It felt like a hunger, one that could only be sated by Avery's promise to stay with him forever. The old maid couldn't help with that.

She stared at his reflection in the vanity mirror. "Well, he will come again next week."

"They're talking about sending me back to the hospital." Carlos waited to see what she'd say. "The doctor mentioned bad spirits might be affecting my recovery."

Dolores's lips pursed for a moment, her version of a shrug. "I think you need to relax and let go. Be at ease, and at peace. Do not be so quick to anger, or do anything to further upset Avery."

What was she referring to? Surely, she couldn't know about the whispering woman in the walls, and what he'd asked her to do. Carlos raised both eyebrows, the picture of innocence. "Upset Avery? What are you talking about?"

Dolores turned away from the mirror and looked at him directly. "I'm saying, Carlos, that some of the energies in this house do indeed mean you and your family harm, and it does no one any good for you to encourage them. It lends them strength."

Her words pressed against his lungs like a demon on his chest, shock and elation jostling together. Finally, here was confirmation that the spirits weren't just in his head. Somehow, the whispering woman had power, and she must have scared Avery, just as he'd ordered. Carlos wasn't surprised that Dolores knew of the ghosts; after all, she'd been close to Lolo since she was a teenager. He must have said something to her about them. But for the first time since the accident, Carlos felt a sense of power over his surroundings, a feeling he'd always taken for granted. He was bedridden, sure. But the spirit had reached out like an extension of his will to remind Avery that he still existed.

"I'm tired, Dolores. I think I do need to rest," he said. He turned his head—the movement easier now than it had been a few weeks ago—and closed his eyes. Her footsteps sounded across the room, and then down the hall, and only then did he crack open his eyes.

Carlos had no idea how to call the woman in the walls. "Hello?" he grated out as loud as he could. "Are you there?"

"Hi." It was the little Pinay he'd seen before, wearing an old-fashioned white nightgown, hair split into two braids. She was barefoot.

"Hello." He liked kids well enough, just didn't want his own. "Have you seen the woman that usually speaks to me?"

"She Who Creeps Between?" The little girl switched to Tagalog and pulled at a braid.

"Is that her name?"

"That's what we call her, 'cuz she's always sneaking through walls and under the floor and stuff. You shouldn't talk to her."

"Who is 'we'?" he asked. "That's kind of a long name for a kid to think of."

"I forget who thought of it. One of the adults."

"Are there lots of people here?" Was one of them his grandfather?

The girl shrugged. "Not a lot, but enough. Some fade away."

"I'm looking for an old man who's been here at least ten years." Unless his grandfather had only come back to the house this summer so Dolores could see him. "Has anyone new come into the house?"

She eyed him. "Only the Broken Man."

Carlos blinked. "These are kind of scary-sounding names, you know? What's yours?"

"I can't tell you. I'm not supposed to talk to strangers." The girl looked over her shoulder, back toward the hall.

"Okay, well. Do you know about any bad gho—" At the last moment, Carlos remembered Lolo teaching him that it was taboo to speak to spirits about the dead. "Bad...guys...that might want to hurt me? Keep me from getting better, that kind of thing?"

The Pinay frowned. "I don't think you're gonna get better."

A chill shivered through him. Maybe he didn't like kids that much after all. "Can you call an adult for me, do you think? Someone who can answer some questions?"

She shrugged her skinny brown shoulders. "I can try to see who'll come."

"Thank you." Carlos watched her skip down the hall, dodging the young woman who had begun her pacing down to the last door.

His family and the doctor could talk about him as if he weren't there. Avery could avoid him beyond the most basic of interactions. He had to get better, and if the obstacle was spiritual, then he'd ask the damn ghosts himself.

CHAPTER TWELVE

Avery

She'd loved birthdays, once. There was something about the day that seemed ripe with possibilities, like a Christmas just for her. Though not rich, her parents had lavished their children with presents and attention on these days, and this only intensified after her sister Noelle had passed, as if they were more determined to celebrate the children who remained.

Avery's future had turned from sparkling potential to a barren doom with traitorous inevitability. She didn't mind getting older, barely noticed the deep crease above her nose where she constantly furrowed her brows. If her body was a temple, the ability to conceive, to carry a healthy baby to term, was the treasure she risked everything for. It was a goal at the end of a long tunnel, but each failed month felt like the walls on each side moved inexorably closer, pinching off her only path and crushing her little by little.

Aren't I a ray of sunshine. The new hairbrush Fatima had bought was too soft for Avery's thick hair and just served as a reminder of the awful things she'd seen crawling through her old brush's bristles and making nests within her loose strands of hair. Avery took the effort to put makeup on. It was to brighten her mood, she told herself, and not at all because she wanted to see

Carlos's reaction. They weren't talking much—she was too tired to assume the cheerful attitude she'd maintained for six weeks—but there was so much her husband conveyed with his eyes that her heart fluttered each time she thought of him.

It made her feel slightly ashamed, given his vulnerable state, but the attraction she felt for him was undeniable. His bed baths had become, at least for her, tense with anticipation, Carlos's eyes locked on hers when they weren't fluttering closed. She didn't do anything intimate—she couldn't be sure he was oriented enough or that he was able to consent, but lust for the man beneath her husband's skin, whoever he was, had infiltrated her dreams, despite her exhaustion, until she wanted to punch the walls in frustration.

It had been years since she'd felt such a physical pull—for anyone, really. Her infertility had made their lovemaking a source of anxiety and tinged the act with a sense of reluctant duty, like an annual Pap smear. And of course, now that her urges had returned with a vengeance, she couldn't sate them. Not with her husband, and not in this house, where the silence watched and the shadows whispered.

Resentment followed her lust like a dark shadow. Her needs, like her need to have children, were again pushed aside for Carlos's.

When she went to see him this morning, he was holding a small mirror in his hand. He'd been slowly getting stronger—*too* slowly, according to Dr. Chen—and every small step of progress made Avery take a step back from despair.

But she was still so close to the edge.

The physiotherapist hadn't been able to get him to stand, or move on his own, but the exercises kept his muscles from atrophying further.

Avery stayed in the hallway, though the basin of soapy water was heavy, and watched Carlos for a minute. He stared at his features like he was studying them. It wasn't the careless look he'd once given himself as he groomed, the quick assessment before heading out the door. The look on his face as he stared at his reflection was like he was relearning the contours of his cheekbones, the straight ridge of his nose. Like they were strange to him.

"Good morning, Carlos," she said as she pushed the door fully open. He dropped his arms to his sides and smiled at her. He was more responsive now that they'd cut his morphine dose down, and he slept less.

She rushed through his care today—teeth, bath, breakfast—trying to be clinical like a nurse, barely meeting his eyes or looking at the body she cared for. She was supposed to meet Tessa for a late lunch, and maybe afterward she would be able to make sense of her feelings.

"I'm going to meet Achi Tessa for lunch," she told him. "Because I don't want to spend my birthday alone."

She intended to hurt him, despite the feelings she felt growing between them, which might very well be one-sided. It was as if her resentment had died and came back to possess her, or maybe she was just hurting so much she wanted to make someone else suffer too. Whatever the reason, Avery was unprepared for the look of sorrow that filled Carlos's eyes. Was that sadness meant for himself, that he was being left alone, or for her, that she should spend her thirty-seventh birthday in this awful situation? As usual, she couldn't tell. The uncertainty about his thoughts and feelings twisted inside her, adding fuel to her cruelty. Or maybe it was the constant whispering sensation in her ears, the tickle of imaginary bugs on her skin waking her from sleep, the malevolent energy of this tomb-like house.

"I wish you'd do more than just lie there," she snapped, and then immediately regretted it. Her feelings for him were a complicated maelstrom of contradictions, of half-swallowed words and fervent apologies. "I'm sorry. I'm sorry... I just—fuck. I know you can't help this, babe. I'm just...fucking exhausted."

As Avery fled from the room, ashamed of her outburst, it occurred to her that maybe his sorrow was for the both of them.

Tessa had sent Bernie to pick her up. On the drive, Avery looked out the window at the country her parents had come from, at the place that was rapidly feeling like her home. She tried to imagine her mom sitting in the bicycle rickshaw at the stoplight, the pedicab outmaneuvering the larger motorized vehicles. Most of the cars here looked like older models, boxy and ungraceful, but well cared for. She pictured her dad walking in a light-brown business suit in the sweltering heat, his hair still styled in the seventies' side sweep she'd seen in the family photo album.

Avery leaned her head against the window, as if she could join this world if she only moved close enough. She wanted to absorb this change in environment—God, how long had it been since she'd seen so many people?—but the relief of leaving Salcedo Drive was like taking off a painfully tight dress. Despite the misty condensation blasting from the car aircon and the heavy perfume of diesel oil combined with melting asphalt, Avery fell asleep.

She woke up when the car stopped. Tessa had asked her if she liked sushi, so Avery had expected a Japanese restaurant. Instead,

Bernie pulled into another gated property. Were the fancy places to eat also secured like Fort Knox?

"Avery!" squealed Tessa, bounding from the front door to meet the car. Her hair was newly shaved on the sides and swept back like an ocean wave in the middle. "Happy birthday, Sis!"

It felt good to hug someone. Instead of letting go after a moment, Avery found herself clutching harder. Was this what the rest of her life would be? Holding embraces long past the point of politeness just to feel human contact?

Her sister-in-law had started to move away, but tightened her arms around Avery. "I know, girl. I know. You're doing amazing. We're so grateful for you," Tessa murmured against her shoulder, and Avery had to step back from her to—*what a surprise*—wipe away tears.

"It's just really nice to be out of the house for a bit," Avery explained, suddenly embarrassed. Before she and Carlos moved here, she'd only met her sister-in-law twice. What must Tessa think of her?

"No one's gonna judge you here. Come on in, get yourself together." Tessa took the lead and walked through the front door.

"Is this your place?" Avery asked as she followed. "I thought you lived in a condo."

Tessa spun away from the entrance so that Avery stood alone in the doorframe. Avery had a half second of warning to school her expression before people jumped out of doorways.

"Happy birthday!"

Carlos's parents, grandmother, and Father Michael beamed at her. Tessa clapped her hands together at the smile Avery plastered on her face. "I didn't want to let your birthday pass without some sort of celebration."

"Thank you so much," Avery said, still grinning. She couldn't think of anything she wanted less. She wanted a break from tension and from talking about Carlos, and now she was going to be interrogated by the very people who blamed her. "Are we all going out for sushi?" In public, she might be safer from prying questions and accusations.

"Even better." Benji gestured to a doorway behind them. "We've hired our own private sushi chef for the night."

"How wonderful," Avery responded. "Did he bring any sake, by any chance?"

The night hadn't been so bad, especially with alcohol. The sushi was amazing, the chef a wonderful showman. Evelyn, perhaps forewarned by Tessa, or suppressed by Father Michael, didn't bring up Carlos, but neither did she speak very much to Avery.

Benji matched Avery cup for cup and fell asleep in his seat, cheeks flushed pink, before the last course was served. Michael and Tessa bantered good-naturedly until Avery giggled herself to hiccups.

She found herself smiling as Bernie drove her home, playing some eighties music that reminded Avery of her childhood. It was spitting rain, and she stared at the droplets on her window, vibrating in place until they melded with another drop and streaked down the window like a tiny comet. That was her and Carlos, she thought. They'd been stable alone, and once they fell in love, they'd melded together and pulled each other down. The somber thought stole the joy she'd tried to hoard inside herself, and when Fatima opened the gate to Salcedo Drive, the delicious fish and alcohol she'd eaten this afternoon turned sour in her stomach.

Avery walked unsteadily from the car past the front door, carrying leftover cake and sake. She leaned against the closed door, staring down the hallway that felt like a tunnel deep underground. The house was just as shadow-filled and claustrophobic as the first day they'd arrived. The dark rectangle where the picture frame used to hang stuck out like a hole in the wall. The atmosphere settled over her as if she carried a corpse on her shoulders, and try as she might, Avery couldn't remember a single joke that had made her laugh hysterically just an hour ago.

"Ma'am?" Fatima loomed close. In Avery's inebriated state, the maid's face was distorted, like the maid wore a fishbowl over her head.

"Why don't you and Dolores take the night off?" Avery murmured. "I'm just going to see to Carlos and go to bed."

"Do you need help with Kuya?"

Avery cleared her throat and tried to look sober. "No. We'll be fine. Enjoy your night."

She waited until she heard the maids leave. Moving carefully, she put aside enough cake for them and Carlos. Avery grabbed a fork and a glass before sitting at the dining table with a slice for herself and her phone.

She typed in any search term that came to mind, looked for any explanation to explain old houses that made their inhabitants feel watched, that filled them with dread, that threw picture frames to the floor and made noises like footsteps on the creaky hardwood and incessantly whispered like an invisible buzzing fly. Houses that kept sick people from recovering.

She skimmed the links as she scrolled, pausing every so often to eat more cake, gulp more sake. Vampires that separated at the waist and fed upon the living. Angry ghosts that stole the vitality of humans. Witches that used insects to commit their foul deeds. Curses placed by jealous neighbors so all in a house would suffer.

Hell, any one of these could explain what she'd experienced. Avery couldn't pretend any longer. In this old land of superstition and folklore, where everyone seemed to believe in God or spirit or fate, why couldn't such impossibilities be true?

A link to an episode of *Convince Carlos* slid on the screen as she scrolled. The temptation was too strong tonight, and finally Avery succumbed to the desire she'd been fighting since Carlos's accident. Tapping on the link, she shoveled the rest of the cake in her mouth and emptied the bottle of sake. The clear liquid burned as it slid down her throat, a welcome warmth that felt like she'd swallowed sunlight.

Her thoughts weren't nearly so bright. To see her husband on the episode, grinning with his easy charm and moving so effortlessly—she had taken everything for granted. She drank in his gestures, the confident way he spoke, which she had started to find so pompous. What she wouldn't give to have this strong version of him back, where she could roll her eyes and be honest with him without feeling like she was breaking his heart.

Carlos and his crew were in a historic restaurant, where patrons and staff had sworn a man with a cane stomped up and down the stairs and a ghostly barmaid rattled the hanging wineglasses before she faded away.

"They say that the trick to seeing ghosts"—her husband turned to the viewer and lowered his voice huskily, as if he were imparting a secret—"is to recreate the conditions where they were first seen. Was there a loud party before the sighting? Had everyone been drinking?" His expression turned solemn. "We've heard of a case in a hospital where only the dying could see the spirit of a nurse."

Avery turned off the video and rubbed at her eyes, not caring that she smeared her makeup in the process. Seeing Carlos healthy emphasized how far he'd deteriorated, and how far he had to recover.

She swirled the clear sake in the glass and contemplated her choices: She could abandon Carlos and spend the rest of her life hating herself, or she could stay and spend the rest of her life hating him. It was seeming more and more unlikely that her husband was going to return to the man she knew—as small a chance as her conceiving, at this point. A voice whispered in her ear, or maybe it was in her mind: *What use is your life, when everything you wanted from it is gone?*

There was a third choice she could make, one that seemed to hold the least suffering. Avery stared upward at the ceiling, as if she could see past layers of plaster and wood and wires to where Carlos lay. Beside him were bottles of morphine he no longer needed; enough morphine to ease her own pain. She was so tired, and the sudden plan to escape became a yellow-brick road, gleaming with promised reward.

Was it another insect buzzing against the shrouded mirror, or a voice whispering, "Do it?"

Still holding her glass, Avery stumbled upstairs and to Carlos's bedside table. She stuffed two nearly full prescription bottles of morphine into her pockets. At the doorway, she turned around to peek at her husband. He lay still, of course, chest rising and falling steadily. Avery gazed at Carlos's high cheekbones, fine brow, full lips, and her resolve weakened. She loved him so much it scared her, so much she'd consider giving up everything she wanted just to stay at his side. Her suffering was the grief of losing the future she'd dreamed of, but it was also grieving for Carlos's future. He was only forty, fit and healthy before the accident. All the tests had come back clear. Why wasn't he healing?

Dr. Chen's words crossed her mind then. Angry spirits stealing his energy, preventing his recovery. It was ludicrous. A medical doctor should know better than to spout such bullshit in front of a desperate family. And yet…she *had* seen a picture frame leap from the wall. She'd seen someone walk across the bathroom when she was in the shower.

What was it that the yellow-toothed medium had said about sensing ghosts? It wasn't just mirrors and candles. It was a different way of seeing, like the rods and cones of your eyes becoming aware of another wavelength of light that wasn't visible to everyone else. She'd remembered that, because she'd just watched a nature documentary about bees, and how some orchids had ultraviolet colorations on their petals, like landing strips, that the human eye could only see with special instruments. But it drew the bees.

To get the same effect, she'd have to reproduce the same conditions. Avery pushed the rest of the thought through the despair closing around her. The shower had been hot, the shower glass steamy.

Slowly, as if in a dream, she exhaled into her glass and watched her breath fog the sides. She raised it up to her face, but her eyes wouldn't open. *I can't.* She lowered the glass back to her side and stared at Carlos. There was nothing there. She was acting irrationally. Of course there was nothing supernatural near him. But then why were her knees trembling; why was sweat tickling a trail down her temples?

Avery fogged the glass again, clenching her eyes shut. She steeled herself, raising her right hand up to her face. She blinked open one eye and gazed through the blurred glass as if looking through an old camera.

God almighty!

She jumped back so far she almost went over the stair railing in the hallway. Avery scrambled away on her knees and one hand, still clutching the glass with one sweaty palm. There *was* something squatting on Carlos. Something grayish and ephemeral, like a corpse made of dandelion fluff. Something that didn't quite fit into his frame, but lay half inside his body, the other half suspended in the air.

Whatthefuckwhatthefuckwhatthefuckwhatthefuck—

Avery ran into the bathroom and gripped the sink with both hands. She retched, keeping as quiet as she could, to avoid waking Carlos. That was it. That was the last goddamn straw. There was quite enough reason to end things with a half-dead husband and a grim future. This fucking…ghost possession was just icing on the cake. She was out. Not playing anymore. Let someone else deal with this shit.

Her hands shook so badly it took her a few tries to open the childproof cap on one of the prescription bottles. Avery filled the glass with water from the sink and poured a handful of pills into her palm. She tried to hold on to happy memories, to leave the world with a smile, but the despair around and inside her was too thick. It was too heavy to be hers alone; it was the despair of many decades of suffering, like lead paint layered thick over the walls. Poisoning her.

And through it all, there was the incessant whispering voice she heard in her sleep. It seemed to come from the sink drain. "Do it. Swallow them all."

A shuffling noise came from the hallway behind her. Dolores and Fatima had left an hour ago, she was sure of it. Another slither of sound behind her, the slide of cloth against wood. She glanced at the small mirror above the sink, but no one stood behind her.

Just her reflection in the bathroom mirror, watching her. Daring her to be brave, for once. The very walls leaned in, begged Avery to take her life, to escape. Die quickly now, or face decades of slow death within Salcedo Drive. The voice from the sink goaded and mocked her cowardice.

Fuck this. Avery jammed the first handful of pills into her mouth and raised the glass full of water.

A strong hand grabbed at her wrist, scaring her enough to lose her grip.

Glass shattered on the new white marble. Avery turned to see who clenched her arm.

It was Carlos, supported by one arm, legs sprawled behind him on the bathroom floor. His eyes were wide with fear.

"Don't," he wheezed.

CHAPTER THIRTEEN

Avery

She spat the pills out into the toilet. The import of what she had just tried to do filled her with a sense of shock. *What the hell was I thinking?* She thought of her parents, grieving another lost daughter, of Claudia and Henry losing another older sister. Avery raised a shaking hand to her mouth before she turned to look at the floor.

"How did you get here?" Avery asked her husband. "How did you know?"

Carlos slid himself away from the broken glass with effort. He was panting, so out of breath he couldn't answer.

"Let me help you." Somehow, with her taking most of his weight and with frequent rests, they were able to return Carlos to the bed. She collapsed beside him, the room spinning from exertion and drink. Sudden giddiness, inappropriate under the circumstances, pushed away the memory of what she'd seen through the fogged glass. "I can't believe the catheter didn't fall off. I should put my tube taping skills down on my resume."

He smiled wanly beside her, and at the sign of him responding to her silly joke, despite what she'd almost done—she began to sob. It didn't matter how he'd known, whether ghost or God or otherwise: She was just overjoyed that Carlos had stopped her. And not only stopped her, he'd moved without any help.

Carlos raised his hand, still trembling from his efforts, and reached out to cup her cheek. She smiled through her tears at him, and closed her eyes as his fingers stroked the line of her jaw. His breath tingled on her face like a blessing.

From the day they'd met, Avery always felt they'd had a magnetic attraction between them, like her very cells pulled toward his, simultaneously energized and soothed by his touch. They'd been fighting so much before they'd moved here that the draw she felt toward him had become muddled.

This moment of reconnection, after months of resentment, and after each of them had been pulled from the brink of death, was like falling back in love. Human words were too clumsy to describe such a miracle.

And it *was* a miracle: Carlos had fought past the pain, the weakness of his injured body, and the house's influence to stop her. She sensed the effect of Salcedo Drive now, the suffering that seeped from the building itself like a gas leak, poisoning them all. Looking into Carlos's alert eyes, feeling his fingers tremble against her face; it filled her lungs with fresh air and chased the corruption from her bloodstream. Her proud, aloof husband had dragged his weakened body across the floor to act as her savior. The very idea filled Avery with wild regret and an equally intense joy—it was her fault he'd had to go to such an extreme, and yet she couldn't ask for stronger proof that he loved her more than he loved himself.

It was an act more powerful than wedding vows, more important than their fights. Carlos's gesture tonight branded her heart, claiming it as his own forever more.

They gazed at each other, held each other as if afraid of letting go. For the first time since his accident, Avery slept within Carlos's arms, and not a footstep, not a dream disturbed her.

Weak sunlight reached the bedroom window, illuminated a square of dark curtain, but did not penetrate the room. Dawn had tiptoed in, and for a moment Avery worried that what had happened last night wasn't real, that she'd crawled into bed atrociously drunk and accosted a sick man.

"Carlos?" she whispered, suddenly afraid. He looked so still, so peaceful, she couldn't see him breathe. He couldn't be—

His long eyelashes fluttered and he blinked his eyes open. He smiled upon seeing her, like he had so many mornings before the accident. Avery kissed him. He hesitated at first, lips tensing, but after a moment he kissed her back. His hands slid up her back, and she moaned at the caress, every sensation intensified because she hadn't believed she'd ever feel it again.

He pulled back.

"You don't feel ready?" she asked him, trying to hide her disappointment. *Eager much?* "I understand. I'm sorry, I've just missed you. I was so scared."

Carlos's brows drew together, and he cleared his throat. "I've missed you too." Pain flickered across his face as he spoke, and his voice was hoarse, but she heard him clearly. Somehow, her husband had returned to her.

Avery sent a group message to the Tams: HE'S BACK TO NORMAL!!

She stared at her husband, filled with a gratitude that beat back even the sobering effects of the house. He looked better than she'd ever seen him, as if something had happened last night that had pushed him past whatever blocked his path to recovery. "Avery, there's something I have to tell you."

There was such a look of *wonder* in his eyes when he looked at her, like she was the only woman in the world he could ever want. "Is it good news or bad?"

Carlos hesitated. "It's unbelievable."

The front door shuddered with loud knocking, interspersed with doorbell rings.

Avery waited for Fatima's or Dolores's footsteps before she remembered she'd sent them home. How quickly one grew accustomed to help.

Her phone buzzed. Open the door! Tessa messaged.

"Your sister is here," Avery told Carlos, moving to check her reflection before remembering the mirror was covered. "I'm going to let her in."

He nodded. Was she ever going to stop marveling at his merest response? After six weeks of drought, she couldn't stop appreciating the sensation of water on her parched tongue.

"My parents are right behind me," Tessa said by way of greeting. She kicked off her sandals and ran upstairs without bothering to put on slippers. Manila air followed her in, moist and warm.

Avery stepped onto the front porch to wait, but spied Fatima closing the gate. She waved at the young woman and headed inside, leaving the doors unlocked before hurrying back to Carlos's side.

Tessa hadn't done her hair or makeup, and the woman looked younger with a clean face. She had plopped beside her brother at the head of the bed, squeezing one of his hands. Carlos held a protein shake in the other, the plastic bottle shaking slightly in his unsteady grip.

"What happened? Why the sudden improvement?" Tessa asked.

Avery's cheeks heated. She didn't want to talk about what she'd almost done last night, what Carlos had saved her from.

Carlos met her eyes and cleared his throat. "I just…felt better," Carlos whispered. She felt a rush of gratitude for her husband. He took another sip from his shake.

Rapid footsteps thudded up the stairs, and Carlos's parents appeared. Evelyn was still draped in gold. Perhaps she slept with her jewelry, but her permed hair was smashed flat on one side. Unlike Tessa, she looked older without makeup, but her face lit up when she saw her son and years fell away. Benji gave a glad shout at the sight of Carlos propped upright on pillows, and the Tams began speaking in rapid-fire Hokkien.

Avery slipped out the door to give them time to catch up. She went downstairs to the den, a room she'd only been in once, when they'd first moved in. It looked small, maybe because the three walls were lined with large sofas, and a large-screen TV dominated the last wall. The three remote controls were confusing to her—there was one for a stereo system that played the television audio and another for streaming movies. She managed to turn on the television for some background noise. There was a Filipino telenovela playing, the Tagalog unintelligible to her, but who really cared about watching a soap opera when she was living one? Tucked neatly against the corner of the couch was a bundle of white cloth. Avery unfolded it, curious. A vivid rainbow of thread colors fell into her lap. Someone was embroidering a beautiful garden scene.

Dolores passed by the room, holding a cup. She did a double

take when she saw Avery and then came in, setting the drink in front of her. "I was looking for you. Here is some coffee."

"Did you have your coffee? Why don't you join me?" Avery was overcome with gratitude this morning, and she wanted to share her joy. Judging from the way Dolores raised her eyebrows, this was an unusual request.

"I will get my drink." The older woman returned and, rather than sinking into the deep leather couch, sat on the edge of her seat.

"Are you comfortable?" Avery wondered if Dolores was here because she saw Avery's invitation as an instruction rather than a request. There was so much she didn't know about living here, and she didn't know if she was breaking some etiquette between employer and employee, even one who had worked for the Tams longer than Avery had lived.

Dolores sipped her coffee. "Comfortable enough. At my age, if I sit too far back, I can't stand up again."

"You've worked for the family a long time." Avery smiled. "I remember seeing you in Carlos's childhood photo albums."

"Almost my whole life. Kuya and Ate took me in when my parents died, raised me as one of their own children. I am a year older than Evelyn." Dolores threw a glance at Avery's direction before returning her attention to the television.

"In Canada, most people retire in their sixties. Is that an option for you?" Avery didn't want to see Dolores go, but if it was a matter of money…

The old maid shook her head. "I retired years ago. When Kuya got older…he asked me to come back, to watch over his family. Over this house."

"But surely now that everyone is grown and independent... When are you allowed to rest?"

Dolores drained her coffee. "I made a promise to Kuya, and I will do my best to fulfill it, even if I die trying."

What the hell kind of blood oath did Carlos's grandfather make his maids sign? Avery looked away from the grim expression on Dolores's face.

"Is this your needlework? It's beautiful. I've always wanted to learn."

The old maid shrugged. "I can teach you. It just takes practice."

Tessa's voice echoed through the halls. "Avery?"

"Here, Achi," Avery called.

Grunting, Dolores stood up. "I will start making breakfast. Do you want anything special?"

"Whatever you feel like. Salamat, Dolores."

Tessa breezed by the old maid, pausing to give her a peck on the cheek. "I miss seeing your wrinkled face. Always reminds me to take my prunes."

"And when I see you, it always makes me want to drink." The old maid tsked and pretended to spank Tessa before both women broke into laughter. Avery's sister-in-law plopped down in the spot Dolores had recently vacated. "My parents wanted to pray the rosary with Carlos. I said I'd do mine later, after breakfast." She yawned. "And maybe a nap. Oh, yeah. Carlos wanted me to ask you to text some guy on his show to make sure the crew in Manila is still getting paid while he's recovering."

Avery froze. "What?"

"Do you know what he's talking about?" Tessa asked.

"Yes, but..." But Carlos never thought about his crew, not here and not in Canada. They were there to support him, not the other way around. For him to mention paying them as soon as he regained proper speech...that wasn't like him. She shrugged the thought away. "I'm glad I have this moment to talk to you alone, Achi. I don't know if your parents mentioned what Dr. Chen said, about Carlos and spirits?" She had to tell someone about what she'd seen coming out of Carlos last night.

Tessa shrugged. "Maybe they mentioned something, but it doesn't matter now. Oh look, I love this commercial! The model looks just like you."

It was a pretty poor attempt at changing the subject, but Avery played along and looked at the screen. A pregnant woman wearing a maternity dress smiled down at her swollen belly. Avery thought that nothing could have ruined her good mood, but she was usually so careful to avoid these images. She watched the commercial, heart aching, until it changed to an ad for skin whitening cream.

Tessa stared at her, no doubt waiting to see Avery's reaction at the similar-looking model. "What's wrong?" Her eyes widened. "I didn't mean it as an insult, I think the woman is beautiful, like you."

Avery forced a smile. "Thank you. If only she and I could be similarly blessed." She placed a hand on her flat stomach.

"I'm sorry," Tessa said. Her voice was subdued. "I didn't realize you and Carlos wanted children."

"It's not important. Not now, anyway. I really wanted to ask what you know about spirits and how they can affect recovery." Avery didn't know how much of their personal lives Carlos and his sister shared, but there was no way she could talk about her infertility with anyone. Not without crying, and stealing the joy that had filled Tessa's face since she'd seen her brother this morning. And right now, the strange, bone-gray glow she'd seen fitting poorly inside Carlos's body was more important.

But her sister-in-law would not be deterred. "In a way it's good you don't have children. You're busy enough helping Carlos recover. But once he's better, you should focus on kids. The older you are, the harder it is. That's what I've heard, anyway."

"If it were up to me, we would have had a kid two years ago." Avery tried to keep her voice light, but she couldn't ignore Tessa's unsolicited advice. As if focusing on conceiving was all that was required. "Even with specialists and medications, it isn't always so easy."

"Oh girl." Tessa reached over to pat her hand. "I had no idea. You should have told me, I know so many people who swear by Chinese herbs. And acupuncture's supposed to help, too. And I'm gonna start praying a novena for you today."

A dozen conflicting thoughts raced through Avery's mind. She'd come to Manila for exactly this hope, that Chinese traditional medicine might help where hormone injections and pills could not. But what was the point in starting all that now, when Carlos hadn't fully recovered? And Tessa's offer to pray for her...it was no different than the other platitudes Avery had heard since arriving here, things that annoyed her but she'd swallowed graciously. Today was different. She was hungover, emotionally wrung out, and couldn't understand why Tessa wouldn't answer her question about spirits. Despite her earlier desire to protect Tessa's happiness, Avery's self-control broke.

"Only the uneducated or the very gullible would believe that muttering words into the air will change an outcome," she said, trying and failing to keep the bitterness from her voice. "If you believe there's a God, and that he is all-powerful, then you must also believe that he's the one who put you in that situation in the first place. Why would he cure anyone he's chosen to die?"

Tessa's eyes widened. "Whoa. Avery, I have a feeling you're talking about more than babies right now."

Evelyn appeared in the doorway, eyes snapping with anger. *Oh shit*. The sight of her mother-in-law was enough to shove Avery back from her outburst, and the roiling anger inside her cooled. She couldn't think of anything else she might have said that would make her religious mother-in-law hate her more. Awkward silence invaded the room like an unwanted daughter-in-law.

To dispel the tension, Avery scrambled to explain. "I'm sorry, Mom. I know your family is very devout. My parents are too. But when my older sister got leukemia, prayers didn't help. Nothing did. And I hated when people told me to 'have faith' that Noelle would get better. As if it was our fault when she didn't. As if she died because we didn't pray hard enough, because our faith wasn't strong enough."

After so many years, her well of tears had dried up, even if the grief was an ever-flowing river streaming inside her. Avery had only ever said these thoughts to Claudia or Henry, and in front of her in-laws, it felt like she was admitting to a shameful crime.

Evelyn's face softened in sympathy, and she stepped over Tessa's legs to sit in the space beside Avery. Her mother-in-law took Avery's hands, the gold rings cool and heavy against Avery's skin. "I lost my sister when I was young, too. She was sick for a few weeks, and we did everything we could."

"It's hard." Avery spoke past the lump in her throat. Perhaps the well of tears hadn't run totally dry. "Most of it happened in the hospital, and I was in school, but what I remember…and near the end, when all we were doing was waiting, and praying…" She shook her head. "It's hard to explain how bad that time was to people who haven't lived it. If I didn't have my sister and brother…I don't think anyone else would understand."

Her mother-in-law frowned. "My mother refused to let us talk about it. It was too painful for my parents, and she didn't see the point in dwelling in bad memories. And my brothers are the same. In a way, you're lucky, because you had people you could speak to."

Avery's eyes filled with tears. Suddenly the woman before her wasn't the disapproving mother-in-law she could never please—it was her own mother back in Canada, mourning Noelle privately, unable to share her grief. Would Avery's guilt for not being able to comfort her own parents be assuaged if she helped Evelyn? "You can tell me, Mom. I'll understand."

"It's better to forget." Evelyn withdrew her hands from Avery's grip. "No sense in reopening old wounds." And yet she didn't leave. She waited, her posture stiff, as if waiting for Avery's response. As if waiting for permission.

Avery tried again, the way she should have done with her own mother. "I still dream about Noelle dying. And before, when I woke up, it used to feel like I needed to mourn her all over again. Do you ever dream about Estelle?"

Evelyn's lips pressed together, but she nodded.

Avery leaned closer. "Now, when I dream of her, I tell Claudia or Henry, and they do the same with me. And then it feels less like I'm grieving for her death alone, and more like I'm remembering her life with people who loved her too. Like she's visiting us from wherever she is to say she's still thinking of us."

Tessa threw her arm over her mother's shoulders. "Maybe it's like cooking. No amount of vegetables or salt is gonna cover up the taste of bad chicken—you have to get the meat out of the pot."

Evelyn didn't lean into her daughter's embrace. She stayed rigid and upright, but her gaze went distant, as if she could see through the dark wood-paneled wall. "We sat vigil by Estelle's bedside. We never left her alone. How many nights of sleep did we lose, just watching for every breath? This was Manila in the sixties—half the time the electricity didn't work. No phones, no television in her room, the aircon off so she wouldn't get a chill. I watched the minutes pass on the clock, while the heat made me drowsy and the mosquitoes buzzed against the window screen. I didn't know how to help her; I was only thirteen. So I'd brush her hair, over and over, because she used to like it when I did her hair. None of the doctors knew what was wrong, or why she wouldn't get better. And then my father left us, desperate to find a cure. He was gone when she..." Tears flowed down Evelyn's cheeks, and she grimaced. "I try not to think about that time, but I do dream about it so often. I feel like I never stop losing her, that she's still here in this house."

"Will you tell me about your next dream of her? To see if it helps?" Avery asked.

Evelyn took a tissue from Tessa. "Maybe. It feels strange to finally talk about her. Like letting her into my life, after so long."

She straightened up, and Avery watched her mother-in-law regain her composure.

"Mom!" Tessa threw her arms around both of them, sniffling. "Why didn't you talk to us? I would have listened!"

"I know, anak. But it's different when you haven't had the same loss."

They stayed for the rest of the day, lowering their voices when Carlos slept and taking turns to sit with him when he was awake. The tension between Evelyn and Avery had been replaced with the bond of shared trauma—at least, that was how Avery felt about things. She'd never been good at knowing what other people thought or felt. But she understood now why Evelyn had limited her visits until Carlos was on the mend.

Avery wanted to ask them about how spirits could affect healing, but she didn't want to ruin the mood. She suspected Tessa was holding back with her own questions about infertility, judging by the way she kept looking at Avery.

Right before Tessa ran upstairs to say goodbye to Carlos, she pulled Avery aside. "I'll come by tomorrow after dinner, okay? We can talk to the spirits. But Dolores cannot be in the house!"

Avery wanted to refuse Tessa's suggestion. Her mind filled with the horror movies Carlos had once loved: The hauntings always worsened when people dabbled in the occult. And yet, Avery needed to know what was happening in this house, and with her husband.

She pressed her lips together and nodded. What else could she do?

After her in-laws had gone, the house rang with emptiness. Avery tried to hold on to the afternoon's laughter and conversation as she went upstairs, but it slipped through her fingers like sand. The gauntlet of bedrooms awaited her, and though the setting sun filled the first two rooms, casting slanted rectangles of light across her path, it did nothing to ward away the gloom. Dread crawled over her shoulders to settle around her like an old shawl, and as always,

Avery fought the urge to hurry through the narrow hallway. She was passing Tessa's old room when the creak of wood stopped her. It was rhythmic and high-pitched, and coming from Lolo's room.

Her first thought was that Carlos had somehow pulled himself into his grandfather's rocking chair, but he hadn't recovered *that* much. She peeked through the crack in the slightly open door. The dark curtains cut the light that filled the other two rooms, but she couldn't see anything beyond the wall. The creaks were definitely coming from here, grating like an off-key violin.

Avery frowned. Dolores often visited the room, which was her choice, but this noise would wake the dead, never mind Carlos.

She pushed open the door to ask the old woman to be quieter, but the words caught in her throat. Dolores wasn't even in the room. The empty chair rocked back and forth. As Avery watched, frozen and disbelieving, the chair slowed to a stop. She might have stood there the whole night, her limbs shaking and disobedient, but the door slammed closed, hard enough to hurt, and she stumbled out of the way.

Whatever errand had sent her upstairs was long forgotten. Avery scrambled on hands and feet toward the stairs, calling for Dolores and Fatima as if they could save her from what she'd just seen.

CHAPTER FOURTEEN

Carlos

It was about time his family visited for longer. Their presence lifted the oppressive gloom in the house, chased it back with Tessa's loud laugh and his dad's lame jokes. Even his mom's voice, bossing Dolores around imperiously, was familiar and comforting.

When they were here, She Who Creeps Between was silent. Carlos wasn't entirely happy about that—something had shifted last night, and even if he hadn't felt the change in his own body, Avery's cheerful mood this morning made it obvious she'd sensed it too. Carlos suspected the spirit would have the answers. He didn't know her name, didn't know how to summon her. Whenever he'd asked what her name was, she'd sidestep his question.

The little girl hadn't come back, nor sent someone to speak to him. He'd even tried calling for the young woman pacing in the hallway, but she ignored him. Other ghosts passed his line of sight through the open doorway, like fish darting from beneath lily pads.

Carlos stared at Tessa's charm, still hanging on the door hook. Over time, the palm fronds had dried and turned rigid. He wondered if he wanted the thing to fall off, if he could get answers faster if the spirits were allowed in the room. Though he was making progress, he wasn't strong enough yet to leave the room whenever he wanted.

A few times a day, when he was sure Avery or the maids wouldn't catch him, he crawled across the room, painfully slow. In bed, he practiced basic motor movements—pick up the clock, push the pillow. The efforts unraveled him, making him foggy with exhaustion until blinding light took over his vision, a precursor to him losing consciousness, but he was determined to improve. He couldn't spend his life stuck in a room, simultaneously resenting Avery while depending on her. He'd behave himself, use her love for him, until he didn't need her anymore.

"Is anyone there?" he rasped. The pain still made him flinch, but he was getting louder. He'd managed to call Dolores in a few times when he'd heard her footsteps thumping past, but she never stayed long, and she'd turned strange since his accident, alternating between telling him to rest or encouraging him to keep moving. As if he had decided to be bedridden.

"Hello?" Tessa said from the hallway.

Finally. "Achi, come in here."

Tessa came in, wearing her headphones and holding her phone. "You rang?"

"What's everyone doing?" he asked.

She didn't answer at first. He was preparing to repeat himself when she spoke, voice thoughtful, eyes resting on the wedding photo Avery had placed on the night table, as if Tessa preferred to see the way he used to be. That made two of them. "Avery and Mom are bonding over losing a sibling. I think it was really good for them."

They should have been bonding over caring for him. "Will you stay with me for a bit, Achi?" Carlos asked. "I'm lonely."

His sister fell silent, a concerned expression on her round face.

"Fatima, the new maid at the house, found broken glass in the rice container when she was scooping rice. She cut her hand pretty badly, and she's convinced it's one of the ghosts," Tessa told him.

"Something probably broke when they were packaging it in the factory," he said.

"It's the second time this happened, and Dolores, the other maid, made sure this bag was safe when she poured it into the container."

He frowned. "I know who our maids are." Was this a new way for Achi to tease him?

Evelyn's voice called up from the stairs, and Tessa turned to look out the door, pulling her headphones away from one ear as she listened to their mother. "Sorry, we're going now. I'll call you when I get home, okay?"

Carlos sighed. At least they'd stayed for a few hours this time. "Thanks for your support," he said, but his hoarse voice didn't convey the sarcasm. "Don't bother calling me."

She was still talking as she turned her back to him and left. Carlos thought his sister was speaking to an older man in the middle of the hallway. His features were blurred at this distance, but he looked familiar. Maybe a cousin he hadn't seen in a while.

Tessa walked right through him.

She didn't flinch, even as Carlos did. He might have grown accustomed to the spirits in this house, but something inside him reacted to the wrongness of the living intermingling with the dead. In *Convince Carlos*, witnesses spoke of cold spots, places in rooms where the temperature inexplicably dropped. It was believed that humans could sense the close proximity of entities in this way, but

Tessa's lack of reaction suggested something much worse—that ghosts could surround someone, even pass through their body or follow them home, and the person would have no idea.

Carlos pushed past his instinct to cower, which always came when he saw a spirit—even now, when they'd proven more constant companions than the living. He waited to call out, afraid Tessa would overhear. Feeling a bit foolish, he tried waving to get the man's attention. For the first time, Carlos understood his grandfather's strange gestures that seemed to be aimed at nothing.

As if the thought had summoned the man, the spirit moved closer until it stood outside his grandparents' bedroom. Carlos recognized him. Lolo, whom Carlos still had nightmares about. Who'd predicted that Carlos would share the same fate as him, long before his car accident. And who watched him now, while he lay helpless on the bed.

He couldn't help it. The instincts of his childhood took over: Carlos turned his face away and clenched his eyes shut as stars exploded beneath his eyelids. If he could have managed it, he'd have pulled the sheets over his head as well until the source of his childhood fears left him alone. He could still hear the whispers in his room telling him to hide when his grandfather came near.

Was Lolo the Broken Man the little girl had mentioned?

Carlos blinked awake sometime later, hours or minutes; it was impossible to tell with the sunless sky. Every blackout ended the same way: One moment he squinted against the bright light he remembered from the accident, whether that was from the moment he'd died or from the intense operating room lamps as they performed emergency surgery on him, and in the next moment he was conscious. Just like the first time he woke up in the ICU, he took mental stock of his surroundings and his body. The pain was fading, but strength hadn't yet come in to replace it. He was in his parents' room, alone, as usual.

The episodes were changing as he recovered—happening less frequently but lasting longer, following stressful events or too much exertion. Carlos peeked through lowered lashes at the hallway. There was no one there. He clenched his fists weakly in frustration. He was so vulnerable here. What could Lolo have done to him while he lay unconscious? Would Tessa's charm keep out the owner of the house?

"Is he gone?" A whisper from a crack in the wood-paneled walls. Unlike the other ghosts, who were sometimes silent but always visible, he had no idea what She Who Creeps Between looked like.

Caution made him choose his words carefully. He didn't know how allegiances worked between the dead in this house, and decided feigning ignorance was safest. "The old man? Yeah, he's gone. Who was he?"

"A cruel man. An evil one. The one who trapped me here. His name was Roberto."

Carlos's blood turned into ice. His grandfather had murdered a woman in this house? Did his Lola or mother know? Of course not; they'd never have stayed. And yet, they'd always treated him so deferentially, as if afraid of his displeasure. Wasn't there some story about Lola swearing she'd never forgive him for something? Maybe that was the reason Carlos had always distrusted him, had been so eager to avoid him, even as Tessa and Carlos's other cousins begged their lolo to tell them stories, or to play. What if that whispering voice he'd heard each night as a child was his own subconscious, trying to protect him from Lolo's wrath? "How did you know him?"

"I didn't. He found me in my home and dragged me here." A hissing sigh that seemed to slide beneath his skin like a razor blade. "I've been in this place ever since."

Some of the things he'd learned from his show bobbed to the surface of his memory. "Why don't you move on? What keeps you here?" At least, that's what mediums promised.

She Who Creeps Between paused. "When I was a girl, I found a small hurt rabbit in a field. Beside it were two birds dying on the ground. It was obvious that they'd been fighting for their prey—their talons were bloody, feathers flying everywhere, and there were deep scratches on both of them."

"Okay..." He wasn't seeing her point. Maybe the fact that he was talking to the ghost of his grandfather's alleged murder victim was distracting him.

"What would you do if you were one of the birds? Stop fighting, in the hopes that the other would let you live, or would you try to kill the other so you could escape?"

"I'd keep fighting."

"And so here I remain," the woman whispered. "Fighting until one of us is gone first."

A beat of silence, but he didn't know how to respond. She could be mistaken, or lying, but too many memories were fitting into place now. Why Lola never dared say a word against Lolo treating Dolores so well. The rumors of Roberto being haunted, of Salcedo Drive becoming unlivable sometime after he'd taken possession of the property, the unreasonable fear Carlos felt when he thought of his grandfather. Was that the future he predicted Carlos would share?

I'm no killer. I'd never hurt anyone on purpose.

"I want you to see what's in another room," she said. "The dark one, near yours."

Considering he'd just seen the old man's ghost standing outside of it before he'd passed out, he could very well guess who he'd find inside. There was a shrouded mirror in there, he knew, one that Lolo would stare at all day, as if he could see unspeakable visions. He'd gone in as a child once, when no one else was there. It's not like they'd ever forbidden the kids—just that Lolo was almost always inside. Carlos pretended he was a pirate, exploring an abandoned ship, while the excitement of being discovered thrilled through his frame.

Inside the closet, he'd found a little metal box, intricately carved and wrapped with rosary beads. It had looked like a pirate's treasure chest, but made to fit into his hand. He'd heard Lola at the base of the stairs, and in fear of getting caught where he shouldn't be, hurried with his scavenged loot back into his room.

The metal box held nothing exciting, no gold doubloons or precious gems. There'd only been some gray powder inside it that had spilled on his bedroom floor. He remembered sweeping it under his bed, shoving it into the cracks in the floor to hide the mess. What had become of that little toy?

He shook his head to focus. "All the ghosts here," Carlos paused when the woman hissed. *Never speak to spirits about the dead*, he remembered. "The people here. This...Roberto...trapped them all?"

"Some were here before. They don't talk. There was a new one, but he found someplace he likes better." Was that glee, or a warning, in her voice? Was this spirit the Broken Man that the Pinay had told him about?

Carlos frowned. "Can…people like you…do that? Just find another place to stay?"

"Move buildings? Not so easily. Move bodies, though?"

He shivered, suddenly cold. His culture was stuffed with warnings about the soul leaving the body. If that happened, could another move in? Was that why his own body felt so alien and weak, why he was losing bouts of time?

"If you're saying what I think you're saying, that's impossible. If you can't get in, then how could anyone else?"

She tittered. "I can't get into the room, true. That's because when your lovely wife hung up the charm, I wasn't already inside."

Oh God.

He understood now what was happening, why he wasn't recovering as the doctors had expected. Spirits could sap health, drain energy. Tons of his clients had complained of feeling tired once paranormal activity started. He'd been so grateful that Tessa's charm was keeping ghosts outside of his room, but what if it had also trapped one inside? Inside with him, while he lay near death?

But that couldn't be the case. Father Michael had blessed this house. Surely no evil spirit could withstand a servant of God. And yet, he'd seen plenty of evidence otherwise. Hell, he was speaking to one. But maybe a full ceremony was required—were exorcisms only for demons?

"Is there someone who knows the new one? Or anyone who could help me?" Carlos asked. He searched the room, looking for a sign he wasn't alone. Avery slept here at night—he'd thought her tossing and turning natural, but what if a spirit were whispering nightmares in her ear? What was it doing in his body whenever he lost time?

In the meantime, he'd tell Avery. No, not Avery; she'd send him back to the hospital for brain scans instead of believing him. For a moment, his fury overcame his fear. If his wife wasn't so fucking skeptical about everything, she could have helped, and now she was another obstacle he'd have to work around.

Dolores then, or Tessa. Fuck, he'd tell the whole world if it meant someone would get the asshole out of him. He stilled. What if the bastard was poking around in his head and could hear his thoughts? Carlos waited, but nothing happened. Would it be able to follow him out if he moved to his parents'? Resentment, always banked, flared at the thought. They really let their only son stay in this ghost-infested house without a fight.

"I don't know. I could ask the others, I suppose. But not when *he's* around. I don't like *him*." The whispering woman meant his grandfather, he guessed.

"Okay, thank you. Just...please. And I could help you, somehow. Once I get better."

"I accept your help. You have a deal," the voice whispered.

He pictured Avery, lounging around the house with *his* family, while he was trapped here like a prisoner with a dangerous cellmate. "And in the meantime, I'd love if you could scare my wife a little." Maybe if she came to him, crying about the scary ghost haunting her, and he acted as her loving protector, she'd be easier to convince and more willing to help him.

The woman gave a low chuckle. "Oh, I know *just* what to do to her. And using your strength, I can."

"What's...what should I call you?" he asked. He'd asked before. Maybe this time she'd give him a real name.

"You can call me...the last thing you'll ever see."

Carlos stared at the doorway, at the scant protection suspended by an ever-more-fragile palm frond. No, he was sure now. Despite whatever was in here with him now, even more dangers lurked outside. Tessa's charm had to stay where it was.

CHAPTER FIFTEEN

Avery

It was only as Fatima was closing the gate behind the Tams' departing cars that Evelyn's earlier words struck Avery. It sounded like Lolo had left just before Estelle died. What kind of cure was he searching for? One that the doctors hadn't known about, clearly. And he'd obviously returned after Estelle's death. Avery hadn't picked up on anything but love when Tessa spoke about her grandfather, so different from Carlos's fear. The family seemed devoted to Roberto Sison, and Dolores's sighting of the old man's ghost had prompted even Carlos to come home after decades away.

He was long dead, so there must be a reason their grandfather had returned. Avery could no longer deny that Lolo's ghost haunted the house: Dolores's sighting of the old man, his picture flinging itself from the wall, and then the rocking chair in his room moving of its own volition were irrefutable evidence. The very idea of ghosts existing sent a thrill of fear up Avery's spine every time she thought of it, and made the nocturnal footsteps and whispering from the walls all the more terrifying.

Carlos was in no shape to find out why, so the task fell to Avery. Solving this problem might soften the blow when she left her in-laws for Toronto. *If* she left, she corrected herself as she walked through the hallways toward the maids' room. The house was still trying to get rid of her, one way or another.

"Why don't you and Fatima take tomorrow night off, Dolores?" Avery suggested. She felt like a teenager again, trying to fool her parents out of the house for some misadventure or another.

"You just gave us last night off." The old maid squinted at her.

"I...I'm not used to having so much help back home. And you two work so hard, you deserve it." Avery flushed. This was *worse* than when she lied to her parents, because back then she could justify it. Dolores had been nothing but kind to her.

"I have four children of my own, you know," Dolores said. "Not to mention raising Evelyn's siblings, and her kids."

"Mmhmm?" Avery widened her eyes to look innocent. She was supposed to be the boss, damn it. She should have just told Dolores instead of asked. Upstairs, something smacked against the floor. It could be Carlos, of course, but things moving or dropping to the ground wasn't unusual at Salcedo Drive. Both women ignored it.

"There are rules in this house for a reason, Avery."

Oh God. In a second Dolores would say, "As long as you're living under *my* roof..."

"Never mind," Avery shrugged. "I thought you'd want the night off, maybe see your family, but it's not a problem if you don't." Tessa could surely find some room with a locked door to do whatever occult thing she had in mind.

Dread settled heavier in Avery's chest as she went upstairs, as if she were climbing a mountain and the air was thinner. Carlos was asleep in the room, and she closed the door tightly to muffle the sound of Fatima singing downstairs before she took his phone to find his production company contact. Avery texted him a quick message with Carlos's request to pay the Manila crew.

She stared at the sharp line of his nose and the lush curve of his eyelashes. Thought about the strange fluff she'd seen half floating out of his body last night and tried to explain it rationally.

The door unlatched on its own and swung open a few inches.

Fine. The damn house was haunted. Now what the hell was Avery supposed to do about it?

The next evening, neither maid left. Dolores let Tessa in and led her to Avery, who was researching spiritual possession on Carlos's laptop. There was another woman with her. Avery shook the stranger's hand, wondering why she looked so familiar.

"This is Winnie, a close friend of mine. She was at the house blessing the other day."

Ah. "You came in with the rest of Carlos's crew," Avery remembered.

"I recommended her to Shoti. She's a hell of a writer and knows as much as him about the paranormal." Tessa grinned, and Winnie looked both embarrassed and pleased.

Dolores moved to leave them but looked over her shoulder before she left the study. "Do you know the saying about playing with fire?"

"Something about roasting marshmallows, right, Ate?" Tessa grinned, but the old maid didn't return her smile. "Relax! Look, I'm empty-handed." Dolores gave Tessa a careful once-over before shaking her head and wandering back to the kitchen, muttering to herself.

Tessa wagged her finger at Avery. "Sis, you had *one* job tonight."

Winnie readjusted the duffel bag on her shoulder. "Are we in trouble?"

"Not if she doesn't catch us." Tessa winked at Winnie as she led them out of Carlos's office. The air was redolent with a creamy, nutty smell and freshly cooked rice. "Mmm, smells like her famous kare kare. I hope there's enough ulam for all of us."

They ate a quick dinner of the peanut-based stew and steamed rice, and there was more than enough to fill their stomachs. While Dolores cleared the plates away, Tessa led them upstairs. They stopped to say hi to Carlos, and Winnie, who hadn't seen him since the night of the accident, burst into tears and knelt by the side of the bed.

"See, Achi? I'm as handsome as a boy-band singer. Women cry when they see me," he joked. "It's nice to see you again, Winnie. Thank you for coming to help with our little pest problem." He didn't *seem* upset that a colleague was over unannounced, but he'd always been a good actor. Normally, Avery would learn exactly how he felt when everyone had gone home, but since his accident, she no longer knew what to expect.

Winnie responded in Tagalog, and Carlos smiled. "Winnie says I look good, but she's obviously lying because I'm her boss. You should have seen me a few weeks ago, Winnie. My wife is a miracle worker. Or maybe just my angel."

Warmth filled Avery's solar plexus at the praise, and she beamed at him. "Flatterer."

"The car crash put some manners in your head, hey, Shoti?" Tessa asked. "You're replacing me as official translator?"

Avery's smile faded as she realized Tessa had highlighted yet another change in her husband. She wanted to think he was transforming into a better, kinder man, that his brush with death had given him a new appreciation for everything he had. And yet it was so drastic, so noticeable, that she couldn't believe this was the man she'd spent the last ten years with. *It's because he's been replaced by someone else*, Avery admitted. If she could accept that Lolo's ghost was real, it wasn't that far a step to believe that another one was residing in Carlos's body. He stared at his own features too much, acted too considerately, treated Avery too well, but there were also shared memories and private jokes he remembered that made her question if all his changes really were because of the accident.

His unpredictability made her feel nervous, but in a good way, like anticipating a new boyfriend's reaction to a pretty dress. The overworked, salted earth of their relationship had been covered with fresh soil, the ruts and bumps smoothed, and in some places, Avery found flowers blooming.

"What kind of things have you been experiencing?" Winnie asked. "There are different types of paranormal events."

"I think ours is the one that wears a white sheet and says 'Boo.'" Avery gave her a nervous smile.

"This is the same stuff you told me before, right?" Winnie had her notebook out, filled with careful handwriting. "This is the house you grew up in?"

"It's worse, somehow." Tessa shrugged. "More malevolent."

"Hey, Winnie, remember the night at the bar? Before my... That story Manny told us about seeing his own face in the elevator and believing it was his ghost from the future trying to warn him?" Carlos rasped. "Did you believe him?"

She nodded. "I've heard weird stories like that before."

"Like Ebenezer Scrooge?" Tessa suggested. "He was visited by the Ghost of Christmas Yet to Come to show him what his future held."

"Yes." Carlos's face brightened. "Exactly."

"There are people who think psychics can predict things by tapping into their future knowledge." Winnie cleared her throat. "Is that what you think is happening here? That the spiritual presence is trying to warn you?"

"I don't think so. The energy feels more…threatening than protective." Tessa rubbed at her arms as if cold and answered for her brother. "That's what I'm hoping to find out, what's making the house feel so angry."

"What if we were to do the stuff in here?" Avery asked. Maybe they could talk to whatever she'd seen coming out of Carlos.

"Bad luck, I think." Tessa squinted at her brother. "We don't want to attract spirits to a place where someone is sickly. Maybe the bathroom? That door locks."

"Cold floors," Carlos said. "My old room? You could jam the chair under the doorknob like I used to."

Tessa nodded. "I'll go set up." She gestured at Winnie, who unzipped her large bag and handed Tessa a plastic bag. "Good thing Dolores doesn't know you well enough to search you."

Avery waited until her sister-in-law had left the room and then pulled Winnie away from the bed so Carlos couldn't overhear. "Is there any way you could see if there are…spirits in this room?" She flushed at the request, but Winnie didn't hesitate.

"The fastest way would be to see if there's a temperature drop." She pulled a black gun-like device with a small square screen from her duffel. "It's not the nicest model, but if you feel a cold spot then I can see if it differs from the rest of the room."

"The whole top floor feels cold to me," Avery looked around Carlos, trying to remember if there was a place that was colder than others.

"We can do something simpler then." Winnie took out her cell phone and set it to camera mode. She took photos around the room and then swiped through them before stopping at one. "Here, you see?"

Avery leaned in to look. Carlos lay on the bed, grinning cheesily at the camera. Did he know what Winnie was doing? "What am I supposed to be seeing?"

"That small distortion in the picture, it looks like a ball of light right by his head? Ghost hunters call those spirit orbs, and it's supposed to mean that there's a ghost there, invisible to the human eye."

Invisible, except if one looked through fogged glass. Avery had tried to dismiss it as a drunken vision, but she hated bullshit and couldn't do it to herself. She hadn't been able to bring herself to try again.

The orb was floating near the bed. "Could that be a glare from the lamp or something?"

"Sure, it could be. But then look at this picture." Winnie swiped her phone screen again. This photo had caught Carlos mid-blink. The orb was still there, even though the camera angle was different. "If it's a trick of the light, it shouldn't be sitting in one place when I take different pictures like this."

Avery walked around the bed to see what might have caused the orb. There was no reflective surface here. On the wall close to the floor, a large crevice separated the wood planks. Something moved beyond the crack. Heart pounding, breath held, Avery squatted to look inside. Shiny-backed insects skittered away from her phone's light.

"Guys, come on," Tessa stage-whispered from the hallway. "Before we get caught."

A small ring of tea lights flickered on Carlos's old bedroom floor, the Ouija board placed in the center. Since the rest of the lights were off, the light wood board seemed to glow and undulate with the candlelight.

The women took careful seats inside the circle, all within reach of the planchette. "Don't knock any candles over," Tessa warned. "Dolores will kill me if she sees any burnt wood."

"We could just turn on the light." It was a suggestion Avery would have made before, before the accident, but now the motivations were different. She didn't like the way the shadows seemed to have a physical presence in the room, crowding around them. She stretched the tension from her shoulders.

The closet door kept drawing her eye. The attic hatch above it was worse; it seemed to throb with menace. Avery had grown to dislike such games as a schoolgirl. At sleepovers, she'd always felt hopeful when someone pulled out a Ouija board or some other occult object, hoping she'd see Noelle again. Her sister never visited her, and Avery knew that it was because these things were useless toys, because her sister would definitely come back to her otherwise. Noelle loved her family and knew how much they were all hurting, how they couldn't even go back to the Philippines to visit their relatives because her parents couldn't bear to remember when their eldest was toddling in their old house, or smiling at strangers in jeepneys, or trying turon for the first time, her face and hands smeared with syrup and smashed plantains.

It was different this time. Now, Avery *feared* that the board would work, and this house had no happy ghosts to call.

"Place your fingers on the planchette." Tessa waited until they had. The wooden triangle skimmed over the board, smooth and light. "Is there a spirit here?"

No response. The planchette continued to glide aimlessly around the board, powered by their hands, wood sliding against wood the only sound. "I guess that's our answer." Avery wasn't going to admit to the relief that calmed her pounding heart, not out loud, but she allowed herself a small sigh.

Winnie spoke. "No, hold on. You're not supposed to ask nicely." She raised her voice and closed her eyes. "If there is a spirit here, reveal yourself."

A moment of held breath passed. Another.

Maybe they exhaled at the same time, because the candles flickered all at once as if diving for cover. Darkness blinded the women before the flames recovered a heartbeat later.

"That was creepy," Tessa laughed. "I thought...well, you know."

The planchette began to move faster, jerking this way and that, making their hands blur in the unsteady light. "Stop pulling at it." Avery scowled at the others. "Stop playing."

"I'm not doing anything," Winnie protested.

Avery could barely keep her fingers on the stupid thing. It was changing directions and speeds so abruptly, she imagined a bucking horse trying to rid itself of its rider. She glared at the other two, looking for some obvious sign that one of them was behind the movement. Her childhood memories superimposed on the present moment, old feelings surging in like mournful ghosts.

"Who are you?" Tessa called. "I mean, tell us who you are."

The planchette swerved from letter to number, spelling out nonsensical words, stopping in the blank spaces, before returning again and again to "Goodbye."

Winnie removed her hands. "If you're going to be disrespectful about it, I'm not participating."

Avery was glad she hadn't been the first to stop—it had always been her in the past—and folded her hands back in her lap. "I wasn't doing anything." She fought to keep the anger from her voice. Just like years ago, she wouldn't give them the satisfaction of a reaction.

Tessa ran her fingers through her hair. "Well, it wasn't me either. Does this mean that there aren't any ghosts here?"

"No, it means one of you is wasting our time." Winnie was staring down at the board, but Avery felt the words directed at her. "I came as a favor for Tessa. I'm not here for some immature prank."

"Winnie, I swear I wasn't moving the planchette." Avery leaned away from the Ouija board. Cast another glance at the closet door.

"Wait a second." Tessa's eyes were fixed on Winnie's face. "You're not mad. You're scared."

Untouched by any of them, the planchette skidded off the board. Avery lost sight of it once it left the circle of candles, but she heard it smack against the far wall.

Fear was a pheromone. It froze them for a heartbeat. Then the three women scrambled toward the bedroom door, breath hitching and panic building as the chair beneath the doorknob got caught. There was the certainty that *something* was gaining on them, that young and alive and healthy though they were, the things in the darkness with them meant them grievous harm, and worse, had ways to exact it.

Intangible hands reached toward them, unheard voices

screamed in their ears, unseen horrors shrieked for their attention. The absence of sensory information wasn't soothing, for it didn't signify emptiness. Not here, not in this house. On the contrary, the very air groaned with malignant energy, and Avery had no idea when and where it would strike, like persistent footsteps approaching in a foggy night that suddenly go silent.

An instinct in their hindbrains made the three of them freeze in the process of opening the door and stop wrestling with the damned chair. The same instinct that made a fleeing animal freeze, hoping to go unnoticed.

Something yanked hard on Avery's hair, snapping strands and searing pain at the back of her scalp. She screamed, and the panic in her voice broke them out of their paralysis and forced them to stumble over each other once more in their haste to escape.

The women ripped the chair away from the door and ricocheted off the hallway banister, which didn't feel far enough away, and they fled farther, running wordlessly to the safety of the room where Carlos waited. Winnie paused, her face shiny with terror, and took a picture of the dark room before she fled. She didn't stop when Tessa and Avery did, leaping onto the bed, barely considering Carlos's legs beneath the thin blankets. Instead, Winnie grabbed her duffel bag and thudded down the steps. The front door slammed.

"What the hell? How would she make it through a whole season of *Convince Carlos*?" Tessa gasped. She was texting on her phone, cursing as her shaking fingers made typos.

The sharp pain in Avery's scalp throbbed, but her hands came away unbloodied when she tentatively poked at the area.

Carlos raised one of his eyebrows at Avery. "What happened?"

"Nothing. Well, we tried to talk to the spirits in the house, and it didn't work. Then the planchette flew across the room and Avery screamed," Tessa's eyes were wide, face gleaming with sweat. "What happened to you?"

"I think…my hair got caught on something." Avery prodded at the raw area of her scalp again.

Carlos cast a stricken look at her. "Are you all right?"

His concern seemed real. There was no hint of the old mockery in his face, no ridicule in his voice. He just looked worried. It made her feel like she could be honest in her reaction, instead of hiding irrational fear or swallowing skeptical words. This new Carlos accepted her without condition.

"Maybe there's a reasonable explanation why the board didn't work." Avery had to say it. Despite knowing she should be honest, the skepticism felt comforting, a shelter she could hide in while the quaking in her bones subsided. "Maybe we were all just pushing the thing at the same time."

Carlos didn't make a face at her wet-blanket realism like he usually did, but merely squeezed her hand tightly and looked thoughtful. If there was a rational explanation, there was no reason to be scared. And no reason to wonder why Noelle hadn't answered her attempts all those years ago.

Avery's scalp throbbed again where the hair had been ripped away. There'd been nothing near her as she fled, she knew that. Just like she knew that there was no way the planchette should have skidded across the room the way it had. Her teeth chattered. *I wanted to see something spooky, didn't I?* God, ignorance was bliss. Now she wished she could forget.

Tessa's phone buzzed. She stared at the screen—it was some image—and wordlessly showed it to her brother.

He stared at the phone and grunted. "Winnie took this in my old room?"

"Right after the planchette was thrown against the wall. It could have taken out an eye." Tessa's recollection was already growing more dramatic.

"So this is the reason the board didn't work," Carlos said.

"Because there weren't any ghosts?" Avery guessed. Hoped.

He turned the phone around. There were light orbs of all sizes, from deep in the room to right in front of the camera.

"No. Because there were too many of them."

CHAPTER SIXTEEN

Avery

"You're really embracing the lady of leisure role, aren't you?" Carlos smiled at her. Only it wasn't his smile, not the practiced, empty one she'd come to know before the accident, anyway. This one basked her in sunlight, warmed her from within, like she lay in a field surrounded by wildflowers.

"Dolores is teaching me to embroider." Avery poked the needle through the Aida fabric. "But it's harder than I thought. My fingertips are getting sore."

"That's what thimbles are for, maybe." He paused. "Dolores taught me a little bit about sewing, once. You see how it's easier to push the needle through a hole that it's already been through?"

"I don't think pushing a needle through the same hole a thousand times is going to get this project done." Avery set it aside. "I didn't know you sewed. What other hidden talents have you kept from me?"

He winked at her. "Like every treasure, you're going to have to discover it." His expression turned serious. "I'd like you to do something for me."

She raised an eyebrow. "You *are* recovering fast."

God, it felt so good to see him laugh again. It felt like they'd gone back in time to the honeymoon period when they were still madly in love. It was so wonderful that she kept waiting for the other shoe to drop. "Not that fast, I'm afraid. I want you to do something for me, but you're not going to like it."

Unease uncoiled inside her. "What is it?"

Carlos reached out his hand. It shook slightly. Avery grasped it with both of hers to steady him. "I'm asking a lot, I know. But this is very important to me. *You're* very important to me."

"Just say it. You're making me nervous."

"I want you to go back to Toronto."

She pulled her hands from his grasp. A few weeks ago she would have rejoiced to hear these words. They would have felt like a pardon from a life sentence. Now, though, the idea of leaving Carlos when she felt like she'd finally refound him was unthinkable. *What if it's not him anymore?* This was the proof she was searching for, wasn't it? The man she'd married would never let her leave, not until he was tired of her and had wrung from their relationship every last drop of joy. "You want me to leave?" Avery repeated dumbly.

He grabbed for her hands again, and she let him. "I don't *want* to ever be apart from you. But more than what I want, I *need* to know you're safe."

"Safe? From what?" Avery tensed, afraid to hear his answer.

"From everything. I've got some recovering to do, and some unfinished family business in this house. And I can see this place is affecting you. The other night…if I hadn't stopped you…" Tears filled his eyes, ran down the sharp edge of his cheekbones. "I need to know you're well and safe. I can do anything as long as I know that."

Avery chewed on her lower lip. She'd never seen him cry. Once, she'd accused him of not caring enough about someone else to cry for them. "I can't leave you, Carlos. Not when you're not recovered."

"Then move. You can stay with Tessa, or my parents. A hotel. Any place you want. Just get out of this house."

"I don't understand. What are you so afraid will happen to me?" He was usually so dismissive of things; his concern was scaring her.

"I don't know. That's the worst part. I have no idea what might happen beyond this point. There's a lot of bad history in this house, and I don't want you wrapped up in it."

She didn't like feeling this way. Ever since she'd seen that gray fluff squatting in his body, the world had become untethered. Unsafe.

Her cynicism kicked in, familiar and reassuring, and she brandished it like a weapon. "Is this about your grandfather? You didn't even want to talk about him in the house before. You didn't even tell me the real reason we moved here. Now suddenly I'm in danger and I have to leave?"

Carlos tightened his grip around her fingers as if afraid she'd pull away again. "I was wrong not to tell you, Avery. I was afraid you'd laugh at my family, at me. But I need you to listen." His eyes searched hers. "It's really important to me that you don't dismiss everything just because it can't be immediately proven. Especially in this house."

Before Manila, they had the same outlook about the supernatural; how strange that they'd both become believers since moving. She frowned, wondering again if the man inside Carlos's body was still her husband, and if so, what had made him abandon his skepticism. "You've spent your life disproving hauntings. And now you want me to believe in them?"

He hesitated before answering. "I know better, now. Ghosts and spirits do exist, in this very building, and I can't protect you from them if they mean you harm. Please, even if you don't believe in the paranormal, believe in your husband. Get out, and be safe."

It was hard to refuse him anything, now that he'd returned to her. And hadn't last night's Ouija board fiasco shown him how much she'd changed? She shivered at the memory, the fear climbing up her back the way she'd been afraid a shadow might, as she fled from his room. *Think of something else.* "Will you come with me?"

He shifted in the bed. "I can't. I have to find out why Dolores saw Lolo before I can move on." His brown eyes looked down at his lap. She figured it was because of Dr. Chen—Carlos was worried he'd never recover fully if angry spirits kept slowing his healing.

"I already decided I'd help you with this," Avery said. It had been the deal she'd made with herself: She would figure out why Lolo's spirit wasn't at rest, and in exchange she could leave Manila and return home without guilt. Of course, things had changed. *Carlos* had changed. "Why can't I help you with it now?"

"Because I don't know how it'll end. And I don't deserve your help." Carlos took a deep breath. "Avery, I've got something to tell you, and you're not going to like it."

Here it came. The other shoe. She shook her head. "No."

"No?"

"Not now. Please. I feel like we've—like *I've*—been through so much. Frankly, I can't handle anything more right now." Her eyes prickled. She didn't want to cry in front of him—she wanted to be positive, to keep his morale up. "I know you're probably going to tell me something that will make me leave you. And I promise we can talk about anything you want. Later. Let's just focus on your recovery first. Okay?"

He nodded.

"It's settled. I'll help you figure out what's going on with your house stuff, and we'll leave it together." She forced a smile, while curiosity and dread gnawed at her heart. "It's been years since I've had to research anything. Do I have to make a poster board at the end?"

"Only if you wear a pocket protector and pull your pants up to your armpits." He cast his new smile upon her again, and she wiped his tears away with her fingertips. "I was thinking we can figure out from my family if there was a reason he'd come back, or what he was doing when Dolores saw him. That sighting is what brought us here, and everyone's been too afraid to ask her about it."

Avery saluted. "Got it, chief." Maybe Dolores had seen Lolo standing outside his room, looking for his family. Was it his footsteps she heard pacing the halls and over the bedroom every night?

Carlos grabbed her hand again and brought it to his mouth for a kiss. Her stomach fluttered as his soft lips brushed against her skin. "You know my family and Dolores are true believers, Avery. Can you *please* try not to offend them?"

She was saved from answering when Fatima came in. "Did you call me, Ate?" The maid looked at the windowsills, then around the room, eyes searching.

"No, I didn't, Fatima. What's wrong?" She hardly ever saw the young woman upstairs, despite her initial claim that the ghosts in this house were kind. Perhaps Avery could start her research by asking Fatima what she'd heard about Roberto Sison.

"Ate Evelyn called to ask how Kuya was doing, and I was on my way up to check when I heard you whisper my name." Fatima took a step back into the hallway, eyes still darting around.

"We were talking to each other, just now. Maybe that's what you heard?" Avery followed Fatima out of the room, away from Carlos's ears, to ask her next question. "What are you looking for in here?"

"Ma'am?" Fatima cast a longing glance down the hall, and Avery, not wanting to interrupt the young woman's work, accompanied her to the stairway.

"You looked at the windowsills and in the corners of the room, then down on the floor. What were you looking for?"

Fatima relaxed the further they descended the stairs. "It's something Dolores taught me when I first came. To always check for insects, especially if someone is sick."

"Insects? Like the ones we found on my hairbrush? He doesn't have one." Was the old woman that worried about uncleanliness? Tessa had told her it was their grandfather who'd been afraid of bugs.

"I didn't ask, Ate. But I didn't see or hear any insects. Only whispering."

Avery nearly missed the next step. "Whispering? Or buzzing?"

Fatima wrinkled her forehead. "I think whispering. But I can't make out any words. It's louder and more frequent upstairs. Near Kuya."

A chill shivered beneath Avery's skin. Like the light orb in Winnie's picture lurking too close to Carlos, Fatima's words seemed to confirm that the gray, glowing thing floating out of her husband's body was no illusion.

It was probably a smudge in the sake glass, or a trick of the light from the bedside lamp. She told herself forcefully. *I was so drunk and sleep-deprived, my brain could have made up anything.* And yet Avery hadn't dared try again. She *liked* this version of Carlos—more than liked it, if she wanted to be honest, and she didn't want to think about what that glowing fluff might be.

But Avery's excuses did not dispel her dread. It was a cold anchor pulling at her intestines, slowing her feet. She left Fatima and hurried back up the stairs, ears straining. She heard nothing except Carlos's steady breaths. He fell asleep so quickly, slept so heavily now. Like the dead.

There were no insects in the room, none that she could see. Nothing vibrated or moved to explain what Fatima had heard. The black shrouded mirror beckoned in Avery's peripheral vision, but the memory of those giant cockroaches in the hallway mirror made her hesitant to look. And worse than those cockroaches, the fingerprints she'd been unable to wipe away.

It's just bugs, Avery. What're you so afraid of? And yet, she was afraid. She didn't know why, couldn't explain it, but she did not want insects anywhere near her husband.

Gripping the bottom of the heavy cloth, Avery slowly uncovered the mirror. No insects. She shook her head. The house's atmosphere and everyone's behavior was getting to her.

She took a last look at Carlos, thinking about his request. There were too many questions and not enough answers in Salcedo Drive. Avery went to make a phone call.

Avery's phone rang as Fatima led Tessa into the sitting room, Father Michael returning her call. Her sister-in-law gave Avery's arm a quick squeeze before heading up to see Carlos.

"Hi, Father. Thanks for calling back." Avery settled on the couch, keeping an eye on the stairs.

The priest's voice was low and calm. His Filipino accent seemed more noticeable than in person. "I'm happy to hear from you, Avery. How are you doing?"

"Mostly better, now that Carlos is improving. It's just everything else that seems to be worse." Even though he couldn't see it, she gestured to encompass the house.

"I'm listening."

"I don't know where to start." She played with the hem of her loose skirt. The mood in the house worsened every day: The footsteps grew louder, lasting all night, small things kept moving from where she left them, and she kept sensing the angry presence in the corner of their bedroom staring at her while she slept. While she undressed. But even that wasn't her main concern. "Of course I'm happy that my husband is awake and getting stronger. But he doesn't seem exactly the same."

"How so?" Michael asked.

"He's kind again, the way he first was. He stares at me like he can't believe I'm with him. As if the last few years of fighting haven't happened. He isn't reacting to things the way I expect him to. He's just...*different*."

"Carlos—and all his loved ones, including you—have been through a very trying seven weeks. Trauma, such as nearly dying, tends to reprioritize things. I'd be more surprised if he didn't change at all."

Tessa's footsteps started down the stairs. Avery lowered her voice and spoke faster. "The other night...I think I saw something...supernatural in Carlos. Father, what are the signs someone is possessed?" She felt ridiculous asking it, but the question sprang out of her mouth. Carlos had acted differently ever since they'd arrived in this house, and changed even more dramatically since the accident. What if someone had taken over her husband's body?

Michael didn't answer right away. "The Catholic faith believes that only demonic forces can possess a person. In that case, your husband might be sensitive to religious symbols. He might have supernatural strength, or speak in tongues, or know things he has no way of knowing. I understood that you're a bit of a cynic, Avery. What was it you saw that changed your mind?"

"Shoti's sleeping," Tessa reported, flopping into the nearby armchair. "He's looking great though. Praise Jesus."

"Oh, Achi Tessa is here, Father. I'm so sorry, but I've got to go." Avery ended the call, thoughts racing.

Someone possessed would have unexplained knowledge—was that how Carlos had known to stop Avery from swallowing all those pills in the bathroom? And yet, he wasn't strong. Were the whispers she—and Fatima—kept hearing in the house emanating from him?

She realized Tessa was staring at her, waiting for some response. "Thanks for coming on such short notice, Achi."

"Anything you need, I'm here." Tessa held up another plastic bag. "Plus I brought some incense to try to cleanse the house."

"I want to help Carlos investigate why your lolo returned from a peaceful rest." Avery picked up the notepad and pen she'd placed on the coffee table. "You've mentioned a few times that the energy feels different than when you lived here. How did it change? What have you heard about the house and your grandfather? Why would he be angry that Carlos came back?"

Tessa hopped to her sneakered feet. "Why don't we go out for a late lunch?"

"Why doesn't anyone want to talk about the supernatural in here?" Avery narrowed her eyes. "You, Carlos, Dolores...what are you afraid will happen if we talk about your grandfather's ghost?"

"I thought it was just superstition too," Tessa answered, her voice low and urgent, "but after what happened with the Ouija board the other day—"

"Do you think it was your lolo who pulled out my hair?"

Tessa looked pale. "No, he would never hurt anyone. But Winnie said there were so many spirits, and any one of them—"

Loud bangs and a shriek made them both jump.

"What the hell was that?" Avery asked, pressing a hand against her chest like it would slow her heart down.

"The kitchen." Tessa ran from the sitting room, yelling for Dolores.

When they reached the kitchen, the screen door was just slamming shut. Fatima stood outside, both hands covering her mouth and nose, eyes wide in terror. Every cabinet door and drawer gaped open.

Dolores slammed cabinets closed, grumbling under her breath. "Whatever you are doing in the other room, please *stop*," she ordered.

"We weren't doing anything, Dolores." Tessa slid a nearby drawer closed. "We were just talking."

"Go talk outside, or you're going to have to find a replacement for Fatima."

Avery and Tessa obeyed the old maid and stood beneath the meager shade of Wilma, her boughs heavy with ripening mangoes.

Fatima darted in soon after they left the kitchen, brushing off Avery's apology with mumbled prayers.

"We don't talk about ghosts in the house because it's supposed to make the activity worse." Tessa hugged herself as if cold. "But it's never actually happened before. I didn't think it was true."

"Ah. Gotcha." Avery nodded, looking to see if the cockroach carcasses were still visible. "Someone could have told me that instead of shushing me every time."

Tessa gave her a look. "I love you like my own sister, girl, but it's pretty obvious when you think something is bullshit. Kind of makes it hard to ask you to play nice."

Avery's face heated more than the weather warranted. It wasn't just the embarrassment of being called out by someone she genuinely liked; it was also the knowledge that, after everything she'd experienced in this house, Avery's skepticism had been proven wrong, and she felt like a fool. Carlos would once have gloated to hear her admit fault, but his sister wouldn't, which made the apology easier to say. "I'm sorry I had such a shitty attitude. I didn't mean to be rude."

Her sister-in-law shook her head. "Don't worry about it. The important thing is that now you understand what the rest of the family is talking about."

The rest of the family. Tessa had included her so nonchalantly that it touched Avery. Despite their differences in upbringing and personalities, Tessa still considered her family.

"I don't even know when I first started doubting everything," Avery confided. "Maybe when Noelle kept getting sicker, even after all our prayers."

Tessa tsk-tsked in sympathy. "After what you've gone through with your sister—I don't blame you at all. That kind of stuff affects kids forever. Look at my mom. She's emotionally distant because she can't take losing another loved one. At least, that's my theory after watching Dr. Phil. It used to drive Carlos crazy. Kids need love, or they turn into…well, my brother."

Kids needed love and attention. What became of children who didn't get enough of either? Would Evelyn and her brothers have grown up differently, even after losing Estelle, if her parents had paid closer attention? Or had Lolo and Lola been eaten alive by their own grief?

"What do you know about your grandfather?" Avery asked.

From the house, Dolores passed Fatima a laundry basket. The young woman began to hang up wet clothing on the lines stretched across part of the yard. Avery watched her work while Tessa gathered her thoughts.

"There's always been weird stuff in the house. But the way the energy feels now is…not what we grew up with." Tessa hugged herself tighter. "We all hated living here, and moved almost immediately after Lolo died."

"Why didn't you sell the house right away? He died before I met Carlos, I think?" At least, Avery couldn't recall him mentioning any death in the family.

Tessa rolled her eyes. "Don't get me started about that. He refused to come home, even when my mom offered to cover his flight. I don't know if you noticed, but Carlos always needs to be the center of attention, otherwise he can't be bothered."

Two months ago, she would have been the first to agree. Now she had to suppress the urge to defend him. "Go on."

"It was almost ten years ago. In May of 2013. And we didn't

sell for a while because Mom didn't want to. I guess she'd promised Lolo before he died that she wouldn't sell the house or the three mirrors. But now Mom's getting old and she doesn't want to leave a mess for her siblings or her kids to resolve."

"Three mirrors?" Avery tried to picture each room. "The covered ones, you mean?"

"Yeah. The one in the downstairs hallway, the one in Lolo's room, and...one more." Tessa mumbled to herself and tapped her fingers as if mentally going through a list.

"Do you know why the mirrors are covered?"

"No idea. No one would ever talk about them except to tell us to never leave them uncovered."

"Sleeping in front of mirrors can steal your soul," Fatima offered, clearly eavesdropping.

Tessa pointed at the maid. "I believe that! It's true! Or, at least, that's what Carlos and I used to think after we..."

Tessa stared at nothing, her expression troubled. Avery placed a hand on the woman's forearm. "Achi?"

"I'd forgotten about that," Tessa said, her voice faint. "It was so long ago."

"Forgotten about what?" Avery prompted.

"Carlos and I were playing around one of the covered mirrors. We'd lifted the shroud and made faces at each other. At some point, a third face appeared in the reflection with us, but it wasn't another child's. It was a woman's, and she looked angry."

"Who was it?" Avery asked, more troubled by the fear on Tessa's face than by her words.

"We never knew. I looked behind us, but there was no one there. The woman was trapped in the mirror, somehow. Carlos even drew a picture of her. We thought she played a game like Bloody Mary and got pulled in or something."

Before moving into Salcedo Drive, Avery had snorted when she heard urban legends like this. Now she eyed the tall, dark house with trepidation.

"I don't blame you for blocking that out," she said. "You had to keep living with the mirrors, after all."

Tessa nodded and gave Avery a half smile. "I wonder if Carlos remembers her. But you probably shouldn't ask him right now."

"Speaking of Carlos, maybe you can convince your brother that we should move to your parents' place, or yours, if you'll have us." God, what she wouldn't give for a good night's sleep. Where she didn't startle awake, expecting to see someone at her bedside. Where she didn't hear footsteps pace the hallway or stomping above her. Stomping…*above*…

"Have you ever been to the attic?" Avery asked.

Tessa shook her head. "You've seen how creepy Carlos's room is. He was always terrified of the attic, wouldn't allow anyone to open the hatch. That's what I brought the incense for, to burn a little in each room and open the windows to shove out the bad energy. When do you want to move to my place?"

Avery sighed. "As soon as you convince Carlos. He just asked me to move out and leave him in the house. Of course I won't do that. But I'm worried about him." And he was clearly worried about something he wasn't sharing, something Avery wouldn't let him share.

"Let me talk to my parents. Maybe I can call you before dinner, try to convince Shoti then?" Tessa asked.

"Sure. Are you leaving already? You just got here." Avery wanted more people in the house with her, not less.

"Uh… After the kitchen cabinets, I am not going in there unless I have to," Tessa said. "I'm too scared. I'll convince my stubborn brother to leave, and we can abandon this house to the ghosts."

Avery waved Fatima away and pushed the metal gate closed herself. The metal was tacky in the heat, and her fingertips slid over ridges of dried paint trails as she slid the bolts closed.

A nap wouldn't be bad. In the daylight, she could pretend the noises and whispers around the house were from Dolores or Fatima. Avery climbed the stairs once more and heard whispering. She checked on Carlos. He was still asleep, and Dolores, who sometimes kept him company, was nowhere to be found.

Perhaps a fly buzzing, then? Avery remembered Dolores's strange instructions to Fatima about insects and checked the windowsills. She lifted the black shroud over the mirror perfunctorily.

Holy shit! She backpedaled so far that she hit the bed and fell on top of her husband. She couldn't scream if she tried; her throat was clenched too tight to breathe.

"Darling? What is it?" Carlos murmured, eyes still closed.

Avery stared at the vanity mirror, her heart thudding out of her rib cage, whimpering. The shroud lay still as if nothing had occurred, but terror froze her limbs. *It's all Tessa's fault.* Her sister-in-law was putting images in her head.

"Carlos, wake up," she said. She couldn't leave him here until she checked again.

"I'm awake," he said, before snoring softly.

Avery grabbed her phone like a cudgel, feeling safer with a weapon, and forced her stiff body past its prey-instinct panic to approach the vanity again.

She checked again, peeking beneath before she lifted the

shroud. Nothing but her own frightened face, and Carlos sleeping soundly behind her.

There was no sign of the unfamiliar woman who'd glared at her from behind the mirror the first time she'd looked.

And yet, fury simmered in the air, making it hard for Avery to breathe.

More proof to weigh down her already flattened skepticism.

This house was full of ghosts, and they were all angry.

CHAPTER SEVENTEEN

Avery

Before we go further, I want you to do something for me." Avery handed Father Michael a clean glass. "Fog this up and look at Carlos. Tell me what you see." She braced herself for his reaction.

"What…am I supposed to be looking at?" He handed it back to her. "I just see your husband."

"Nothing around him?" When Michael shook his head, Avery took the glass back and fogged it up herself, waiting for the glass to turn translucent enough to see through. She held her breath as she looked again. Carlos napped in his bed. There was no bone-gray glow hanging halfway out of him, like a lobster molting its shell. Had she imagined the whole thing? Dreamed it? Or had the entity succeeded in fully possessing him? She shook her head. These were not the rational thoughts of a skeptic, but then nothing that had happened since they'd come to this house was rational. "Let's just keep going."

Carlos's childhood room was a time capsule, a period of innocence that was both precious and poignant for its fleetingness. She took a good look at it in the daylight. It was clean, but pictures he'd taped to the blue wall hung faded and sagging, like overstretched skin. In one corner, there was the planchette they'd abandoned. Apparently, the maids didn't enter this room too often.

"This has to be the first Spice Girls poster I've seen in a couple of decades," Avery said. "Were you ever a fan?"

Michael gave her a considering look. "I preferred *NSYNC."

"I loved Backstreet Boys!" Tessa said from the phone, where she was video chatting with them. She hadn't dared to come back and sent Michael in her stead, with the promise that priests were protected from most things she was vulnerable to, like nightmares and dust allergies.

Avery had to admit that Michael's calm demeanor was preferable to Tessa's nervous energy. She felt safer with him here.

The attic hatch was right beside Carlos's small closet, a square inset into the ceiling. "Shoti hated his room when he was younger. He'd always try to sleep with my parents or me."

"If he was so scared when he was younger, why choose to do a show like *Convince Carlos*?" Michael shook his head.

"Who knows why people do anything? Brains are weird. Maybe he disproves paranormal events to make himself feel better," Tessa said.

"And now that he's back in this house?" Father Michael asked. "Has he disproven anything?"

"Quite the opposite, I think," Avery answered. "He believes not only that there's something in the house, but also that it may cause us harm."

"And even then, he will not leave?" The priest sounded incredulous.

"Don't even get me started," Tessa said. Her attempt last night to cajole, command, bully, and finally, guilt-trip Carlos into staying elsewhere had been unsuccessful.

Avery and Michael set up the ladder. Being so near to the closet made her feel…not scared, exactly. Watched. She could imagine someone peeking from within the dark silhouettes of dated clothes.

"I can go up first," Michael said. "It might be stuck, the panel."

Another time, Avery might have argued. She was strong, and not too much shorter than him. After what she'd seen yesterday, though, she was happy to let someone else take the lead. She'd spent the night cowering in the bedroom, staring at Tessa's charm and googling what else people might use to protect themselves from otherworldly entities. She'd searched for anything to explain the woman in the mirror: First, she looked for reasonable things like warped glass or tricks of light, and then she found herself wandering back into superstitions about hungry mirrors, Filipino witches, shape-shifting creatures. If spirits could communicate using sound waves and electricity—electronic voice phenomena and flickering bulbs—couldn't that mean that light waves—reflections—were within their arsenal as well?

Maybe she was affected by mass hysteria from living with true believers. Or…could Dolores be behind this all? The old maid had seen Lolo's ghost after Evelyn decided to sell the house. She'd been strangely close to Lolo, the rumored medium. Perhaps he'd taught her how to fake the presence of ghosts. Avery's mind rationalized things, but her body reacted out of reflex and instinct anyway. It was like her struggle with conceiving all over again: Her mind was determined to succeed, science could find no problem with her, and yet her body failed her, again and again.

Focus, Avery. There'd be time enough to mourn for lost chances once Carlos was better. A part of her worried they'd go back to the way they had been, sniping and resentful, after he recovered. That the sacrifice she was making to stay with him would seem like a mistake once they'd fallen into their old patterns. Yet what choice did she have? She couldn't leave him now, not when he needed her more than children who were not yet born. Not when she could never love another man as much as she loved him.

Unlike the rest of the room, flies crawled and buzzed around the attic entrance as if trying to get in. Michael reached the ceiling and pressed his palms against the hatch, shooing away the bugs. He pushed upward, and a cloud of white plaster flurried around him, settling on his black high-collared shirt like dandruff. The dark specks of desiccated insects who'd managed to wedge themselves in the tight squeeze between door and border fell faster, like hail. Avery clutched her phone, holding her breath both in anticipation and so she wouldn't inhale the ancient particles.

The white panel squeaked as it moved upward, until a layer of insulation and unstained wood appeared. Michael pushed farther to move the square out of the way. From his pocket, Tessa was breathing loudly, clearly as nervous as Avery.

"Let Tessa see first, Father. To make sure it's safe." There'd been news of a Japanese woman who had lived in a man's storage space without his knowledge. Was a squatter the source of all the whispers and footsteps?

"Ah...okay, listen. I'm going to hit record as you put your phone up, but I'll cover my eyes, okay? You can rewatch the video to make sure there's nothing there." Even through the video chat, Tessa was pale and sweaty. "If I see, like, hanging legs or a scary face, you're going to have to deal with my ghost too. 'Cause I'll just die."

Michael turned on the flashlight function on his phone. "I think I'll be okay."

"What if something attacks you?" Tessa squeaked.

The priest shrugged. "Then it's God's will."

Avery caught herself just as she was about to roll her eyes. If his faith gave him courage, the way her cynicism gave her comfort, were they really that different? "I'm here if you need me."

"I appreciate that, my friend." He smiled down at her before his head and wide shoulders squeezed into the dark mouth of the attic door.

Avery tried to peek, but all she could see was shifting light as the priest twisted to look around the space. He whistled, and then he sneezed. "Not the worst attic I've seen." Michael moved farther up the rungs, disappearing in increments, so that it looked like he was being devoured headfirst.

Her turn. She gripped the cool metal of the ladder and climbed upward, the rungs vibrating beneath her palms as she moved. There were no windows up here, no space at all to let light through. The darkness was so complete it felt solid, like their phone lights were knives carving Vantablack flesh from a giant being, only to have it regrow as soon as they moved away.

"Is there a light?" Michael whispered to Tessa. Avery was glad he'd kept his voice down. This was a place of silence, not the quiet reverence found in a church or at a wake, but a scuttling, cowering, hoping-to-avoid-notice gloom.

"I don't know. I've never been up here." Tessa, too, was murmuring. Her face was so close to her phone that only her over-wide eye and part of one cheek were visible.

The attic had wood floors and was cluttered with boxes and misshapen lumps of other items, stored and forgotten. The air was musty, with an oppressive wet heat. The acrid smell of mothballs tinged the air.

Avery held tight to her phone and to Michael's arm, grateful she wasn't alone. *So much for being a skeptic,* she mused. Even before she believed in spirits, she would have admitted that there was something threatening about the total darkness here. The potential danger within it, the way it hid as much as it covered.

There, in the corner, a long black shape that did not fade as she shone her light toward it. It stood as tall as her, merging with the shadows. Her light traced the curved silhouette of a neck sloping downward, ruffles of black material hanging from the shoulders straight down to the floor. She couldn't see a face—was the person facing the corner, or looking down?

Avery squeezed Michael's arm, trying to show him that they weren't alone. The light from her phone moved weirdly against the figure, making shadows shift and stretch on the wall, until she was sure she could see the person breathing. No, it was her own hand that was trembling, creating the inconstant light.

Whispers hissed in the darkness. Metal clinked right above them. "Susmaryosep," Tessa hissed.

"Something brushed against my face," Michael said, and the calm in his voice was a ragged thing, seemingly held in place by the last shreds of his willpower—as if he was trying not to scream.

Perhaps his faith did give the priest a divine courage, for Avery would have run for the ladder instead of what Michael did next. He switched his phone to the arm she clutched and aimed it upward, sweeping the ceiling for movement. There was a length of thin ball chain hanging down, no thicker than the clothing lines Fatima had used the other day.

He reached up with his free hand, slowly, and pulled on the metal chain.

A bulb flickered on above them, as pale yellow as the others downstairs. It cast a weak light in the center of the open space, creating humps of shadow that fled toward the walls, collecting in the corners.

Avery whipped her gaze and her light toward the headless figure she'd been staring at and nearly collapsed with relief. It was a tall, freestanding piece of furniture, shrouded in black. What she'd mistaken for a person's neck and shoulders was likely the top of an ornate frame. This must be the third mirror Tessa had mentioned.

The memory of what she'd seen in the other mirror made her cautious, and Avery kept her distance, especially because the shroud seemed to be moving. As she watched, a fly from the entrance drifted across the room and landed on the mirror. There was movement around her, a subtle shift in her peripheral vision, and she grabbed for Michael's arm to keep him still.

Sweat trickled down Avery's face, pasting her hair along her cheeks and against her neck as she stared at the shadow-painted walls. There was nothing that should be moving in this windowless space, nothing whatsoever that should cause the unfamiliar shapes on the wall to contort or stretch. And yet…

"Something's moving," Avery whispered, shining her phone in front of her.

"Maybe the bulb I turned on is swinging," Michael said, but Avery knew he didn't believe his own words either. If the light source swung, all the shadows would shift, including their own.

Her own phone light showed aged wood planks, rough and unpolished. They scanned each wall, but nothing moved in the circle of light.

Avery aimed her phone toward the ground, and darkness devoured the walls once more. The shadows undulated around them, as if squirming to reach them, and Avery fought to breathe, her heart thumping loudly in her ears.

"It's not the shadows moving. It's the walls." Michael's voice was thick with disgust.

As soon as she heard the words, Avery understood what her eyes couldn't make sense of. The dark spots on the walls that shifted incessantly and fled the light were insects—hundreds of cockroaches and beetles amassed on the wood like a plague.

They weren't dangerous, though. Just gross. Avery stepped farther into the attic, careful where she stepped, in case the infestation covered the floors as well.

"What's that?" Tessa whispered. "Where you pointed the light just now, Father."

It was a lump on the otherwise smooth floor. As they approached it, details grew clearer. Ragged fur. Tiny sharp claws. A long, leathery tail.

"Just a rat," Michael reported. "Probably why this place is full of bugs."

"We're lucky it doesn't smell," Avery said. The rat was huge, and with the moist heat trapped in this space, she'd expected the sickly sweet odor of rot to filter into the house. Her skin prickled, as if insects climbed over it, and the feeling of being watched grew stronger.

"It's probably been here for years." Tessa squinted at them from behind the screen. "There's another lump over there."

It was a dead bat, and then another rat, a short distance away. Then a small bird, its beak pointing deeper into the attic like an arrow.

"I don't like this," Michael muttered. "It feels like we're being led." He was whispering too. As if he also sensed people in the room, drawing closer as they moved.

"We've come this far," Avery urged. "Don't make me do this by myself." She thought of Carlos's warm eyes, and the trust she saw there when he looked at her. It didn't stop her trembling, but she clutched onto the memory of his face like she was a child with a stuffed animal.

The next lump was the largest and, unlike the others, wasn't desiccated with age. A large cat, its body still rounded, eyes glassy with death, wearing a pink collar with a gold bell. Poor thing. A paw twitched, claws unsheathed, but Avery saw the writhing underneath its skin and heard the dry buzzing noises of the insects within the carcass. The cat was long past voluntary movement.

"Over there," Tessa said, her voice sounding too loud. Avery fought the urge to shush her. "Something glinted on the ground."

It was the metal clasp of a ragged book bag. A few feet away, in a space of its own, was a small metal container, about the size of a book. It was intricately decorated and placed within a circle of white grains.

"What is that? Rice?" Michael leaned down to touch the ground.

Avery slapped his hand away. "Have you ever seen a horror movie in your life? Don't mess with things in salt circles."

There was a clump of fur near the salt. No, not fur—a lock of long, dark hair, ragged at one end. It hadn't been removed with scissors; that would have left a clean, sharp edge. Avery's hand reached up to touch the smooth, hairless area at the back of her scalp. She'd never wondered where the hair had gone. Was there any point in taking it now, after someone had taken it up here for nearly two days, and done God knows what with it? Avery thought of the stranger who'd visited Estelle, and her throat tightened. She bent down and took it anyway. In case something could be done, and because it was hers.

Out of the corner of her eye, something on the floor moved. A whisper of cloth, followed by a clack of metal on wood. "Oh my…" The flap of the book bag, clasped when Avery's eye had first skimmed over it, was now unfurled like a tongue on the floor, revealing a pit-dark maw. Her stomach dropped like a man on a noose.

Michael followed her gaze, bringing Tessa with him. "What?"

"The bag," Tessa panted, taking the words right out of Avery's mouth. "Holy shit. Sorry, Father. Holy crap. Get the hell out of there, you guys!"

Was this what was causing the house's activity, what was draining Carlos's strength? Avery's mouth was sandpaper dry, but she forced herself to take a step toward the old book bag. *If it moves again, I'm fucking out of here. Forget the ladder; I'll just jump.* She crouched down, stiff with fear, her clothing sticking to her sweating skin as she moved.

"For Carlos," she muttered, and reached inside the canvas bag. There were a few papers inside. She stood up, holding the documents carefully; they were stiff with age. "Anything else that might be helpful?" Avery asked Michael.

When the lone lightbulb burned out with a sudden pop, drowning them in darkness once more, it felt like an answer from something else in the attic that might have heard her.

Their panting breaths sounded loud, frantic as heartbeats, intertwined as if seeking comfort. Somewhere, an insect flew past, its buzz sounding like a whispered *psst*. There was the slither of moving cloth, and a floorboard creaked.

"I guess that's our cue to leave," Tessa whispered.

Shuffling sounds, as if something changed position. A quiet tinkle rang, growing closer to them, sounding exactly like a small gold bell on a pink collar.

Avery, clutching Michael for dear life, forced her feet to move. She focused on the tiny sliver of light from the open attic hatch like a diver surfacing for air, instead of trying to count the number of people breathing beside her, ignoring the scratch of claws and tinny bell at their heels.

They didn't speak again until they reached the square exit. The ladder was a welcome sight, and the sunlit room below even better. Avery and Michael exchanged glances.

His face looked different in the scant light. Colder, angrier. He stabbed a finger toward the exit. "Ladies first."

Avery would usually argue out of politeness. Right now, she almost wept with gratitude. "Thank you." She moved as quickly as she could, but the priest hopped onto the ladder before she'd finished climbing down, almost kicking her in the face. Avery couldn't blame him. At least he'd remembered to grab the hatch door as he came down. She shuddered at the thought of leaving the attic open, at the insects picking away at the salt circle, crystal by crystal, at the cat's corpse waiting, insects acting as the very muscle and ligament and nervous system they'd devoured.

"I'm on my way to get you guys," Tessa said, her voice returned to normal volume. Her short hair was spiky with sweat, and she was flushed pink. "We can look through everything together, but not in the house."

"Yeah, I need to get out of here." Avery hesitated. "Do you think it's okay to leave Carlos here after what we just did?"

"Ask Dolores to sit with him. She'll figure out what to do if something goes wrong."

"How would she know?" The maid was competent and experienced, but what could she offer in a situation like this?

Tessa beeped her car horn furiously as she drove, the video call still connected. "Lolo taught her."

They sat at an outdoor table, too chilled for the arctic levels of air-conditioning in the restaurant. Living in the Philippines seemed to be a perpetual cycle of sweating and shivering as one moved from outside to inside.

Avery had ordered a halo-halo, both because it was something fun to look at and because it gave her hands something to do, but she didn't consider that it would make her colder. She jabbed her spoon through the crushed ice, mixing ice cream, beans, and leche flan with the condensed milk. Tessa had ordered a hot bubble tea, and Father Michael sipped only black coffee. The staff greeted Tessa by name and the service was astounding, with staff hovering nearby, smiling and refilling their glasses of water after every sip.

"If we wanted privacy, we've come to the wrong place," Avery muttered.

"They're just trying to impress," Michael said. His face had melted back into its warm lines, until Avery couldn't believe she'd ever witnessed his cold fury in the attic. "It's not every day their boss visits."

"You manage this place?" Avery asked Tessa, impressed. It was full of customers and was beautifully decorated.

"No way. I can't handle the stress. I own this store and two other branches." Tessa shrugged and spoke to the nearest waiter. The line of smiling employees dispersed and returned to their tasks.

"Okay. Okay. What the hell was that?" Tessa asked. The drive to the dessert place had been a silent one—Tessa had asked them not to talk about it while she drove, afraid it would further distract her. That was fine with Avery, who needed to collect her thoughts. She'd stared out the window at the Manila landscape, at the people, which had become both familiar and comfortable to her, and rubbed her fingers against the smooth patch of skin on her scalp.

"The bag was closed. When I turned around again, the bag was open," Michael cupped both hands around his mug as if he could absorb the heat. "Did anyone see it move?"

"I thought I saw something in my peripheral vision. But isn't it more reasonable that we made the bag slide open when we went in there? By…vibrating the floorboards when we walked by, or… maybe the fresh air from the attic door? Oh, what if there was a mouse living in the bag and we scared it away, but it knocked the flap of the bag open when it left?" Avery was babbling. She wanted to share all the ideas she'd thought of during the car ride. If her friends agreed, that might ease her shaking.

"Maybe? But what was that white circle? Who left the trail of dead animals?" Tessa's expression said she was placating Avery. *Is that what I look like when people bring up praying?*

"I think it was salt. That's what it looked like, anyway." She didn't have an answer for the animals. Avery spooned some halo-halo into her mouth and wished she'd brought a sweater.

"You wouldn't let me touch it," Michael said. He assumed an exaggerated hurt expression. "You smacked my hand away."

"I'm sorry. I just—in Carlos's show and in movies, ghosts aren't supposed to be able to pass over salt."

"Oh, like vampires," Tessa volunteered. "They have to count all the crystals. So you carry rice or salt in your pocket in case you're being chased by one."

"I thought the rice or salt was to scatter over the waist if you come across legs," Michael laughed. He was far too cheerful to have just had the scare of his life. And yet, wasn't adrenaline surging through her body too? Avery couldn't stop looking around her, savoring the sweetness of the dessert, as if it were the last time she'd experience this. The ball of her own hair seemed to pulse in her pocket. Perhaps it was the last time she'd feel this way.

"Don't keep us in suspense. Let's see what was in the bag, girl." Tessa snapped her fingers.

Avery pulled the plastic bag from her lap. She'd been gripping the documents in her sweaty hand until Tessa had unearthed an empty bag from the glove compartment. "They're probably pretty fragile. Put them in here."

Avery swallowed another bite of halo-halo. Her mouth was pleasantly numb, a state she wished would spread to the rest of her. "There's something else. In the attic, near the salt. I found a clump of hair, and I think it was mine. From the…from the night of the Ouija board."

Father Michael leaned back, hands clutching his hair. "That isn't good."

Tessa gazed at Avery with sympathy. "Oh, girl. Oh no."

"How much time passed between the visitor at the door and Estelle getting sick?" Avery asked. "How much time have I got?"

Tessa shrugged, brow furrowed with worry. "I don't know. Days, maybe? Oh my God. Maybe we can find a protective charm for you."

"Do those really work?" Father Michael protested.

"Do you have any better ideas?" Tessa asked.

Panic filled Avery. "We figure out who it was that visited Estelle, and why. And we figure out how to stop her."

She reached into the bag and took out the first thing that came to her hand. A yellowed newspaper clipping, brittle with age, the photo far too blurred to be useful. "What does it say?"

"It's an advertisement for healing tonics and revenge spells," Michael translated. "From a mangkukulam. A witch."

"Are witches common here? They come up a lot when I research Filipino folklore." Avery wondered if a witch could protect her from whatever was coming.

"They were more common before Western medicine became established. In the smaller communities, they might still use old-school remedies if they don't have easy access to doctors, or if doctors haven't helped. What else is in there?" Tessa said.

"A paper with writing on it." Avery tilted her head, trying to read the scrawl. "Mala…malaking…"

"It's Lolo's handwriting. Let me," Tessa took the sheet of paper, stiff and flaking at the edges, holding it at arm's length. "It's a list of some kind: *large mirror, silver container, white candles, unused blade*. Then what looks like an address, but it's too faded to read."

Michael looked disturbed. "That sounds like a list for a ritual. What else is there?"

Avery dipped her hand into the bag again. "Another newspaper clipping." It wasn't the ragged rectangle of the previous but cut carefully and folded neatly. She scanned the Tagalog and saw a familiar name. "Roberto Sison. That's your grandfather."

Tessa skimmed the article. "It looks like in March of 1963, a witch was accused of killing a man and his wife, leaving only their child alive. Lolo spoke to the victims and led the authorities to the witch's home, where they found plenty of evidence. The witch died in prison shortly after."

"How did Lolo speak to the victims before they died?" Avery asked.

Michael cleared his throat. He looked uncomfortable. All of them leaned toward each other, their words clipped with stress. "I presume they asked him to speak to their spirits after their deaths were discovered."

Avery played with her dessert some more, but she'd lost her appetite. Had they really jailed a woman based on the information provided by ghosts, or worse, a man who professed to see them? Was her stomach aching because of the condensed milk, or because the curse that killed Estelle had been cast on Avery?

"That's awful," she murmured. Someone had lost their freedom without an investigation or evidence, merely the word of one man. It made her heart ache to imagine what had become of the surviving child, if anyone had taken them in, or if they'd been left to beg for food the way she'd seen so many children here do. Avery's anxiety drove her to take the last document from the plastic bag.

A faded brown-and-yellow photograph featured an unsmiling woman gazing into the camera. Behind her were the blurred outlines of trees and sky. The picture could have been taken anywhere. Avery froze, staring at the faded photograph. She recognized the woman. The sullen expression was burned into Avery's brain, even though she'd only seen it for a second.

Glaring out at the world from the reflection of a shrouded mirror.

CHAPTER EIGHTEEN

Avery

Avery shivered and rubbed at the gooseflesh that sprouted over her arms and legs. It was impossible. She had seen a distorted reflection of herself in an old mirror, and now her brain was playing tricks on her. How often had her mother confused her and Claudia at a quick glance? Dark hair, tan skin, and features that many Filipinas shared. And yet she couldn't deny the jolt of recognition that had struck her body at the sight of this picture.

Now that she looked more closely, she could see this woman didn't look much like her at all—the stranger's nose was flatter, her eyes larger, her long, straight hair split in the middle, while Avery's was flipped on the side. The woman in the photograph looked older as well, with crow's feet at the corners of her eyes and deep lines at both sides of her mouth so that she looked like she was frowning.

"What? Do you know her?" Tessa asked. "Let me see."

It was both a relief and a difficulty to pass the photograph over. Avery didn't want those large, dark eyes looking into hers anymore, as if the image was a window instead of a photograph, but at the same time, she didn't want to stop analyzing the features. If she let it out of her sight, would the features be unrecognizable when she looked again?

"I saw her." Avery took a deep breath and tried to organize her thoughts. "This is going to sound…unbelievable, I know. But yesterday, I heard whispering in Carlos's room, and I thought it was the cockroaches against the mirror again, like downstairs. And your mom had asked Fatima to make sure there weren't any bugs around him, so I checked under the mirror cover."

But Tessa wasn't listening. The woman clasped a hand tight over her mouth, her eyes so wide the whites of her irises were visible all the way around her pupils. Tears welled.

Michael looked from one woman to the next. He scooted his chair closer to Tessa's and put a hand on her shoulder. "I've got you. What's wrong?"

Tessa shook her head, the tears spilling over her cheeks and dribbling over her hand, still clasped tight against her mouth. She pointed to the picture.

The priest wrinkled his forehead. "You know this woman?"

"That's who Carlos and I saw in the mirror when we were kids," Tessa gasped.

It wasn't just Avery, then. The idea that someone else had seen—had recognized—the same woman in the mirror was a comfort, and yet it raised more questions. If she was seen, decades apart, by different people, that was independent confirmation, wasn't it? She wanted to show Carlos the photo, without Tessa present. If he recognized her face as the one he'd seen in the mirror, that was proof to Avery that this was real. And yet, how could it be?

"Why is she with these newspaper clippings?" Avery asked.

"Is this the witch, then?" Things were coming together. If she suspended all rationality, she could almost trace the timeline of events. They'd moved into this house full of covered mirrors and footsteps that paced the hallway and above her head all night. Carlos wasn't recovering as he should be, and the doctor thought it could be due to an angry spirit affecting his energy. Strange things happened in the house that she couldn't explain: a dark silhouette in the bathroom, whispers from empty rooms, dropped objects, things that moved as she was looking at them. And she followed the footsteps to the attic, where they'd found the third covered mirror, the bag with these papers, and a metal box ringed with salt. "The objects were all separated," she murmured, half to herself. "In the attic. They were spaced out." As if whoever had taken them up there had been afraid to keep them together. But why would Lolo have brought home the items of a dead witch? Avery shook her head. "I have to talk to Carlos. He knows more about this stuff than I do, and my mind is jumping to conclusions."

"What are you thinking?" Tessa wiped at her eyes and took frantic gulps of her bubble tea.

"I'm thinking that your lolo…was responsible for a woman's death, whether or not she was truly a witch. It's so strange to me that he kept souvenirs of her." Avery gestured to the news clippings and photo. "And now his grandson is being punished by her angry spirit." It sounded like a bad horror movie, when she said it out loud. To find out, after all this time, that a man everyone respected had helped murder a woman based on some voices he'd heard… Maybe Roberto had deserved to be haunted, but Carlos hadn't even been born then. And what had Avery ever done to the ghost, except stare defiantly into a haunted mirror?

"The fact that it came from you, the skeptical one, terrifies me," Tessa said. "Because that's pretty close to what I'm thinking too."

"We could be jumping to conclusions now based on a picture and some articles," Michael said.

"Okay, let's present this stuff objectively to Carlos, and to Dolores, who was there when everything went down. Let's see what they come up with." Tessa took a deep breath and stood up, tucking cash underneath her cup. "And figure out what we're going to do about it."

"I've got evening mass," Michael said as they walked to the car. "But someone please update me after."

"Thank you so much for coming with me, Father," Avery turned to look at him in the back seat. "I could never have gone up to the attic myself."

"God doesn't present challenges you cannot overcome." He grinned at her frozen expression. "Ah, getting better, no eye rolling. You're welcome, my friend."

Avery and Tessa were silent on the way back, lost in their own thoughts, and Tessa waved goodbye as she backed out of Salcedo Drive's lot. Apparently, when she said "we," she meant Avery would do everything in person, while Tessa called in remotely, still not willing to go inside the house.

Fatima let her in. As always, entering the house seemed to siphon all the sunlight from the day, until she felt like she was in a tomb underground. If only Carlos would agree to leave this place, she was sure he'd recover more quickly. But he was so determined to find out why Lolo was back and what he needed. She'd never seen him help another person to the detriment of himself. It was amazing and altruistic, and for once Avery wished he'd return to the selfish man she knew him as.

The plastic bag stuck to her clammy palm, already peppered with small holes from where she'd nervously poked her index finger through. Her hair felt filthy in her pocket, pulsating like a malignant mass, sapping her health.

Upstairs, Dolores sat on a stool beside Carlos, just as she'd left them. Avery took a deep breath. "Dolores, I'm on the phone with Tessa. We're going to show you a few things, and then I'm going to ask you some questions. Carlos still can't walk out of this house, and I know that you don't like talking about things inside, but I think it's time to be honest with each other."

Dolores gave Avery a wary look before she glanced at the door, clearly tempted to leave.

Avery pulled the ripped lock of hair from her pocket and held it out with a trembling hand. "I found this. Based on the story you told me on the balcony, about Estelle, I think my life may be at stake."

The old maid seemed to age before Avery's eyes. "It can't be. Where did you find this?"

Avery sat beside Carlos on the bed and showed him the photograph. "Do you recognize this woman at all?"

He leaned over to kiss her cheek before taking the picture. His eyes widened. "I know this face, but I don't know from where."

Don't say the mirror, she pleaded with him silently. If he could explain why Tessa knew her as well, Avery could go back to pretending the face in the mirror was an illusion. "Was it a teacher you had, or a neighbor?"

"Someone I saw as a kid. I think Achi was with me." Carlos handed the photo to Dolores. "Achi, do you recognize her?"

"I do. Remember, we had just seen some scary movie?"

When Avery turned the picture to Dolores, the old maid threw it away from her like she'd been burned. They watched it drift like an ember onto Carlos's bed. "You've been in the attic," Dolores moaned. "What else did you touch?"

Avery had never seen the woman so distressed. "Nothing. But there was an old backpack up there too. It slid open and so we thought that was a sign—"

Dolores hissed in annoyance. "Are you normally so gullible?"

"Tell me who this is, Dolores. Please. I think she's the reason why Carlos isn't healing, and that's where I found this clump of hair," Avery pleaded.

"Your hair… But she is not a problem anymore." Dolores glared at the covered vanity mirror. "Kuya Roberto made sure of that."

Avery's stomach clenched as she realized where the old woman had looked. "You've seen her too. In the mirror."

"We don't talk of these things in the house." The old woman wrung her hands together and moaned in distress. "How did she get your hair?"

"I'm sorry, but I think Carlos deserves to know. It's his health and his grandfather, after all." She turned to her husband—was he really still her husband, though?—and took his hand. "Your lolo was asked by police to help them investigate a young couple's death, by talking to their ghosts. I believe that, without concrete evidence, he blamed a local witch. The witch was arrested, and this article we found says she died shortly after, in prison. We found a list written by your grandfather that includes a mirror and a silver box, which we also found in the attic. I think your lolo did some sort of ritual on the witch—I'm not sure what—but her spirit has haunted the house ever since. That's why I keep hearing footsteps in the ceiling, why you're not healing, and why I saw her face in the mirror. She wanted me to discover what he did, why she can't be at rest."

"Bullshit!" spat Dolores. The old woman leapt to her feet, eyes blazing.

"Now, Dolores, I know that Lolo took you on when you were young and had a close relationship with you. It's normal to feel a strong loyalty to him," Avery said. "You had nothing to do with what he did, and you don't have to protect—"

"It's so typical of a North American, to come in here and assume you know everything." Dolores began to curse in Tagalog, words Avery had only heard her mother say a few times. Tessa tried to calm her, but Dolores just spoke louder.

"Ate, if you know Avery is wrong, then you must know what really happened." Carlos was using his charming voice, the one he used to interview frightened people on his show. "Is Avery in danger?"

The old woman caught her breath, face flushed with anger. "I do know what happened, and what will happen again. But I won't waste my breath trying to explain to someone who sees Kuya as the villain, instead of the hero." She strode away, shoulders squared with anger. "I am going to the market."

Avery fought the urge to grab the old woman and shake the truth out of her. Guilt churned with her frustration and shame, as if she'd been scolded by a beloved teacher.

A loud thud shook the house, rattling the windows and eliciting an involuntary yelp from Avery's mouth. From the main floor, Fatima screamed. Rapid footsteps pounded up the stairs, and she appeared at the doorway, eyes wide and terrified. She threw herself into Dolores's arms, her wailing Tagalog muffled by Dolores's shoulder.

"Fatima was sweeping when all the chairs around the dining table rose into the air, up to the ceiling, and crashed to the floor," Carlos translated.

Avery shuddered. Whatever was causing the haunting seemed to be getting stronger, and more violent. She wished fervently that they'd return to the days of small objects moving, when her skepticism protected her like a shield from the terror now riding her body. Avery exchanged a long look with her husband, who looked as shaken as she felt. What would happen next?

"See what happens when you don't respect the rules?" Dolores glared at them as if Avery were responsible for Fatima's terror as she led the younger woman away.

"Take Fatima with you to the market," Carlos called out to the maid. "I worry about her having a heart attack if she's walking around in this state, and I don't even know which maid I'm referring to."

"Well, that went well," Tessa said from the phone screen. "Did we learn anything at all?"

"Only that Dolores is weirdly protective over Lolo. She's willing to let Avery suffer just to defend him." Carlos wrinkled his forehead in confusion and picked up his phone.

"We knew that though. That's one of the reasons Mom hates her. Dolores always took his side, and Lolo seemed to love her the most. Even sent her to school with his own kids."

Carlos huffed in frustration and dropped his arms into his lap. "Finding a picture of this woman doesn't explain why Lolo's spirit appeared though, does it?"

"Sure it does. Lolo doesn't want us to sell the house with an angry spirit inside it," Tessa said. "Or maybe he wanted us to know what he did to her, and needs to, like, be forgiven. I have to look up charms to protect Avery first, though. That's most important. In the meantime, all of you should pack to get out of there. Today it's the chairs. Maybe tomorrow it's Carlos's bed."

"Thanks, Achi." Carlos looked at Avery. "In the meantime, I need to talk to my wife."

Avery ended the call and turned to Carlos, dread pooling in her gut at the anguish in his eyes.

"You've done so much for me, even doing the job I came back home to do. Things will no doubt become even stranger, and now your safety is at risk. We can't delay things any longer, Avery," Carlos said. "I've got something to confess."

CHAPTER NINETEEN

Avery

"Can't we just put it off until you're better?" Avery begged. This secret he kept bringing up, the look on his face when he did: She could already tell it wasn't something she wanted to hear, and it was going to break something between them. She knew this, just as well as she knew the secret would force her to do something horrible. "I told you, Carlos, I can't deal with any more problems."

"You won't have to deal with any more problems," he said gently. "Because you're going back to Canada."

She recoiled. Fear slithered through her exasperation, sharpening her words. "I told you already. I'm not leaving you."

"Avery, this is way more than you signed up for. And things have changed so much… *We* have changed so much. Maybe, across an ocean full of salt, thousands of kilometers away, this curse can't reach you."

She stared at him incredulously. "I'm staying to see this through, Carlos. What if something happens to you? You're totally helpless."

"Avery." He shook his head. "I don't want you here. I want you to leave."

No. It couldn't be. "Are you…are you breaking up with me?"

After everything they'd been through, now that he was on the mend and she was in danger, now he was pulling this shit?

Carlos's eyes widened, and he reached his hand out to her before letting it drop back on the blanket. "Never. I mean...it's not about me. You're everything I could ever... I'm not the man you came here with, the man you married. And there's things that you don't know about me, things you'll never believe."

Human nature was such a ridiculous thing. She knew he was possessed, maybe had been possessed since the moment he'd come back from the dead. And yet now that Carlos confirmed that she'd been right all along, all she wanted to do was argue. She took a deep breath. Whether or not he was her Carlos didn't matter, did it? Her feelings for him were the same. Stronger, even. It was as if she'd shoved all her old feelings into a ball and buried it deep into the earth. She'd expected it to remain a barren grave, and instead a new flower had emerged, a fresh, strong love for the him-that-was-not-him.

"I know what you're trying to say. But I already know. I knew from the moment you opened your eyes that you were different. Maybe that made me distant, at first. Like I didn't want to be around you. And it was a big decision to step away from trying to conceive in order to prioritize you. But I've fallen back in love with you, Carlos, or fallen in love with you for the first time." Avery laughed, suddenly giddy now that the truth was finally laid bare between them. "That sounds so weird. But it's true. I love you. And I know you're gonna figure out how to help me, but not if I'm stuck on a plane somewhere."

He clenched his eyes shut and shook his head. That wasn't the reaction she'd expected, and a worm of misgiving squirmed inside her.

"Avery. I… You have to leave me. Go home. I didn't mean to turn this into a declaration of our feelings. I just want you to leave, and live your life, and be safe and happy. Please, just go."

A pit opened in her guts, infinitely deep. So deep it might swallow her, soul and all. She didn't understand. The way he'd looked at her, the way he'd *kissed* her… "Carlos, I just told you I've fallen in love with you. I'm not going to leave you. We're going to go home together."

Carlos opened his eyes and stared at her. His expression was so bitter, so full of hatred, that she leaned away from him. It was as if the husband she'd known before had returned, and the contrast between the features she'd grown accustomed to and the ones she wanted to forget was like running through soft, thick grass and falling onto jagged rock. "You know why you could never conceive, Avery?"

She couldn't breathe. She braced herself as if he were going to hit her. "Don't."

His face flickered with too many emotions for her to identify. "I had a vasectomy. Before we met."

"You…what?" Time froze. A thread of pain sliced through her, thickening and snarling between heartbeats.

"You heard me. I had a vasectomy."

The room spun. Her heart broke. Two years of appointments and ultrasounds and injections and side effects. "You *watched* what I went through. You let me go broke trying to afford treatment. Refused to go to any appointments. I thought it was my body that was failing me. And all this time, it was you?" There were no tears, no lump tightening her throat. Crying was a corporeal reaction, and Carlos's words had destroyed her to mere atoms, a million of them, all vibrating with the same frequency of pain.

Moving slowly, she stood up and went into the hallway. Her limbs moved heavily, weighed down like a synaptic signal innervating dead flesh. The pit in her guts consumed Avery, until she sat at the bottom of a deep hole she would never climb out of. Emotions crashed against her, drowned her particles in unbearable agony.

"Why did you bother stopping me the other night?" she whispered. "You should have left me to swallow those pills. It would have been more merciful than this." Now she welcomed the curse taking hold of her, sure no suffering could ever touch the depth of her current pain.

"Avery, wait." Carlos reached out for her, fear in his traitorous, beautiful face. "God, I'm such an idiot. I shouldn't have told you like that. I've imagined this moment for so long, and it still came out so badly. Please, come here."

He'd lied to her. For *years*. And now that she'd finally found her way back to the man she loved, he was breaking her heart all over again. "How could you do this? You told me you loved me. You don't do this to someone you love." She took a few steps toward the bathroom before her legs gave out, and she slid to the hallway floor.

Despair buffeted her. Rage flayed skin from bone and stripped Avery from herself. Carlos had been the center of her life, her anchor, her guiding star. Her religion. She was ether without him, a ghost ripped from its mortal container.

Something heavy thumped from the room. Carlos had pulled himself from the bed, no doubt determined to torment her further. No more. She wouldn't let him take anything else from her, not one more second of her life.

She had to use the wall to stand again. The graininess of the wood beneath her fingertips helped ground her, bring her back to herself. Avery didn't have the strength for a suitcase, but she found herself holding the knapsack she'd worn from Canada. Time was skipping, or she was in shock. Toothbrush, a change of clothing, her phone charger. Her wallet and passport. She tossed them all into the bag without realizing she'd done any of it.

She heard a flat mumbling, a monotonous drone in her ear, before she realized it was her own voice repeating the same words. "You had a vasectomy. This whole time. You had a vasectomy..." as if the words were beyond her control, sneaking past her lips like a curse, like a centipede crawling from her hollowed abdomen.

"Avery," the bastard called as she neared the stairs. He dragged himself along the hallway, the way he had when he'd saved her. He looked so vulnerable, so distraught, that for a moment her separate molecules vibrated with the exact same furious resonance. She turned around and went to him. And the relief in his face filled within her a murderous, violent madness, so that even though he was weak and unable to stand, she bent down and punched him with all her strength.

His head struck the floor and blood seeped from a cut on his cheek she'd made with her wedding band. Avery left him there, afraid that if she lingered he would suffer more injuries, until the blood no longer seeped but pooled. Congealed. Cooled.

She didn't remember descending the stairs, but she took care to lock the front door carefully, as carefully as one might care for a borrowed object, rather than with the casual mistreatment of familiarity. Avery left Salcedo Drive with her small half-filled backpack, her back bent with the weight of a shattered heart, and walked in the humid, dusty streets. There was no one to call—everyone who might have a car was related to Carlos, and she spoke no Tagalog, nor had any pesos.

It occurred to her that it might not be safe for a woman to walk with Canadian credit cards and her passport, alone in a strange country. She considered her danger with relish, as if a robbery or assault might ease the pain of Carlos's betrayal, as if setting the exterior of her house ablaze would soothe the burning agony within.

Each step she took reverberated with a number, a running total of things she had lost since marrying this man. Her stable job. All her careful savings. Her friends. Her sweet, small apartment she'd rented for ten years. The last healthy years of fertility. Her dream of having children.

Avery's disparate particles froze at the last thought. *Children.*

People flowed around her, turning to gaze at her curiously before continuing. Horns beeped and brakes squealed on the busy road nearby. The sun beat through the haze of diesel fumes and seared the top of her head and across her shoulders. Avery was aware of the world spinning around her. Despite her. To spite her.

Atoms converged to reform a thirty-seven-year-old woman, utterly lost and sobbing in the street.

CHAPTER TWENTY

Carlos

Carlos blinked his eyes open and squinted at the late afternoon sunlight streaming through the windows. Another episode of lost time—he had been doing his exercises, keeping an eye out for the blinding light that signaled he was pushing himself too hard, and then…oblivion. Fear made it hard to swallow. Maybe She Who Creeps Between had been telling the truth, and the Broken Man was in his body. What if losing time had nothing to do with Carlos, but instead was the aftermath of a spirit draining his body of energy? He tested his limbs slowly, one by one, as gingerly as he had when his injuries were fresh: Was his arm's heaviness a sign of the ghost inside him resisting? Were the thoughts in his head even his own?

A sound pulled his attention to the hallway. Avery knelt on the floor, just past the bedroom door. How long had she been there? He ached at the sight of her; she looked like a broken doll who'd been dropped and forgotten, all flailing-limbed and vacant-eyed. She was muttering something, and even her voice was distant and dead, like a ventriloquist's dummy.

"You had a vasectomy. This whole time. You had a vasectomy…"

She always had to make him feel like shit. It was emotional manipulation, that's what it was, and he was a damn fool to think that bringing her to a new country would fix anything. His wife needed to work on herself before they could patch up their marriage, but even with a brain injury, Carlos knew better than to suggest that.

Even so, she looked so damn pathetic that his first reaction was to comfort her. That was the problem with their entire relationship—it was so one-sided. Defensiveness followed soon after. Why should he feel the need to apologize for a decision he'd made years before he even met her? As if he'd had the procedure to spite her.

True, he probably could have mentioned it to her when she was seeing all those doctors. He'd figured the fact that he refused to show up to the appointments was enough, that the "specialists" would determine it was likely a sperm issue and stop treating her. And yet they continued to take her money, continued to package hope in fifty-dollar syringes, the dishonest crooks.

If Avery knew he'd been snipped, they'd be arguing about reversing it instead of having romantic dates and long nights of lovemaking. She'd be angry at him instead of trying to stay in his good graces. He shook his head and fought the urge to apologize. Now she knew the truth, and wasn't that a good thing? There shouldn't be secrets in a marriage, and finally everything was out in the open. Both of them should be relieved, actually. The bullet was extracted from flesh, and the wound could heal.

She didn't look relieved. Carlos stared at the woman he'd loved with his entire soul for the last ten years. She looked made of porcelain, her features blank and lifeless. There was a fragility to her face, her movements, that he'd never seen before, not even when she was sobbing at his bedside after his accident. Somehow, out of all the things they'd been through, all the fights they'd had, this one small breach in trust—a mere crack, a hairline fracture—was what had broken her.

It was the house, he decided. The oppressive influence and the constant noise was exhausting her. All she needed was a good night's rest and some time away, and she'd come to her senses, realize that they were meant for each other and no one else should come between them.

Anger, always burning beneath his skin like lava, roiled closer. She was packing her things. Not just for a night away, which he'd always be supportive of, even if it meant she was abandoning him just when he needed her most, but for good if she'd thought to take her passport. She was actually doing what he'd always been afraid of: She was leaving him. So much for in sickness and in health; the moment Avery was tested, she was gone.

If he could just make her understand why he'd had the snip, she would stay. If he could just explain to her how the idea of his wife cooing over their baby sickened him to his very marrow, that he was afraid he'd stop loving her if she made him less of a priority, and yet he couldn't imagine loving anyone else, she'd understand. She didn't know he'd already suffered so much in his loveless childhood. His mom was cold and distracted, and Achi had babied her dog instead of him, and he'd felt like he was always thirsty and could never drink his fill. Until he'd seen her.

Maybe he could still convince her to stay. Maybe she'd grow old with him, sweeping away her own dreams like they were nothing more than spiderwebs.

You're lying to yourself. It left a sour taste in his mouth, but Carlos knew Avery would never have married him if she'd known he'd never share her—that's why he'd lied, wasn't it? Still, some part of her must have suspected; he and his sister had both warned her how selfish he could be. She'd said the vows anyway. And now, even though they didn't have kids, he was still losing her—losing her in a way that was more final and painful than sharing her with children would ever have been.

In their marriage, he'd always been the strong one. The one who decided things. Sure, there was always the chance Avery would get fed up and leave, but he'd been confident that he could say or do the right things to give himself another chance. He'd been confident in her love.

Carlos had done what was necessary to save their relationship. He'd lied to her to keep her with him, stringing her hopes along like they were pearls in a necklace. The anger that always boiled inside him was aimed at both of them: for her selfish desire to have children, and for his selfish desire to keep Avery to himself.

Carlos couldn't see a way out. He loved Avery too much to let her go; he loved Avery too much to make her stay. He needed to have children to keep her happy; having children would make him miserable.

When he was twelve, his father had helped him plant mango seeds in the small plot of soil outside. Two small seedlings had eventually poked through the earth, and Carlos watered them carefully each day and chased away any insects that might nibble on their small leaves.

One day Benji had called him over, holding a sharp knife. "Cut the stem off one of the plants," he told his son.

Carlos shook his head, aghast. "I can't choose between Fred and Wilma."

"You have to, son. We planted them too close, and they'll only get in each other's way. You sacrifice now, or you'll end up with no tree at all."

He'd chosen to cut Fred's stem because it was the smaller plant. Wilma had flourished thereafter.

Was that what he had to do with his own marriage? Cut the ties that bound them, that choked them, so that at least one of them could survive?

Avery yanked the charger from the wall socket and zipped up her backpack, still mumbling about his vasectomy. He could speak to her now, convince her to cool off. And then he'd, what, spend the next twenty years staring at the poorly concealed pain in her face? If he even lived twenty years—who knew what would happen with the Broken Man inside him, infesting his body like an invisible disease.

No. It was time to be strong.

Avery slipped out the room door.

Carlos let her go.

Something crawled from Lolo's bedroom into the hallway, following his fleeing wife. Fear tightened his throat. Carlos considered warning Avery, but the last thing he wanted was to draw the entity's attention to him. The Broken Man had possessed his body; it was likely another spirit wanted Avery's.

The bright light was filling his vision like an oncoming train, removing his need to make a decision. Distantly, the front door clicked shut.

His wife was gone.

CHAPTER TWENTY-ONE

Avery

The sun was setting when Avery finally caved. The blisters from her flip-flops had long since burst after hours of walking, and each step was a slippery burn. She was thirsty, tired of crying, and hopelessly lost. Avery pulled out her phone to call Michael and saw that all this time, there'd been no missed calls. It hit home for her how truly alone she was in this country.

"Kamusta, Avery," Father Michael's greeting brought about a fresh wave of tears.

"I'm sorry, Father." She tried to gulp down the sobs, but her shaking voice betrayed her.

"Oh no. What's wrong, my friend?"

"Something bad happened, and I had to leave the house. I didn't know where to go, and now I'm lost." Embarrassment flared through her—*thirty-seven years old and in this helpless state*—but it was a drop in the middle of a tsunami.

"Do you see any road signs? Or taxis?" The priest sounded concerned.

"I'm in the middle of a long road. There's a…an auto parts store in front of me." She peered down the road. "I think I see a taxi coming."

"If it's a taxi, try to flag it down. What is the name of the store, or an address? I can call Tessa." He didn't question why Avery hadn't called her sister-in-law in the first place, for which she was grateful.

"Please, don't tell her. I… It has to do with her brother."

Michael spoke more urgently. "Avery, you're an obvious foreigner alone in a strange area, and night is coming."

She squinted at the approaching cars. "Are you about to warn me about vampires, Father? I forgot my handful of uncooked rice." It felt good to joke, to pretend her world hadn't collapsed around her.

"Not vampires, no. Worse. Humans who have lost their way."

Avery shivered at his words.

There *was* a taxi. She raised her hand, worried it wouldn't stop, that it was occupied. Hell, was this even how they flagged taxis here?

The driver pulled over. "I'm putting you on speakerphone, Father. Can you please tell this man where to go?"

"First, check to see he has a picture of himself and his name posted in the back seat." He did, and Avery spelled his name out loud. Michael and the driver spoke briefly in Tagalog before the driver gestured impatiently for her to sit down while horns complained and cars swerved around them. "He's going to take you to my church. It shouldn't take long."

"I don't have any cash. Just my card."

"Don't worry about that, Avery."

"Thank you, Father. I'll see you soon." She ended the call and stared out the window, determined to focus on anything but Carlos's confession. The driver was playing sappy love songs, and she fought the urge to ask him to turn the radio off. If only Carlos had told her earlier. If she'd found out before his accident, before he'd looked at her with such…such awe… It would have been painful, but also the last nail in the coffin. Now, it felt like a double betrayal, because he'd made her fall back in love with him first. Or had she fooled herself into thinking he was different? When had he ever given her the idea that he wanted to stay together? She'd kissed him, and he'd pulled away…and she still hadn't gotten the hint. How could she have misread his gestures so badly?

She was thinking about him again. Avery swiped at her wet cheeks and cursed the day she ever met Carlos Tam.

Sooner than she expected, the taxi pulled up to a large gray church. Father Michael sat on the steps, hands clasped loosely together. As the driver stopped, the priest jogged toward them, taking bills from his pants pocket as he did.

Avery got out of the cab and walked toward him. He looked at her solemnly, forehead creased in concern. "What do you need from me right now, Avery?"

"I could use a hug." She tried to smile. "If you don't mind sweat and tears on your shirt."

"To provide a friend comfort, that's a fair trade." He folded her into his arms, gently, as if afraid she'd break. Avery sank into the hug. He was keeping her in one piece with his embrace; only the priest's kindness held her separate atoms together. Long before she felt ready to leave the warmth of his body, her pride reasserted itself and she straightened up.

"Thank you, Father. You'll have to tell me how much I owe you."

"You were so close to my church already, it was nothing," he said. "You might have reached here on your own if you kept going." He gave her a searching look. "Did you walk all the way from your house?"

She nodded, and he winced in sympathy. "We can talk inside, before the mosquitoes join us," Michael said.

Her phone buzzed as they walked into the basement of the church. Avery glanced at the screen, hoping against hope that it was Carlos. *Why? What would you say to him?* It was Tessa. Avery's first reaction was to end the call, to ignore it, anything to avoid speaking to her sister-in-law. That wasn't fair though. Tessa had been nothing but kind to her since they'd arrived, going out of her way to visit and make sure she spoke with or texted Avery every day. She didn't deserve any ill treatment.

"Hi, Achi."

"Hey, girl. What are you up to?"

Avery looked at Michael, who nodded. She inhaled. "I'm at Father Michael's church."

"Father's… Why?" A hesitation. "I don't want to pry, but…did you and Shoti fight or something? What happened?" Tessa asked.

"Can I…can I call you tomorrow or something, Achi?" She didn't have the strength to defend herself from Carlos's family tonight. Not without saying things she was sure she'd regret.

"No way. I'll be there in twenty minutes." She hung up before Avery could protest again. Tessa was the opposite of Carlos: aggressively generous where he was selfish. Was having a selfless sister the reason why her husband had turned out the way he had?

Father Michael's apartment, the rectory attached to the church, was smaller than the one she'd rented in Toronto, the furniture mismatched but solid. There was a main room, which had a small table and two chairs against one whitewashed wall, and a patched brown love seat set in front of a small television. A kitchenette took up nearly half the space. There were two doors that led from this room, one of which looked like a sparse, clean bedroom.

"Have you eaten?" Michael asked her. "I have a little rice and opu, or some lugaw?"

"I'd love some water, if you don't mind." Avery sank into one of the dining chairs with a groan of relief and accepted the offered glass.

"The water has been boiled, so it's safe to drink." The priest brought out a plastic basin from the second door. A bathroom, then. He filled the basin with water before placing it on the ground in front of Avery and returned with soap and a towel. When he kneeled before her, Avery flushed with embarrassment and tucked her feet further beneath the chair.

"You don't have to do that. You've done so much already."

He shook his head. "I'm just doing what Jesus would have done. Please." He gestured, and she reluctantly put her feet in the water. It was warm and soothed the burning pain of her raw blisters. She leaned back against the wall in gratitude.

"For your hand." Michael spoke above her. Avery blinked her eyes open and realized she must have nodded off.

"My hand?" she repeated, confused. Her eyes skimmed over her right hand first and then widened when she saw the knuckles of her left. They were swollen and red. Two of them had split open, though the blood had long since dried. The thought of her husband, crawling on the floor toward her, and what she had done to him when he couldn't defend himself filled her with shame. It was the first time she'd committed an act of violence, and she'd chosen a victim at his most vulnerable. She lowered her head and stared at her lap. She didn't deserve to accept the priest's kindness, not after what she had done.

Michael placed a cold, wet cloth wrapped around an ice pack onto her hand. "You're a good person, Avery."

She snorted, her sore eyes burning with tears once again. "You wouldn't think so if you knew what I did."

"Everyone is capable of sinning, but not everyone is capable of remorse." Michael lifted her left foot and gently rubbed soap over it. She hissed as the blisters burned. He rinsed the lather off and placed her foot on a towel.

"I'm full of remorse, all right. I'm remorsing the last ten years."

Michael's phone buzzed. He finished washing her right foot and placed it on the towel as well, drying both carefully before checking the message. "Tessa is here. I'll be right back."

He stepped out of his apartment. Avery had no right to feel this good after what she'd just experienced. Her feet tingled instead of ached, and she felt cared for. Might as well revel in this feeling before Carlos's sister found her.

Tessa burst in, a sheen of sweat on her face. She gave Avery a once-over, and her expression clouded with concern when she saw the ice on Avery's knuckles, her damaged feet. "Who did this to you? Is this about the girl in the picture?"

Avery blinked. She'd completely forgotten about the attic and Dolores's anger at her. If only it was something as simple as a fight about a murderous grandfather. Avery was too exhausted to justify why she'd left her husband in such a circumstance. Tessa would take her shoti's side, so what was the point in wasting energy trying to convince anyone? "Long story short, I've been seeing specialists to try to have a baby for the last two years. Carlos confessed tonight that he'd had a vasectomy before we even met, and didn't bother telling me before I spent all my money and two of my last fertile years trying."

It was easier when she said it like that. Lifeless and empty, like her uterus. Michael clucked in sympathy, bending to hold her right hand in both of his.

Tessa shook her head, frowning. "What? What are you saying?"

Avery didn't repeat herself. She knew her sister-in-law had heard every word. Michael refilled her empty glass. Both of them were waiting for Tessa to understand, to react.

Tessa burst into sobs. "That selfish asshole! That stupid bastard!" She lunged forward to throw her arms around Avery, the woman's tears landing hot and wet on Avery's shoulder, soaking into her already filthy tank top. "I'm so sorry, Avery. I'm so…fucking mad!"

The thin shell of self-control shattered under Tessa's weeping. If her sister-in-law was heartbroken at the news, her tears gave Avery permission to shed her own. They cried together, two women who both loved Carlos and hated his betrayal—Tessa, who loved the boy he had been, and Avery, who loved the man he might have become.

Avery patted Tessa on the back and hiccupped. "I'm sorry, Achi."

"Don't you apologize!" She stepped away from Avery and blew her nose. "Don't you dare apologize. Not when it's my brother who—" Her face crumpled like the tissue in her hand. "I'm going to give that idiot a piece of my mind. Father, don't you leave Avery alone for one minute." She gave Avery a watery smile. "I'll come back and take you to my place after."

As fast as she came in, Avery's sister-in-law departed. Michael took the basin of dirty water and soap back into the bathroom before he dragged the second chair in front of her. "Put your feet up while we wait." He settled on the couch across the small room.

Avery was relieved that Tessa's support had been so quick and unwavering. It brought the anger back again, deepened the sense of betrayal, as if her sister-in-law's reaction confirmed Avery's feelings were reasonable.

Silence settled over them, comfortable and easy like a cool summer night. If Carlos had brought her to a place like this when they'd first arrived, humble and plain but somehow...clean, she wouldn't have minded. "I like the energy of your apartment, Father. It feels like a weighted blanket, somehow."

He beamed at her. "You've come so far, my friend. When I first met you, I would never have guessed you'd speak of a place's energy without cynicism."

"It's just so different from Salcedo Drive." She shrugged, embarrassed.

"I agree completely. Here, as in the Tam home, the energy is related to what is above us. In their case, a nefarious mystery. In my case, God's House. Ah, that's a familiar look on your face. I see your transformation has limits. Would you accept, then, that hundreds of people, every week for years, praying with faith and love, could create such an energy, even if you cannot believe its source is divine?"

Avery hesitated. "I guess living in that house for two months, I can believe almost anything."

"And you've seen things happen in the house you can't explain? What is your stance on spirits now?"

Unless the entire house was designed to fool her with tricks and gadgets, there was no other way to account for what she had seen. "I've found things in a different place from where I left them, and have seen objects move when no one was nearby. Once, I watched a newspaper slide right across my night table. The whole house feels restless at night, even when everyone is supposed to be asleep. And the change in Carlos..." Her voice trailed off.

Michael got up and brought her a bowl of purple grapes. "I find it interesting that Carlos told you about his vasectomy tonight, after keeping it secret for years."

"I don't really give a shit why he decided to tell me, Father. Sorry." She crunched on a grape as if it might temper the rage inside her.

"What were you talking about before he confessed to this?" Michael settled back on his brown couch. "Did it come out of the blue?"

"He was...trying to get me to leave the house. To go home to Canada. I had just told him I'd fallen in love with him..." The humiliation made things worse. She'd expected him to be happy at the news, had made herself so damn vulnerable...but she didn't know this new Carlos.

"And do you believe he loves you?"

Avery shrugged, stared down at her damaged feet. "I thought he did. I don't know what to believe about anything anymore."

"I understand from spending time with the Tams that Carlos has always prioritized himself. Would you say that was true?"

"I'd say today is a perfect example of that. What are you getting at?" She wanted him to change the subject, or to get to the point. Anything to stop poking at a fresh wound. It was fine when *she* did it. She knew exactly how much she could take. This prodding from anyone else felt needlessly cruel.

"I would say, from an outsider's perspective, that it sounded like Carlos revealed this horrible betrayal as a reason for you to leave him. To possibly escape the spell that killed his aunt Estelle, so many decades ago." Michael tilted his head as he looked at her. "You've just admitted that you've changed since coming to Manila, that living in the house has made you more open to supernatural possibilities. Could it be that your husband has also undergone some changes, and has begun to think of more than himself?"

"I don't want to hear about what a hero Carlos is, okay? He's ruined my life. For however long I have left." Avery set the glass down harder than she intended. The sharp rap of glass on the table seemed loud as a gunshot, and the silence that followed was less comfortable than before. Was that tightness in her throat from her crying, or a sign the witch's curse was taking effect?

"I'm sorry, Avery. I didn't mean to make you more upset." Michael rubbed at his face. "It's been on my mind to talk to you about Carlos ever since you asked me about possession."

"I don't care about that anymore. I just want to get out of here and go back to my life without feeling like this."

"Like what?" Michael crossed the room again and slipped a box of tissues on the table beside her.

"Like...*this*." Avery gestured at her face and the tissue box. "I feel like I've been crying for two years. I just want to go back to being happy, and feeling...emotionally stable. I want to walk away from this nightmare without feeling so foolish. Without looking over my shoulder, wondering how some witch is gonna use my hair to torture me." She stared at the ice pack resting on her swollen knuckles. "And without feeling like some villain who assaulted and abandoned her sick husband."

"How can we achieve this for you? To leave here with a clean conscience?"

She sighed. "I'd already decided what I wanted to do, before all *this* happened. We came here to help figure out why Lolo's ghost appeared to Dolores, and we did that. We know it's the witch's vengeful spirit that haunts Salcedo Drive, and we have to get rid of her before the house is safe to sell. And before she hurts me. I need to see it through now, if I'm to ever feel safe."

She didn't want to leave at all, despite everything. Manila was foreign and strange to her eyes, and yet there was something that had grown familiar within it. As a child she'd wake up from long car rides just before her father pulled into their driveway. Somehow, though her eyes were closed and she was deep asleep, her body sensed she was home. That was how she felt here, even if the sights were still new and it was the place of her greatest betrayal.

Her phone vibrated. She checked the screen, dreading—hoping?—to see Carlos's name. It was Tessa.

Avery connected the call. "Hi, Achi."

Her sister-in-law wasted no time. The background noise was loud and muffled. Avery pressed the phone harder against her ear, as if that would help her hear more clearly. "Can you guys come to the house quick? No one is opening the door, and I think something's seriously wrong."

The background noise clarified into distant screams.

CHAPTER TWENTY-TWO

Carlos

The prospect of a life without Avery loomed ahead of him, miserable and unending. Would it have been better if he'd never come back from death, if he'd been mourned instead of reviled?

"I can cheer you up," She Who Creeps Between whispered.

"How? You going to take me out for a steak dinner?" Carlos muttered, too distracted to remember who he was speaking to.

"I don't think a steak would help," she tittered. "Perhaps something a little…bloodier?"

He shivered. "You were going to ask around for me. Other gho—people who might know about the new guy, or how to get him away from me." He wondered how much the spirit, this Broken Man, had drained from him already. Would it shorten the years of his life?

"He's a reclusive sort. Not many have met him."

"Can you get the little girl to come visit? She was going to ask around for me too." He thought he'd seen flashes of her, peeking at him through the crack in the door, but she'd never spoken to him again.

The whispering woman hissed. "Not that one. She's always with *him*."

"Roberto?" Had he answered too quickly? "That was the old man's name, right?"

"Surely even a selfish boy like you knows the name of his grandfather."

She knew who he was, then. Maybe she'd always known. Just because she wasn't speaking didn't mean she wasn't listening. Carlos licked his lips. "Some grandfather. He hasn't even come to see me. He's as bad as the rest of my family. You're the only friend I've got here."

Her whispers moved from the wall to the doorway. "I'll make you feel better, *friend*."

"I just need to know how I can get the Broken Man out of me," Carlos pleaded. "That's all I want." If he could get the spirit out of him, his periods of losing time might cease, and his body might actually start healing properly.

"Get that charm off the door, then," she said.

"Will you…? Am I in danger from anyone else in the house if I can get it off?" The charm was currently beyond his reach. His legs still weren't able to fully bear his weight. Avery was probably on the first flight out of here, but he could ask Dolores, or Tessa when she visited. But not until he was sure he wasn't making things worse for himself.

"The only thing you're in danger of waits in the dark room down the hall," she whispered.

"And whatever is in here with me." Sorrow cut through the fear and exhaustion. "My wife left me today."

"She wasn't much of a wife. She barely spoke to you, I think. Too busy enjoying life with your money, your sister, and that devilishly handsome priest."

If the words stabbed like a knife blade, it was because they were honed with truth. He'd been thinking the same thing. It hurt him to think of Avery returning to Toronto, back to the gray concrete prison where she hated her job and would be alone, but it hurt less than imagining her here, being happy without him.

"Don't worry, apo ni Roberto. I will take your pain away."

Curiosity had him crawl closer to the door, toward her. "How?"

"By passing the pain to someone else, of course." There was laughter in her voice.

She paused as if waiting for him to stop her. As if he had more than mere words to use, when she had the run of the house. Carlos hesitated. He decided that it wasn't fair for him to be the only one suffering on this fine tropical day. "What can you do?" he asked.

A few seconds later, he heard Dolores cry out, and then the heavy, terrible thuds of a body rolling down the stairs.

"Dolores!" Carlos called. There was a pain-filled moan.

"Ate? Ate!" Fatima's panicked voice came to his ears, and he had to admit, it was like music. The skittish waif had ignored him since his accident, acted like she was too good to serve him. Her terror was a poultice to the festering wound of resentment. Things were being thrown, no doubt the work of his friend. He welcomed the crashing sounds of destruction downstairs, waved his hands in the air like he was conducting a symphony, as if the whispering woman was his own instrument, under his control and performing flawlessly.

She was right. It was hard to think of Avery when Fatima screamed so beautifully, hard to dwell on his own pain when he could cause it in others. He should have done this weeks ago: better to be feared than to be ignored, to have servants cower rather than be negligent. This was the power he'd craved since his cousin had ignored the police officer, the sense of being untouchable. *Is this what you wanted, all this time?* Carlos asked the spirit that resided within him. *It turns out that we have similar tastes.*

For the first time since his accident, he wasn't helpless. He'd tear this house down to its foundation, shake the ghosts from its very bones. Carlos roared and lurched brokenly across the room, sweeping surfaces clear of objects and howling in triumph as they smashed on the floor.

Fatima screamed with each crash—tiny, staccato deaths that filled him with euphoria. When it was over, when there was nothing else he could reach or break, he lay panting on the floor. He felt formless. Deboned. He'd been stuck in this house for two months. How many decades had She Who Creeps Between waited here? How much more time had her hatred aged, like a fine wine?

He laughed, breathless and drained, still limp on the floor. "Thank you, my friend. I do feel better."

He heard a sound downstairs, only noticeable now that the destruction above and below had ceased. Someone hammered on the door.

His first thought was that Avery had returned to him. "Dolores, get the door!" he called. But then he remembered again the bone-cracking thumps as the old woman tumbled down the stairs.

Carlos laughed and laughed, until oblivion claimed him once more.

CHAPTER TWENTY-THREE

Avery

She didn't expect her first experience with a pedicab to be under such circumstances, but Michael assured her that it was the fastest way. "There's too much traffic if we take a car," he said. It seemed he was right, though motion sickness sloshed through Avery with every swerve toward the curb or between cars, with every lurch of acceleration or sudden brake.

The priest was crammed beside her in the narrow seat, and a line of heat ran between them, sweat from both of them mingling from thigh to shoulder. Somehow, it was a comfort, a reminder that she was not alone in this strange adventure.

"I'll miss you when you go," he said, during one of the many interminable traffic stops. "But nowadays it is easy to keep in touch."

"Let's figure out Salcedo Drive before we say our goodbyes." Solving Carlos's house problem was a life preserver, something to keep her afloat while the riptide of her emotions tried to overwhelm her. She nudged him. "But I'll miss you too."

She would, she realized. She'd miss Michael, and Tessa, and even Dolores. Most of all, she'd miss the dusty streets of Manila, where horses let loose streams of urine just meters from the finest restaurants, where mangoes and coconuts were not merely tasted, but experienced, where real joy seemed possible even without the trappings of comfort. Or perhaps because there was no guarantee of comfort.

Avery belonged to these people in a way that she'd never belonged to anyone—the children she couldn't claim, all rounded cheeks and prominent bellies, the women selling wares from carts or storefronts, the men with dirty sandos and flip-flops as they ambled down the street, smoking cigarettes. Somehow, they were a part of her, and she realized at some point she'd become reluctant to return to Canada, where everyone was their own, discrete self, busy denying their connectedness with averted eyes and earbuds, with e-readers and iPhones.

For the first time, she walked down the street and she looked like everyone else. She belonged, even if it was just her face. Avery thought of the time she'd gone on a honeymoon cruise with Carlos and had fended off the leering advances of men, the haughty orders of women, who'd seen her brown skin and assumed she was part of the ship's crew.

"We can walk from here." Michael stopped and paid the rickshaw cyclist. She owed him so much, this priest who felt more like a cousin, a brother. They hurried down Salcedo Drive, the walls built high, the trees looming like they were giants leaning over stone and metal gates to observe the two of them. The moon was obscured by clouds, white cotton candy that glowed like the entity she'd seen in Carlos's body.

She wished he hadn't come to mind. The thought came with a sharp pang, a needle through cloth, that matched the cramp in her side. Perhaps if she pushed the needle through the same painful hole, over and over, it would become easier to traverse, a path made smooth by familiarity. *See, Dolores? I learned something from your cross-stitch lessons after all*, she thought, before she remembered that it was Carlos who had told her that.

The Tam property came into view, sooner than she would have preferred. They'd rushed—Avery in socks and borrowed shoes, far too big for her—the echoes of screams in their ears, and the journey was safe, even if the destination wasn't. She could have pretended they were accomplishing something, until they actually arrived.

Tessa paced on the porch, alternating between wringing her hands together and pounding on the door. "No one's answering. I heard screaming, but now it's all quiet."

Avery handed her the house key. She felt removed from everything now, a backup dancer instead of the star. She'd do what she could tonight, and then she'd book her flight to Toronto tomorrow. The journey back to Salcedo Drive had clarified things for her. It was no longer her husband trapped in the house, in his body. Instead, a strange, kinder entity had been decent enough to tell her the truth Carlos had never bothered to, had shown the kindness she wanted in a partner. Right before he'd spurned her. She'd fall in love again, or not. She'd have children, or not. But what she wouldn't do was stay in a marriage with a selfish liar. Avery had once believed in Carlos, and only Carlos; now the only thing she believed in was that she deserved better.

Tessa pushed open the front door, key still in the lock. Avery couldn't help but recoil. Dolores lay in a crumpled heap at the base of the stairs, and Fatima a cowering figure beside her. Glass was shattered everywhere, the photos from the wall smashed to pieces on the floor. Every time Fatima tried to move toward them, she stopped with a whimper, her head moving this way and that as if trying to keep track of a mouse. The very walls seemed to draw closer, like a prison. Like a noose.

"May nagtulak kay Ate Dolores pababa ng hagdan," Fatima cried out, voice high with fear. Michael answered her, soothing and calm, both speaking Tagalog.

"Apparently something pushed Dolores down the stairs, but there was no one behind her. Fatima says something comes closer to her any time she takes a step. It's why she couldn't let me in," Tessa translated.

"How do we make it stop?" Avery asked.

"The activity is because of the witch's ghost. She's letting us know she's angry. We have to figure out how to give her peace, and only then will she settle." Tessa held up her phone. "Shoti says he's fine, but a little tired."

Avery swallowed hard, as if that would make the words go down easier. He had his phone, and he was capable of sending messages, and *he hadn't reached out to her*. She wished she were on a plane speeding away from here, a jet fast enough to abandon her husband and her soul and her heartbreak all for one low price.

"We'll do a séance, figure out what the witch needs to move on," Tessa decided. "No running away this time."

"You're sure that will work?" Michael turned to her, resignation in his voice.

"I don't have any other ideas, Father. Do you?" Tessa asked.

He shook his head. "Where, then?"

"The upstairs hallway," Avery heard herself say. "Or maybe the bathroom." Hadn't someone told her once that mirrors were doorways? The bathroom and master bedroom mirrors were the only ones uncovered. Although whatever haunted Salcedo Drive was already inside.

"First, we need to get Dolores looked at," Tessa said. "She's moaning, which means she's breathing, but for a fall at her age, she needs a doctor."

The old maid spoke, her voice muffled against the hardwood floor. "The only thing I need is to be rid of this house. If you're going to try to speak to the spirits, I'm staying. You can call the ambulance for me later. Fatima has cut herself on glass."

"We don't need an old woman dying on us, Ate," Tessa said. "There are enough ghosts in here."

"Can any of you see those ghosts? Channel them?" Dolores asked, her breath hitching with pain. "No? Then how can one carry on a séance without a medium?"

Tessa whistled. "I *knew* it! Lolo did teach you."

Dolores sniffed. "As much as those Hollywood movies taught you, I'm sure."

Michael strode forward and gently guided Fatima toward the door. The house's walls seemed to squeeze tighter around them, but the priest beside her seemed to give the maid courage. When she reached the exit, Fatima bent to grab her sandals and ran out into the night, not stopping to put on her shoes until she reached the gate. She left bloody footprints on the gray concrete. She didn't leave, as Avery expected, but turned and waited for Dolores.

Dolores called out to Fatima in Tagalog. The young woman nodded and left through the pedestrian door beside the fence. "Can you teach eyes to be nearsighted, or hair to be brown? I was born with this ability. Your grandfather just helped me cope with it. He taught me to keep it secret, to keep me safe." She grunted as the priest pulled her up to stand. The only visible sign Dolores had fallen down the stairs was a large lump on her forehead. "Some bumps and bruises. A strained shoulder, I expect. No more than many infants suffer at birth, though I have a pain reliever they don't." She pointed upstairs with her lips. "The hallway, I think you said? I'll meet you there."

They traipsed upstairs, Avery's stomach fluttering more with every step. She'd struck Carlos with a closed fist while he lay defenseless on the floor. While he crawled toward her, calling her name. Wasn't that why she was here now, instead of at the airport? If she hadn't punched a vulnerable man, if instead, she'd run crying from this godforsaken house, the only true victim, would she ever have come back? This séance was a last gasp to calm the ghosts of past and present that would follow her, rattling chains of guilt and shame. An attempt to convince the witch to let Avery be.

The upstairs hallway was dark and forbidding. A smear of blood gleamed dark against the floor. Carlos's blood.

"Do we need something to talk to the witch?" Avery asked, remembering old sleepovers and bad horror movies. "That Ouija board?"

"Just a candle." Tessa pulled a wide candle and a lighter from a cloth bag. She'd had it in her trunk, in case an emergency séance was required, perhaps. "Or so the internet tells me."

They settled on the cold wood floor in the space where the bathroom, master bedroom, and main hallway intersected, the candle lit between them. Avery wished she'd chosen the dining room, where there were chairs, or the kitchen, where there were snacks, but somehow she felt that this space was the most in-between, and that if there were spirits, they would be here.

Father Michael helped Carlos from his room, the sick man's legs trembling like a newborn calf as he leaned heavily on the tall priest. A bruise bloomed over Carlos's right eye like a night blossom, and the skin beneath the wound on his cheekbone was puffy and swollen. Blood had dried like runny mascara down one side of his face and spotted the shoulder of his T-shirt. He slid down the wall and stared at Avery. She looked down at her lap, unwilling to give him any satisfaction, though her knuckles ached with a sick triumph and shame corroded her guts.

Tessa hissed. Avery glanced at her, and flushed when she saw her sister-in-law's expression, which flickered between concern and anger. "I can't say you don't deserve it, Shoti."

"I deserve far worse." Carlos turned to Dolores, plodding up the stairs. She stopped to take a long pull from a small bottle. "I heard the screaming, Dolores, but I was too lightheaded to come down. Are you okay? Where is Fatima?"

"Don't worry about me. I look better than you." The old woman offered Carlos the bottle and stifled a burp. "You want some?"

It took him two hands to raise the bottle to his lips, but he gulped some of the alcohol before handing it back. Up here, the air was heavy with threat, impossible for even those insensitive to such things to ignore. The very walls seemed to loom closer, the gaps between planks staring outward like empty sockets. Avery shivered and watched Michael rub at the raised hairs on his arms. Malevolent energy circled around them like wolves around prey, making their haphazard circle draw closer together and their eyes dart at the shadows around them.

"What should I ask?" Tessa furrowed her brow and stared at the others.

Dolores leaned forward, her wrinkles made into chasms in the candlelight. "Ask about Kuya Roberto, and what he needs."

"Ask what the witch wants in exchange for leaving us alone," Avery suggested at the same time.

Maid and wife glared at each other.

"Carlos came home because Kuya appeared," Dolores said.

"And Carlos will recover when the angry ghost stops draining him." Avery still refused to look at her husband.

"I can speak for myself," Carlos protested mildly. He considered. "Helping Lolo is more important than my recovery, if it gets Dolores to the hospital faster. And perhaps Lolo knows how to bring peace both to him and the witch. When did Lolo appear to you, and what was he doing?"

Tessa scowled at her brother. "Since when do you care about helping Lolo? You were terrified of him. You literally ran away when he said you'd turn out like him, and you refused to come back."

"My priorities have shifted since dying; what can I say?" Carlos glanced at Avery, and she looked away immediately. More proof he wasn't the man she'd moved to the Philippines for.

"I don't think Dolores wants to help the witch, or me," Avery accused. "She freaked out when I told her what Roberto Sison did to that poor girl."

"That's because you were wrong," Dolores snapped. "And so proud of your ignorance."

"Whoa." Carlos held his palm up, shaking from this small effort. "Let's all calm down. Ate, please don't talk to Avery like that. She's only trying to help."

Dolores pressed her lips into a tight line and shook her head.

"Kuya Roberto didn't want me to tell any of you that he was here. Then to hear your wife make such horrible accusations, after everything he has done for this family. If only you knew the truth."

"Then tell us what happened. Do you think this witch is why Lolo appeared to you?" Tessa asked.

The old woman shook her head again, refusing to answer.

"Avery's life may be at stake," Carlos said. "Please Dolores, help us. Was the article they found in the attic true? Is the ghost haunting this house a mangkukulam?"

Dolores gave a pained sigh. "The mangkukulam, the witch, caused a couple to become very sick, expecting them to pay for a cure. But they couldn't afford her fee, and so they died." Her eyes gleamed in the candlelight. "The local authorities had no leads. The neighborhood was frightened, you see. So someone asked Kuya for help. He went to the house and spoke to the new spirits, who named the witch that cursed them. The couple's teenage daughter helped identify the witch after Roberto found her."

"How did she end up in this house, in the mirror?" Avery asked. She didn't see why Dolores was so angry; her version didn't contradict Avery's theory much.

Tessa picked up her phone. "The woman we saw in the photograph, or in the mirror, isn't the mangkukulam that Lolo helped imprison. Tonight, I found more articles on the case, and some included this picture of an old woman." She held the screen out for the others to see.

Dolores cried out and covered her face when she saw. Avery stared at it to see what was so horrible. The old witch had an unpleasant cast to her eyes and a cruel twist of her mouth, but there was nothing frightening about her countenance. Still, there was a clear resemblance between the picture they'd found in the attic and this woman.

"The photo we have is of the witch's daughter," Michael guessed.

Dolores lowered her trembling hands from her face. "Yes. The daughter, who inherited her mother's dark powers along with her features. This witch had different abilities than her mother. She was a mambabarang. She came to this house after her mother was jailed, seeking revenge. And poor Estelle opened the door."

The lines and creases in Dolores's expression deepened into crevices of old grief. "She bespelled the girl to get your Lola's hair, which she needed for her magic."

Avery shivered, remembering the morning on the small balcony with Dolores. Estelle had said, "She wants Ma Ma." The mambabarang wanted to kill a child's mother to avenge her own.

After that, Roberto had run out to buy a charmed necklace for his wife, but it wasn't Carlos's grandmother who had gotten sick. "Estelle gave the stranger her own hair," Avery whispered.

Dolores nodded gravely. "That is what Kuya thinks happened. Remarkable that a nine-year-old could disobey such a powerful witch. But Estelle should have told her father. By the time he figured it out..." The old woman pressed her lips together.

"What can a mambabarang do? Is it more evil than a mangkukulam?" Carlos asked.

"A mambabarang can control insects and spirits," Avery answered, remembering her long hours of researching folklore. "The victim's hair is tied around an insect, and it burrows into their body. They use their dark arts to torture and kill their victims."

Tessa gasped. "So the reason Estelle died...the reason our grandparents hated insects..."

"Estelle grew so swollen and bruised. Small things crawled beneath her skin—you could see them as they moved. Centipedes crawled out of her mouth. She coughed out cockroaches. Worms coiled in her stool. When the doctors took her blood, little eggs floated in the glass tubes." Dolores crossed herself. "Kawawang bata. There was nothing anyone could do. She couldn't eat, couldn't sleep. And she hated to be alone, she was so scared. Near the end, she screamed until she lost her voice, screamed that she was being devoured from the inside. It was almost a relief when she fell unconscious, because we hoped she couldn't suffer anymore. When it was quiet, all you could hear was the ticking of the clock and the sounds of buzzing from within her. At her death..." She stopped to place a shaking hand over her mouth. "At her death, her abdomen split open, and thousands of creatures spilled out. There was almost nothing left of her beneath her skin, just bone and tendon, everything else taken by the insects inside her."

Avery swallowed bile. Was this the fate that awaited her? No wonder Evelyn had asked Fatima to always check Carlos's room for bugs, why they left no loose hairs where anyone might find them. "What happened then?"

"Call him here. Ask him yourself," Dolores said. "That is his part of the story to tell."

"I'm sorry I accused him of murder before." Avery met the old maid's blue-ringed eyes. "I thought that's what the house was trying to tell me."

"You can't trust wood and stone to tell the truth." Dolores snorted.

"But a house carries memories." Tessa looked at the maid. "You used to tell us that."

"Whose memories? Whose feelings? There are always two perspectives to every event," Dolores said. "Why don't you ask your lolo for his side?"

Tessa took Carlos's hand and gestured for the others to do the same. "Fine, then. Let's get started. Everyone try to relax."

Avery faced Lolo's dark room, the door still ajar. Her back pressed against the wooden stair spindles. She placed her left hand in Dolores's grasp, the other in Michael's. Carlos was slumped against the wall, his legs splayed out on either side of the candle.

The candle flickered, making the shadows shift behind them. Avery felt as if they were surrounded by silent observers, their movements restless and jerky from the corner of her eye.

"Ready?" Tessa cleared her throat and closed her eyes. "I call upon the angry spirit that lurks upstairs. I call my lolo, Roberto Sison."

Dolores cursed. "You and your theatrics. You were supposed to call Kuya,"

"I did!"

"You should have used only his name."

"What's the difference?" Avery shuffled on the floor, trying to get relaxed.

"The difference is that now she has summoned more than one ghost: Kuya and the angry spirit upstairs. But there is more than one spirit that lurks upstairs, and they are all angry."

"Even the..." Tessa licked her lips. "Even the woman in the mirror?"

Dolores's eyes flickered toward each doorway, and down the stairs. Avery tensed. *Don't look at the first door*, she begged silently. That was Carlos's boyhood room, where they'd fled from the attic.

Avery's scalp tingled where her hair had been pulled out, and her clump of hair throbbed in her pocket. Instead, the old maid turned to look into the master bedroom.

Dolores squeezed Avery's hand painfully as the maid's eyes fixed on a point behind Avery's shoulder. "He's here."

CHAPTER TWENTY-FOUR

Avery

Lolo?" Tessa's eyes widened and she looked around. "Where?"

Avery was about to move—to shout, to flee, she wasn't sure—when the stray hairs from her ponytail fluttered against her neck, an errant breeze blowing where there should be none. As if something passed over her shoulder. Dolores inhaled a deep, gasping breath. Her back arched in a way that shouldn't have been possible for an arthritic septuagenarian.

When Avery was young, she loved to watch videos of people performing impressions of actors. Jim Carrey was her favorite. She watched his features shift to channel James Dean, Jack Nicholson, Robert De Niro like magic. In the same way, the maid transformed into a stranger before Avery's eyes. It was the way Dolores moved, the way her features twisted into expressions she normally didn't make, the way the lines of her face deepened into a different life lived. And when she spoke, the timbre of her voice was deeper, the Filipino accent stronger. "Tessie. It's good to see you." She looked at Carlos's slumped body. "You too, Carlos, even in such a manner."

"Lolo? Is that you?" Tessa's voice cracked.

Avery fought the urge to laugh, to pretend this was merely an awful prank, but the looks on everyone's faces were too serious. They clearly believed Dolores, and the deluge of their belief washed away the skepticism Avery wanted to hide behind. She wanted to stop touching the rough, callused fingers of the old maid, but now she was afraid to let go. Wasn't that how people got in trouble, letting go of planchettes or breaking séance circles before dismissing the spirits?

"I have always been here, apo. Since the day I left." The grooves in Dolores's face grew deeper with sorrow, until she resembled an old man.

"What happened with the mambabarang, Lolo? Is she the reason you can't rest now?" Carlos asked.

Dolores's body sighed. "I left Estelle's bedside when no doctor could cure her. I meant to find the witch's daughter and beg her to undo the curse. Even to offer my own life in exchange. But she laughed in my face. I was still gone when Estelle…when I got word that my daughter had…" He shook his head, grief shrinking his frame. "It was a dark, dark time. I didn't return for another four months."

"Your wife was left alone to care for the other children while she grieved." Avery knew something about feeling abandoned in this house. A small part of her cringed at what felt like a farce: She was glaring into the cataract-blue of an old woman's eyes instead of Roberto Sison's.

Dolores seemed to come back to her body. It was a subtle change of posture, a smoothing of her face. "It was important to stop the witch before she claimed more victims," the old maid murmured in a soothing voice. "And you did, Kuya. You used the documents Avery found in the attic to hunt down the mambabarang. You came back with the three mirrors and her ashes, assuring the rest of your children would be safe."

"Is Lolo gone because he didn't like what I had to say?" Avery asked.

"It is difficult for a spirit to be in this realm. Strong emotion shatters a ghost's concentration, and it takes time to collect themselves. And your accusations, when you're not even a part of this family, are beyond insulting." Dolores glared at her and broke the circle by releasing Avery's hand.

"Avery is my wife," Carlos protested. "For now, anyway. She married into this family; she took my last name. She has a right to speak."

Avery fought the urge to meet Carlos's eyes. He didn't deserve her gratitude; hell, it had taken a full-fledged possession for him to speak up for her. "I'll say it, since it sounds like no one else is willing to. He could have said goodbye to Estelle properly. He could have comforted his family when he heard she'd died. You're not going to convince me that wasn't selfish." Avery stood up while anger replaced her fear. It was hard to breathe. She needed fresh air and some time away from the suffocating, furious hallway.

Carlos's voice followed her downstairs. "No wonder Mom was always so weird about strangers. I'm surprised she had kids at all after losing a sister like that."

Avery's shoes crushed glass against wood and skittered broken pieces of debris in every direction. She unlocked the front door and tugged at it.

It didn't move.

A steel band encircled Avery's chest as the remaining urine-yellow bulbs that hadn't already broken died and fizzled out, leaving the first floor in darkness. She pulled at the door again, and a third time. Avery strode to the sitting room, feeling her way in the dark, and clawed aside the curtains, tugging at the window. The steel band drew tighter with each window she couldn't open, until she collapsed, gasping, against the immobile kitchen door.

If houses absorbed the atmosphere of their inhabitants, the people within Salcedo Drive had felt trapped and unable to escape, and they were forced to relive this now. Avery couldn't say she was surprised. She'd felt stuck for so many years now—in her love, in her job, in her infertile body—that physical imprisonment felt like the inevitable next step. But expectations of doom didn't make it easier to swallow when it arrived, nor did it calm the fluttering bird beating against her rib cage.

Avery tried to regain her breath, but with each passing second, it felt as if someone with ill intent approached her. The others eased the ravenous darkness with their presence, though she doubted whatever plagued them cared about witnesses or numbers.

When she returned and explained that the doors and windows wouldn't open, Tessa's eyes widened. "But that's never happened," she protested, dragging Michael downstairs with her. After a few moments, they came back upstairs wide-eyed and sweaty, feigning calm as if no one had heard them pounding on the doors and grunting with their efforts to escape.

Carlos turned to Dolores. "Is it Lolo keeping us in here? Why now after all these years?"

The maid glanced at him and Tessa. "His appearance in this house is not new. I have seen him here since he died. But I need to take steps on his behalf. When your mother spoke of selling the place, I pretended he appeared for the first time." She held up a gnarled finger when Carlos opened his mouth to speak. "Listen to me. Your lolo entrusted me with a task, and now I must pass it on to you. Kuya, come back." She gave Avery a pointed look. "Fools should be seen and not heard."

"A lie? Told by a member of *this* family?" Avery said, refusing to look at Carlos. "How *surprising*." The very idea that the old woman was fine with manipulating two people to move across the world for some weird sense of loyalty to a dead man was no longer shocking, not after learning of Carlos's vasectomy. Avery wished she'd never come. These assholes could strangle in their webs of deception, if they'd just let her go home.

No one bothered joining hands. The spirits were already here; even Avery could feel them. They brushed past, prickling flesh with frigid cold, whispering hateful messages into her ringing ears.

You'll join us soon.

Everyone hates you.

Your life is nothing without Carlos.

Dolores's face and voice changed, and Roberto resumed his story as if he'd never stopped. "I hired a local witch doctor to defeat the mambabarang when I found her." He grimaced. "I must speak frankly of the dead, though it is taboo among us spirits. I needed to be sure that the witch wouldn't escape. So we took her magic and contained it inside a mirror. She was so powerful that I needed three of them: one I had brought, and two taken from her own home. Next, we killed her and burned her body to ashes, which we placed into a metal box the witch doctor ensorcelled to contain her."

"Why did you bring it home?" Carlos asked.

"I was afraid the witch would find some way to reunite body, spirit, and magic." Lolo sighed. "Dolores told me of the day she found the witch's remains in your room and the metal box beneath your bed when you were just a child. You'd tried to hide everything where the maids wouldn't find it, and pushed the spilled ashes between the floorboards. Since then some measure of her spirit has spread through the house like an infestation. Her spirit hides in hidden spaces, like a rat."

Carlos's eyes widened. "Is that why I was always so frightened?"

Lolo nodded. "She whispered poison into your ears, apo, and your young mind believed her. You grew scared of the house, the darkness, even of me."

"Let me guess. *We* have to figure out a way to destroy the mirrors and banish the mambabarang's ghost, six decades after everyone else ignored it." Avery couldn't hide the bite in her voice. She wasn't sure she wanted to. "Why don't we just burn the mirrors then, or hell, the whole house? Carlos's recovery is the priority here, isn't it?"

Lolo's calm demeanor vanished, and anger brought forth Dolores once more. "How dare you even speak about these matters, as if you have a say? You know nothing of our culture. An ignorant person such as yourself can never understand how difficult it was for Kuya. For me."

Avery snorted. "Know what's not difficult? Being honest with people from the beginning and not acting like a damn martyr with some noble secret task."

"Ate Dolores, Avery, please." Carlos pulled at his shaggy hair before turning to face Dolores completely. "I will accept whatever duty you lay at my feet. It's the least I can do for you—you've cared for this family and followed Lolo's wishes for so long."

Avery couldn't believe what she was hearing. For him to agree to something without consulting her, after she'd traveled all this way for him. For a grandfather he never even talked about.

It's not really him anymore, is it? The thought was salt scoured over a fatal wound—it changed nothing, only brought a fresh wave of pain.

"Lolo, what can we do?" Tessa asked.

Lolo smoothed his fingers over his chin as if stroking a beard. "Dolores is terrified the mambabarang will regain power again. With good reason, considering what happened to her parents."

"Dolores's parents?" Tessa frowned. A moment later, she gasped. "She was the daughter of the cursed couple? I had no idea. Poor thing."

Avery thought of Dolores's reaction at seeing the photo of the old witch. What must it have been like to be the young teen, watching helplessly as both of her parents were cursed? The Sisons taking her into their home, their family, must have felt like a life preserver thrown into a frigid, uncaring sea. No wonder Dolores spoke of Carlos's grandparents so lovingly.

It made Avery consider their lolo in a new light: He was not only a man who had abandoned his family in their time of need, but also a man kind enough to raise an orphan as his own. She stared at Dolores, imagining her as a scared young woman, adopted by a man who saved her from her tragic past, who shared the same ability, and understood why the old woman had spent her life near Lolo and defended him so fiercely. To Dolores, Roberto Sison was more than an employer—he was the closest thing she had to a father.

"Why did you bring the remains into your own house?" Michael asked. "That could only attract bad luck."

"To keep watch. And it was my punishment," Lolo said. "For failing Estelle."

Avery bit at the inside of her cheek, imagining the serious man she'd seen in the pictures bringing home the remnants of the witch who'd murdered his daughter. He'd put a shrouded mirror in his own bedroom, knowing every time he saw it, he'd be reminded of his loss. No wonder the house reeked of sadness and negativity.

"You're both ghosts. Force her to leave," Tessa suggested.

"Before I was able to strip her of her magic, the witch had gained control over one more spirit." Lolo's gnarled hands brushed away his tears.

"Estelle," Avery whispered.

Lolo nodded. "She will not let Estelle leave this realm. I have failed my poor daughter three times. I failed to protect her, to save her life, and now I have failed to give her peace." He glanced forlornly at an empty space beside him. "I'm so sorry, mga anak."

If there was a response, Avery didn't hear it, but a small smile touched Lolo's face.

"Estelle says she will be happy here forever, as long as I stay with her." He sighed and shifted his gaze into the master bedroom. "I am not worthy of it, but she grants me forgiveness anyway."

"Can we do something, Lolo?" Tessa asked. Tears trailed down her own cheeks and dripped onto her shorts. "Father here can perform a rite, or something?"

"This house has been blessed so many times, but still the mambabarang will not leave. There was one idea I had—to use my own spirit to break the link between Estelle and the witch, like cutting an umbilical cord, and force the witch to move on." He shrugged. "I cannot risk it. Whether or not I succeed, I can't leave my daughter here alone. I promised never to leave her again."

"So what can we do?" Avery asked. "Judging by what Tessa tells me, Carlos and me being here makes the house's activity worse."

Lolo shook his head and glanced at his grandson. "It's not She Who Creeps Between that is making the house feel this way. Not her acting alone, anyway. The Broken Man is with her and strengthens her with his hate."

Avery caught Carlos staring at her. She broke their gaze immediately, but anger at her own weakness choked her. Her self-control was a tenuous thing, morning dew strung on a spiderweb. Looking at Carlos weakened her position, undermined her fury, made everyone think she still cared for him. Even now, she fought to keep her chin from rising, her gaze from finding his face. This would be the last night she'd see him. Her foolish heart wanted to tattoo the memory of his face onto her cells, braid the sound of his voice into her DNA, sear the smell of him into her amygdala. When she was back home, her body would have a séance of its own, to rekindle these ghosts in memory of the man she'd loved beyond all else.

A gentle hand squeezed hers, the warmth like her childhood blanket, protective and soothing. She clutched Michael's hand and gave him a watery smile.

The master bedroom door, which hung open closest to Avery's right side, slammed closed, almost blowing the candle out. All of them flinched at the sound, their eyes widening. Tessa muttered a short prayer. A crack like a broken eggshell followed. "That sounded fragile." Michael stood up.

"We're in the middle of a séance, Father," Tessa complained, as if she hadn't dragged him downstairs a few minutes ago.

"I'll just be a moment," he said, and carefully pushed the bedroom door open. The priest bent to retrieve something from behind the door.

Tessa's handwoven protective charm, crushed on one side from the impact with the floor.

Lolo straightened up in Dolores's body. "The Broken Man comes."

CHAPTER TWENTY-FIVE

Carlos

Their voices sounded distorted by the time he heard them, as if the words had traveled a long distance, or his ears needed to pop after an altitude change. He lay at the bottom of a deep well, trapped and in darkness.

His wife's voice was like smoke, close enough to sense but offering no warmth. She was angry, but she'd returned to him. He'd let her go, and she'd come back. The confirmation that she still loved him made him almost ready to forgive her for her negligent care during his long recovery.

Carlos blinked his eyes open and searched for Avery. She wasn't in their bedroom, but he found her out in the hallway, sitting on the floor with others. As he watched, she shared a long look with Father Michael and held his hand. Carlos's benevolence evaporated like the last drop of water against the merciless onslaught of a blazing sun. The sight of the priest—the ugly bastard—touching Avery under the romantic cloak of candlelight was too much to bear. Rage filled Carlos until he seethed with it, an intensity that couldn't be tempered even at the sight of Dolores's injured face. Rage that overcame his exhaustion. He slammed the bedroom door shut. His sister's handmade, garage-sale-worthy craft snapped its tenuous frond from the hook and fell to the floor. *Don't take it out on her*. That charm had kept him safe while he regained strength, he was sure of it. But it had also trapped the spirit they called the Broken Man in with him, giving the entity ample time to invade his weakened body.

The door opened and the priest looked in, no doubt to leer at where Avery slept. Michael bent to pick up Tessa's charm, the brittle fronds half-smashed from hitting the ground. As he moved the woven circle from the doorway, something shifted in Carlos, and the hallway no longer seemed so inaccessible.

"The Broken Man comes," Dolores said from the hallway, her voice strangely deep. Strangely familiar.

Carlos surged toward the group. He called his wife's name, singsong and playful, as he moved toward her. There would be a reckoning, a retribution for the slights Avery had imposed on him. But first there was the sweetness of reunion. He breathed on her face, her neck, waiting for her fearful shiver. "Back so soon?" he murmured, triumph mixing with his contempt, his love, a heady bouquet that transported him to memories of drawn-out breaths, gasps, and the slide of flesh on bedsheets.

She didn't move. Her eyes were fixed on the opposite wall, her mouth open in alarm.

"Shoti!" Tessa gasped. "Carlos! Sit up!"

Carlos followed their gaze and saw—

Lolo, somehow returned to his prime, slouching against the wall. The haunted look had left his face, the creases of grief and sacrifice erased, as if they'd never occurred.

No. This man was pampered in a way Lolo never was: clean-shaven instead of Lolo's mustache, an expensive haircut that had grown long, brown eyes that weren't ancient like his grandfather's.

The man sliding to the floor was Carlos himself. Thinner and paler, but there was the scar on his eyebrow from diving into the astroturf during a football scrimmage, the birthmark on the side of his neck that Avery always kissed. It was *his* body drooping weakly to the ground, yet he was somehow outside of it. As untethered as a balloon accidentally set free, as lost as a young boy craving the compass of his mother's love.

He stared across the hall at his own face, disbelieving. *Convince Carlos* had exposed so many mirror tricks and smoke shows. Only here, there was no mirror, no trick of the light. Everyone leaned toward his slumped form, even as he stood right behind them.

Suddenly the night of the accident became clear. His own face, approaching him as he lost consciousness in his wrecked car, and every moment since. The strange sensation of floating above his body in the hospital. He'd thought Avery had been ignoring him, his family neglecting him, but what if he'd never returned to his body after the paramedics had revived him? What if another spirit had seized the opportunity and claimed his flesh at the site of the car crash? Was this what She Who Creeps Between wanted him to see in his grandfather's room—Carlos's own body, lying on the bed?

But that couldn't be true. People had spoken to him, he was certain of it. Surely Avery had responded to him at some point in the past eight weeks… Tessa had looked right *at* him when she slipped into the room the day they'd all visited. And Dolores…Dolores kept telling him to rest…

Carlos gritted his teeth. How strange, that he could feel the tension in his jawbone, the grind of molar on molar, and yet the form lying in the hall didn't clench one muscle. Carlos was a disembodied spirit deprived of his rightful body by some opportunistic parasite.

Grief struck him. How could he be a ghost? He was only forty, for God's sake. There was so much he still wanted to do. The crash hadn't been that bad; he'd been wearing his seat belt. He'd been driving a Benz; surely it was safer than some cheap brand. Carlos gave a wordless scream of shock and rage. The people in the hallway flinched.

"You *can* hear me," he laughed. "You overacting bunch of—"

"They can't hear you," Dolores said, her features strangely blurred. "But they can sense your anger."

"You're talking to me. You've talked to me since I came home."

Dolores nodded. "I tried to get you to move on, to be at peace, even if it meant we would lose you. But instead, you grew angrier."

"Of course I'm angry," Carlos spat. "Who wouldn't be, in my situation?"

"And who put you in this situation but yourself?"

Carlos pointed at the slumped body. "How do I know he didn't cause the crash so he could wear my skin?"

That flaccid corpse over there was *his* body, and Carlos Tam had never been one to share. Whatever spirit had lurked within it could be no match for him. A glass slipper fit only the rightful owner. Carlos ran across the hall and dove into his body, and met resistance. He snarled, and the candle flared high in response to his fury. He would never give up on something he owned. Not without a fight, and this was a matter of life and death.

Carlos prepared to leap into his body once again, determined to claim what was his.

He glanced over at the other faces and stumbled as he recognized the familiar features superimposed over Dolores's. He heard the voice he'd thought—hoped—he'd never hear again.

"Hello, Caloy," his grandfather said, looking right at him.

CHAPTER TWENTY-SIX

Carlos

"Carlos?" Avery said. "There's something wrong with him. We need to call an ambulance." The worry in her voice was a living thing, a fine wine he savored. She loved him still. It gave him the courage to nod at his grandfather, to pretend that the old man hadn't just witnessed Carlos suffering the shock of his life.

"Kamusta-po, Lolo."

Lolo shook his head, his features and Dolores's blurring dizzyingly with the movement, like two reflections in a window. For the first time, Carlos noticed the small, thin girl in pigtails half-hidden behind Dolores's thick body. The old man addressed the others. "If you truly want to help Carlos, forget his body and see this through. My grandson's spirit is here now, standing behind the padre."

Avery scowled. "You think talking to Carlos's ghost is going to save his body? Look at him. He needs an IV, or a defibrillator, or something."

"Wait, what do you mean, Lolo? Carlos is right beside me," Tessa said. "I'm holding his hand."

Carlos's body opened heavy eyelids. "No ambulance. Talking to Carlos's ghost is more important."

Michael blinked. "What do you mean, talking to Carlos's ghost? You *are* Carlos."

"And what do you mean, more important? The damn house will be here tomorrow, you stubborn fool," Tessa protested.

"The house will be here, yes," the impostor in Carlos's body said. "But I may not be."

Carlos crept past—*through*—the bent knees of the priest and his sister. He leaned close to his double's face, trying to see who squatted inside. Was it the Broken Man the little girl had spoken of, with fear in her large brown eyes? Unlike the mismatched features of Dolores and Lolo, the fit between his face and the spirit who hid behind it was flawless.

"Who are you?" he asked, jabbing a finger into the sunken cheek. His finger met a gauzy resistance, like poking ashes found in a silver box.

"You can speak to him now, apo," Lolo said. "The Broken Man is right in front of you."

"I just did," Carlos snapped. "How do I get him out of my body?"

"I wasn't talking to you, Caloy," the senile old man replied, using his childhood nickname. "I was talking to *him*." He pointed a finger at Carlos's body.

"Carlos, this is going to sound strange," the impostor controlling his body said, his eyes focused some distance away from him. "But I've possessed you out of necessity. I am the Carlos Tam you will become, after ten years of suffering and grief."

His family gasped at his admission, staring wide-eyed at the impostor's face as if it would look different to them with this knowledge. All except his grandfather, whose gaze was fixed on Carlos. Carlos, whom nobody else could see.

"I wasn't driving the Mercedes fast enough to hit *Back to the Future* speeds," Carlos sneered. The others in the hallway spoke over his words.

As if they couldn't hear him.

It made Carlos think of something. "Wait, if we're really the same person, he should have the same ability I have. Since the accident, I've been able to speak to spirits. Just like you predicted when I was eighteen. So why can't he hear me?"

Lolo repeated the question so the others could hear, and then he shook his head. "I wasn't talking about seeing the dead when I said you'd end up with my fate, Caloy. I was talking about your selfishness, and how you'd end up hurting the people you most love. And that you'd regret it until the end of your days. You can speak to spirits because you *are* a spirit."

"No, Lolo, you weren't selfish. You were trying to save Estelle. That's why you left, right?" implored Tessa. The need to believe this stripped the maturity from her face, made her look childlike with hope.

Their grandfather shook his head. "Avery was right. After I failed to save my daughter, I should have come back. To be strong for the rest of my family. But I chose revenge. When I returned, the look on my wife's face, my children… I should have been here for them. And when I saw my poor Estelle in the house, a lost little spirit wandering the halls…" Dolores's face contorted with Lolo's grief, and she reached out to embrace the small girl, but her arm passed through the child's spirit. "Nothing I do will ever make up for that regret."

"So the person in this body…" Avery touched the impostor's bruised face with a trembling hand. "You aren't my husband. You haven't been him since the accident. I knew it. I *felt* it." A look of dawning horror widened Avery's eyes. "But Lolo's saying that the real Carlos—his ghost—has been here in this house the whole time?"

This was unbelievable. It must be some prank everyone agreed to play on him. But how could they have found someone who looked exactly like him? He turned to the man with his face. "You're one of the ghosts in the house, I suppose? The Broken Man? Just waiting for a meat suit that fits you?"

Carlos's body didn't respond to his questions, not until Lolo repeated the words to the others. And then his body replied. "I've never been a ghost in this house, Carlos."

His grandfather exchanged a long look with the young girl in pigtails. "You're the one they call the Broken Man, Caloy."

"Bullshit," Carlos muttered, but the whispering woman and the little girl's answers to him clarified into something that felt like truth: He hadn't been possessed by the new spirit—he *was* the new spirit, trapped in a room by his sister's charm. He was the Broken Man, and he would never recover. All this time, Avery hadn't been ignoring him—she'd been caring for his body, which was recovering in Lolo's bedroom, while his own spirit had been trapped by Tessa's charm inside of theirs.

"Tessa, help me sit him up higher." Michael stood up. "His chin is touching his chest. That can't be comfortable."

She shied away. "I don't want to touch him if he's possessed my brother."

"He's saying that he *is* your brother." The priest grunted as he slid Carlos's limp body higher up against the wall by himself.

"Don't touch me, you slimy asshole," Carlos snarled, even as his traitorous body smiled at Michael in gratitude before turning to address the air—to address *him*—again.

"Listen to me, Carlos. I'm not here to take your body forever. I came back for one reason, and one reason only, and since that's done, I'm going to try to help Lolo. You can take your body, your life, back."

"What life? You took the only woman I ever loved away from me." Now things were clicking into place: Avery's absences from their room all day were probably spent in Lolo's room, having intimate conversations with this impostor. Conversations where Avery bestowed the attention that Carlos deserved to this asshole, where they traded jokes and secrets. "That's how she knew about the vasectomy. You fucking told her, even knowing how she'd react."

Dolores's voice repeated his words, tinged with his grandfather's accent.

The candle flame flared higher with his agitation. He wished he could use it to burn the damn house down, and everyone in it. The small flame flared bright enough to make him squint. Careful now, or he'd end up losing time and regaining consciousness hours later.

"Avery would have left you if you'd been honest, Carlos. But it wasn't fair to lie to her."

He knew this. God, how he knew this. It killed little pieces of him every time she asked him to go to an appointment, every time he watched her flinch as she injected herself with some needle. He was trapped by his love for her and his inability to compromise: He couldn't share her affection with a mewling brat, and if he told her that, she'd leave. It was selfish of *her* to hold him hostage like this, to force him to choose between having a child he didn't want or losing his soulmate. And what of the child? He wouldn't wish his childhood on anyone, feeling like he was nobody, nothing, while everyone prioritized their own grief or their stupid dog and never him. Never him.

"This isn't fair to me," he muttered. "You don't get it. Nobody ever did."

Lolo repeated his words to the others, and Tessa groaned with exasperation. "You're so spoiled, Shoti. You always have been. You eat a feast and complain to the beggars about the food. What love did you show anyone, growing up? Where were you when my dog died, or when Mom had nightmares about Auntie Estelle, or when we held Lolo's funeral?"

"I get it," the spirit who invaded Carlos's body said loudly. "More than anyone, I know what you're feeling. All these terrible memories started after you spilled the silver box of ashes, after you started hearing the whispers under your bed, right? Even if I didn't come back, you'd eventually realize how wrong you are, how *loved* you are, but it would have been too late. You've got a long, tough road ahead of you, and you won't come out of it unscathed. But you deserve it. You deserve to suffer, after how you've treated people. And the growth you're going to go through is for the best, believe me."

"So if you want me to suffer, to change, why the fuck did you come back? *How* the fuck did you come back?" Trust his family to turn this moment into an attack session on him. He was the one who'd come home to help, despite how he felt about his grandfather, and he was the one who'd suffered for two months. Hell, he was the one who'd died—

Dolores spoke in her own voice. "A needle that has gone through fabric once will find it easier to re-enter the same hole again."

Carlos's body nodded at the old woman. "That's right. Ghosts return to their past all the time; they don't always stay where they die, but return to homes or objects or people they loved before. Places where they felt safe. When I died, ten years in the future, my life flashed before my eyes. Including the moment of the car crash. And I thought, what if I could re-enter my life at that moment between life and death, enter my body just as they resuscitate it? If I could come back for one pivotal moment, like Manny seeing his own ghost in the doomed elevator, whatever happens to me afterward would be worth it."

"What moment?" Carlos was lost, and angry that he was lost. "Why not appear to me before the crash, or before the bar, or before we got on the plane?"

Lolo repeated the words. The impostor gave a small smile. "There was no entry point then, Carlos. Death is the only way in and out of a body—or a séance with a skilled medium, excuse me, Ate Dolores—and frankly, you weren't worth the effort."

"You're talking in riddles. If I wasn't worth the effort, then why come back at all?" Carlos asked.

His body turned to look at Avery, and his face seemed to glow from within.

"For her."

CHAPTER TWENTY-SEVEN

Avery

If bodies could leave souls behind when they traveled, as Avery's yoga teacher believed, why couldn't souls leave bodies behind when they died? When someone's life flashed before their eyes, were those synaptic signals of remembered experiences reduced to travel signposts for the one who had lived it? Here was when the love of my life got married; there, my favorite child was born; and at that moment, my life slipped away, only for defibrillators to snatch it back within grasp.

Avery remembered how her sister Noelle had gone delirious before she'd passed away. Her mother said she was hallucinating, that her sister thought she was still a child, playing in their old house. Avery had wondered at the time how it could be a hallucination if the events had once been real—what if Noelle's spirit had traveled to a happier place in her life, just like how some people returned to a favorite vacation spot?

Get it together. You're supposed to be the rational one. And yet what about this entire ordeal supported reason? It was a fever dream, a nightmare, where the ghost that had been haunting the house turned out to be her own husband, and the man she'd fallen in love with had turned out to be…also her husband. She wondered what Carlos's ghost—how strange, that she didn't consider the future version of Carlos, the one possessing his body, the ghost—was doing now. Based on Dolores's focus, he was right in front of his own body. Was he trying to get inside it? Pulling the other spirit out?

What would Avery see if she had a fogged glass to peek through? Glowing dandelion fluff pouring out of her husband's body, like the stuffing of a ripped teddy bear?

All of Carlos's small changes, the way her body had reacted to him, somehow her subconscious had known it wasn't her husband, or the one she had known until this point. She was half listening to what he and his grandfather were saying, half removed, as if her very mind rebelled at such improbable events.

And then Carlos's face had turned toward her, and a soft smile touched his lips. "For her."

It was easy to sink into his loving look, to be held in his gaze where time slipped away and only this moment mattered. That's how they'd started their relationship, when the importance of prophecies and discussions of children faded like nightmares in the blinding light of the sun.

"It's not possible," Tessa said, breaking the spell. "If you could do it, why can't everyone?"

"Not everyone has died in their life and been saved," Carlos said. "Not everyone has reason to return."

"I saw you," Avery's voice shook. "Through my fogged sake glass. You were half inside Carlos's body. And then, you disappeared."

"It was harder than I imagined to borrow another body, even if it was once my own. I wasn't able to fully possess it for weeks. And without a soul inside, this body was slow to heal."

"What was the price?" Michael asked. "To come back?" His expression was somber, mouth tight as if he'd already guessed.

"When I died, I found myself in a long hallway. Ahead of me was a bright light that stretched as far as I could see. Behind me, there was my life, flickering like digital photo frames on the walls, like a gallery. The moment I died in that crash…there was somehow room to climb through the scene, to force my way through." Carlos shrugged. "It was an easy choice. Backward or forward. I knew, somehow, that by coming back, I'd given up the rest of my afterlife. Once younger me retakes this body, I'll cease to exist."

"Why sacrifice eternity?" Michael raised his voice, the first time Avery had ever seen him do so. "You could have joined Avery in heaven, God willing."

"I don't need eternity, Father. If I can give Avery happiness in this life, that's close enough to heaven for me." Carlos winked at her, and she found herself smiling through her tears. He'd always been able to find the thread of happiness from any situation, until a few years ago, when he'd stopped looking.

"That night I took your pills," she whispered. "That's how you knew. In your timeline, I'd succeeded."

They stared at each other across the furious whipping of candlelight, choked by the rage of spirits surrounding them, and comfort like her husband's warm arms pressed against her sternum. It was a moment she would always remember, a touch her soul would always feel.

"Losing you to suicide was the biggest mistake of my life, Avery.

The fear that I'd fail you again, and my desperate desire to save you, was what gave me the strength to complete the possession. Even if you leave me, find love with someone new, have a dozen children, it will all be worth it."

She shook her head. This man was the Carlos she'd always hoped her husband would become, a marble statue revealed once the rough stone was chipped away. Sculpted by grief and carved by regret, stripping away his selfishness to the wonder she'd always hoped was beneath. "I don't want anyone else. I want you. This version of you."

Carlos smiled, his eyes glowing with love. "And all I've ever wanted is you. But I never deserved you. Not then, and not now." His face turned somber. "When tonight is over, my darling, now that you know the truth, I'm going to help Lolo and Dolores with the mambabarang. I'll try to sever her hold on Estelle, so she and Lolo can move on. That should nullify the spell she has cast on you. And Dolores can finally retire." He winked at Dolores before he turned to the air in front of him. "Come on, younger Carlos. It's time to take your body back. Let Avery move on to live a happy life. You'll regret it if you don't, I promise you. Hell, I'll haunt you myself."

Avery clamped her lips together to muffle her crying, tried to imprint the sound of his voice and his last words into her brain, an oasis to return to when she needed respite. The impossibility of what Carlos had done for her humbled her. How could she deserve such sacrifice? How could any man compare after this? The sense of wasted time pulled at her. If only she'd known. "Why didn't you tell me any of this sooner?"

He laughed. "My darling, would you have believed a word of it until this moment?" Tears ran down his cheeks, but his expression was peaceful. "I love you, Avery Tam. You are the love of my life, and of my afterlife, however long or short that might be."

CHAPTER TWENTY-EIGHT

Carlos

The look on Avery's face crushed Carlos. It was everything he'd ever wanted, pure love without the stain of resentment. She used to gaze at him that way, before everything turned sour.

Before he'd ruined things. If he'd been honest with her, she would have stayed, or left, and his secret guilt wouldn't have turned into resentment. And yet what was done was done—he didn't have another near-death experience he could use, a reset button on a stacked game. Anger seethed in him, but for the first time it was directed inward as well. Tessa's words hit him hard, even if he'd heard them before. Was he really selfish, and if so, who had made him this way?

If the spirit possessing his body was right, Carlos was doomed. He couldn't become the man Avery wanted, because that man had only come into existence after she'd died, after a decade of suffering. There was no way she'd ever settle for him again, not after fucking Lazarus returned from the dead to possess his body, and yet Carlos couldn't imagine living without her.

I'd have lost her either way. Whether or not his spirit had come back, Avery was beyond his grasp, escaping by death or divorce. The only difference now was that she was alive, and this knowledge would always be a torment to him, a hope for reconciliation that would never die. Like her hope for children, despite his lack of support. The candle near him flared, reaching this way and that for flesh to burn, to make someone suffer as he was suffering.

"I told you she'd hurt you," the whispering woman's voice said from beside him. "All that's left is revenge."

"You don't understand love," Carlos said to her. "I would do anything for Avery." For the first time, he saw She Who Creeps Between, a slice of her face and disheveled hair peering at them through a crack in the wall, like a caged animal. Hers was the face in the attic photograph, the face he'd seen once with Tessa, but wild-haired, and wilder-eyed. He saw things clearly now, perhaps for the first time: It was the mambabarang's ghost that had whispered to him each night beneath his childhood bed or from the closet, twisting his thoughts so he feared his grandfather, making young Carlos feel so unloved.

"Anything except what she most wanted." The voice tittered, and then hardened. "You're like your grandfather. Self-righteous and cruel. Ruining the lives of young women for your own selfish purposes."

The whispered conversations Carlos had heard all his life melded with the pieces of information he'd heard tonight. "You're one to talk. You're the one who cast a spell on my aunt, aren't you?"

"The child gave me her own hair, instead of her mother's." He imagined her shrugging. "I didn't ask her to sacrifice her life."

"People who sacrifice do so voluntarily," Dolores said. For the first time, he realized the old woman and his grandfather could hear She Who Creeps Between as well. What must it have been like for them, to hear the witch taunting them for decades? "They don't need to be asked. It's the ultimate act of love."

"Like you, giving up your whole life to serve this family?" The whispering woman asked Dolores.

Dolores lifted her chin. "Kuya took me in when your mother killed my parents. He and Ate took care of me. Understood me, accepted me even though my ability to see spirits would scare any other family. For them, and for my parents, I devoted my life to make sure you would never hurt anyone else again."

"I'm ready, Lolo," Carlos's body spoke up. Avery had moved beside him and clutched at his limp hand with both of hers. She wept. His wife wept for the him-that-was-not-him.

His grandfather smiled at Carlos's body, and it wasn't the twisted, cruel smile of Carlos's childhood memories, but a benevolent one Carlos vaguely remembered, full of love and gratitude. "Thank you, Apo. Your Auntie Estelle and I, we both thank you."

"Carlos, you can take your body over. I'm already half out. Tell me what to do, Lolo." That explained why his body was sliding down the wall, perhaps. The sense of double vision worsened as the spirit possessing his body slid out, revealing a face identical to Carlos's.

Lolo stroked a nonexistent mustache, a gesture Carlos remembered from his childhood. "Find the witch's spirit and surround her, like a ring of salt surrounds her ashes. Break the connection between her and her magic, between her and Estelle, and force her down the hallway you turned away from. Toward the bright door. Do you think you can find it again?"

Carlos's body nodded. "I think so. It's like popping through the same hole; it gets wider each time." He turned to Avery and squeezed her hand, and somehow Carlos felt her skin against his own. He was slowly taking over his own flesh again, donning it like a familiar suit, heavy and slightly uncomfortable.

"I love you, Carlos," Avery said, and it sounded like a wedding vow.

"I love you, Shoti," Tessa repeated, tears running down her cheeks.

"Wait," Carlos said, waiting for Lolo to repeat his command for living ears. He considered his future without Avery, miserable and resentful. Thought about his insatiable hunger for love, a void that could never be filled. Somehow, this future self was the better version of him: He'd won over an angry wife and a protective sister, the ghosts of his judgmental grandfather and tortured aunt. The only person Carlos had in his corner was the witch who'd murdered a child, and his ever-present rage.

If there was one thing he could do to help ease the pain he'd caused Avery, to make up for his life of selfishness, wasn't it this? To replace the flawed version of him with the one who had already suffered, and come through the gauntlet transformed? He didn't want the life he'd built for himself, the life he'd ruined by himself, at least not without Avery. And he could never be this version she wanted, not while he could hope for her return. His rage was an ardent lover that would never let him go.

"I'll go. You stay. In my body. In this life. Just...make her happy. Or let her go." Either way, it wouldn't be him suffering. It would be this altruistic version of him, who probably liked being selfless and feeling like shit. Strangely, in this moment of sacrifice, Carlos realized it was simultaneously the ultimate act of selfishness as well: He was escaping the repercussions of his actions, a broken heart, a potential heaven or hell. Just a bad roll of character traits, he was hitting game over without having to suffer.

Carlos turned to his grandfather. "Could you...could you tell Avery that even though I messed this up, I really do love her and want her to be happy?" As long as he didn't have to see her happy without him.

Lolo conveyed the message, and Avery wiped at her eyes. "I loved you so much, Carlos. Enough that I considered giving up everything I ever wanted." Her voice steadied. "I loved you so much, I didn't even care that I deserved better."

He brushed his lips past her hair and tried to hold on to her scent, even as his heart broke at her use of past tense. "Well, now you won't have to decide."

Lolo murmured Carlos's goodbye to a weeping Tessa, and then it was time.

Carlos moved through the house, searching for She Who Creeps Between, who had sunk through the floor and gone silent. The crawling he'd been restricted to disappeared once he realized he didn't have a body, wasn't beholden to gravity or emaciated muscle. He started from the first floor, following her taunting whispers. He passed over crevices he used to jump over as a child, afraid long, thin fingers would reach from beneath the floor to grab his legs. There were spirits here, translucent things that ignored him or turned to stare. He checked the faces of each one, looking for a woman who stared through bedraggled hair with her hateful eyes.

"She Who Creeps Between," he asked each one. "Where is she?"

But they didn't know, or they didn't hear him, or they didn't dare answer. He checked beneath the shrouded mirror in the hallway, looking for her reflection, before he slipped into the cracks in the wall, not stopping to worry about how he was able to fit in such a tiny space. The space in between was musty and, like the rest of the floor, completely dark. He was glad for it: The spirits glowed, making them easily visible, and this way he couldn't see the insects crawling around him. Her hissing voice called to him, always just out of sight beyond the next corner or in the next room.

"I almost convinced your lovely wife to join us here," she said. "You could be together for eternity."

"She deserves better than this," Carlos grunted, unsure if the witch could even hear him.

He ascended to the second floor, passing wooden beams and dust-coated wires. The distant star, ever-present in his peripheral vision, flashed threateningly, a sign he was tiring. He had to catch her before he lost consciousness, or he'd be at her mercy without Tessa's charms to save him.

Carlos passed through the master bedroom, where his parents once slept. As a child, he'd run here to sleep when the nocturnal fears overcame him. It was a place of childhood comfort and love; no wonder his spirit had gravitated to this room once he and his broken body were discharged from the hospital.

The bathroom was empty, and he passed over his family members, still sitting in the hallway. Spirits crowded around them, attracted by the candlelight, shouting to be heard. The priest bent his head, leading Carlos's family in prayer. Tessa was weeping, but the Pinay—Auntie Estelle—waved at him, faith in him brightening her eyes.

Lolo's room was as forbidding as he remembered, and he gave Lolo's rocking chair a wary glance as he checked the shrouded mirror, the narrow closets, and beneath the bed. He didn't find the witch's ghost, but a memory found him: feeling safe and warm in Lolo's arms as the old man hummed and rocked him to sleep.

Tessa's room was impenetrable, devoid of ghosts and crammed with Bagua mirrors, rosaries, and lucky red knots. Only Carlos's childhood room remained, where he'd learned the meaning of terror. He gave a cursory glance around the small space, but he knew she wasn't down here. She'd led him throughout the house, tiring him, before retiring to her place of power, a place so filled with malevolence that it seeped through the attic hatch and reached into his nightmares even now.

The square entrance to the attic stared down at Carlos like a baleful eye. He'd spent so many nights watching to make sure the hatch didn't shift, that nothing would emerge from the attic to crawl from the ceiling, and now it was him who had to enter her domain.

He slipped into the space between the walls, pulling his weightless body up wooden slats before emerging into the coffin-like air of the attic. There was no sign of her: no telltale glow, no mocking insults. The space was filled with buzzing and clicking, with the rustle of dry carapaces rubbing against one another.

Carlos passed over a trail of animal remains before touching down on the open book bag like a bloodhound catching a scent. There remained only one place the witch could hide, assuming she hadn't fled to another floor as soon as he'd reached this one.

The last covered mirror in the house beckoned him with a rustle of cloth. He concentrated; weeks of effort to "recover" barely allowed him the strength to raise the shroud. She Who Creeps Between was there, hiding beneath a layer of insects that swarmed over the smudged glass. She smiled at him with long, narrow teeth and slipped out of his reach, tattered gray dress brushing the floor as she floated.

Carlos reached for her. She evaded him. Again and again, darting around like a small fly. Faster than he thought possible. Why wasn't she getting tired like he was? He slowed, the bright light overtaking his vision. He was losing consciousness again.

She Who Creeps Between had wanted Tessa's charm removed ever since Avery had hung it up. She'd fed off him for weeks to increase her power, but stealing his energy wasn't enough; the witch could—and would—hurt him if given the chance. He descended to the floor, trying to gather his strength, fighting to stay alert.

Nails stabbed into his back like burrowing maggots. Incorporeal as he was, Carlos didn't expect the pain to feel so…visceral. He screamed as the mambabarang's fingers dug into him. He turned and grabbed ahold of her stick-thin arms. She fought him viciously, and he was already so tired.

She flung him away from her. Carlos slid along the ground, animals stuffed with insects passing through his body undisturbed. As his momentum slowed, he grit his teeth against the pain of the witch's nails gouged deep into his flesh. And then agony scorched through his body, searing nerves and tearing shrieks from his throat.

He scrambled away from what felt like fire as the mambabarang cackled. She'd thrown him into the salt circle, scattering the tiny crystals and leaving the metal box unprotected. He remembered this box from his youth, but only now did he understand what it truly contained.

Carlos stood up unsteadily, fear cramping his guts and sweat pouring over his skin. There was nothing to keep She Who Creeps Between from reclaiming her ashes. Lolo was no longer alive to stop her, and once her magic reunited with her remains, she would be unstoppable.

Insects flew between them, buzzing bullets flying through his face, blinding and distracting him. She was stronger, faster, and more vicious than him. He would never beat her in a fight. The bright light grew larger, encompassing his vision. He thought of what his future self had said about his death, how he'd seen a bright light and run from it. Hadn't Carlos been doing the same? Maybe the light wasn't his brain injury, but a path beyond the mortal veil.

There was no more time.

It was a Hail Mary, but there was nothing else he could do. He had no more strength, and no more chances. Carlos leapt toward the witch and clutched her as though he was a small child hugging his mother, only this time he wouldn't let go when she pushed him away. Love for his family, and rage at his circumstances filled him. He used these twin founts of strength to surround the mambabarang's ghost and pull her with him as the bright light blinded him to everything but her.

He might have been shoving against a giant oak tree. She was anchored too tightly to the house. Oh God, what if he sacrificed his afterlife and still failed? Lolo and Auntie Estelle would remain trapped. And Avery would know he didn't fulfill his last promise. She'd think ill of him for the rest of her life.

No. Carlos Tam always got what he wanted.

"You wanted an end to this," he gasped at the mambabarang, his body wracked with pain and his energy gone. He could never overpower her, but perhaps he could reason with her. "Two wounded birds in the forest, remember? I'll help you find rest. I promise my grandfather won't touch you."

Her long, brown teeth were clenched, breath reeking of musty mildew and rotting earth. She blinked tears from her dark eyes, cloudy with dust. "I've been furious for so long. I can't just stop. I don't know how."

Rage was something he knew, as intimate as any lover. "You just have to let go. It's just me and you here. There's no more need for anger, or fighting. Just...unclench your fists."

She whimpered. "It hurts."

It did. Carlos's own fury throbbed like a phantom limb that he turned his back on. Slowly, the bonds holding the mambabarang to Salcedo Drive shriveled and fell away, like snipping the stem of a young mango sapling. He moved with her deeper into the brilliant light, and she didn't resist.

"Let's go," he found himself saying to She Who Creeps Between. To himself. "It's time to move on."

The mambabarang, the first person who'd spoken to him since he'd returned to his childhood home, whispered her thanks before they left the realm. At least, he thought she did. Carlos kept Avery's face firmly in his mind as the light transformed into a massive doorway. As peace surrounded them.

And then he knew no more.

EPILOGUE

Carlos

Eighteen months later

"Carlos, did you hear that?" Avery asked.

Carlos snorted. "Was it your voice, asking me a question?"

She nudged him. "Listen."

He yawned. "I do hear it. And it's the most beautiful sound I've ever heard."

"It's your turn to get up." She lay back down on her pillow. "And you better hurry, or Iris is going to beat you there."

Carlos skimmed his lips over Avery's soft shoulder. "For someone who swore she didn't care about children, she sure loves ours."

"I could say the same about you," Avery said.

"I don't know what you're talking about. You're probably remembering an ex-boyfriend or something." He slid his feet into his slippers and went into what was once his grandparents' bedroom. The light here was always gentle dusk, perfect for sleeping babies.

Iris, who moved fast despite her advanced age, already cradled one infant in each arm. She flashed her gap-toothed grin at him. "They're happy with me; why don't you get the bottles?"

He breathed deep, as if the sweet, warm baby smell was fuel to his tired body, and nodded. "Right away, Boss."

The main floor was still dark at this hour, but the shadows rested like dozing pets, harmless and lazy. Salcedo Drive's wood floors absorbed the sound of his footsteps, extending the peaceful silence of the early morning. Out of habit, Carlos looked for the shrouded mirror in the hallway, and smiled at the new family photographs they'd hung there instead. If buildings imprinted memories within their wood walls, enough joy seemed to act as wallpaper, and the house no longer loomed menacingly but hovered like a watchful grandparent.

The roosters were crowing by the time he came back upstairs, holding two warm bottles of milk. He took his daughter and sat in one of the rocking chairs to feed her, while the maid took his son. The Manila sunrise was spectacular but couldn't hold a candle to the love in his babies' eyes.

He whispered a silent prayer of thanks to whoever might be listening—God, Lolo, and most recently, Dolores. These memories would be on his gallery wall as he left this life, he was sure. And no matter what might happen after, for Carlos at this moment, Manila was heaven on earth.

Avery joined him a few minutes later, taking their son from Iris with a smile. "I couldn't stay away." They sat on matching rocking chairs, holding their children and watching the sun peek over metal roofs and slanted palm trees. Her quiet joy was a balm to his heart, however hard-won it was.

After the night of the séance, Avery had grieved the loss of her husband for months. She struggled to understand his final sacrifice but was grateful to the man all the same. Carlos had held her most mornings while she wept.

"I just wish I knew why he did it," she'd said for weeks.

"Whether he was choosing my happiness over his, or because he knew I'd never stay with him after he lied about the vasectomy."

"Does it matter, if the end result is the same?" Carlos had asked her once.

She pushed away from him and sat upright, her expression incredulous. "Of course it matters. One is an act of love, and the other is an act of selfishness. The answer determines how much guilt I take on."

"But both reasons still revolved around you," he told her gently.

That brought an onslaught of new tears, and she pressed her face against his shoulder once more. "How can I deserve this kind of love? I'm not worthy of it. Of you."

Carlos had embraced her tightly, tears coming to his own eyes at the thought of this woman not knowing how wonderful she was, and promised himself he would spend the rest of their lives showing her.

He looked at his wife now, holding one of their children, the picture of contentment, and felt overcome with gratitude.

"The crew's coming by for lunch with some new script ideas," Carlos said. "Places to take the new season."

She arched one of her eyebrows. "What does Carlos want, now that he's been thoroughly convinced?"

He chuckled. "What any man wants. To be convinced again."

They smiled at each other across the room, over the slurping grunts of their babies.

"I had a dream about him last night," Avery said, and there was no need to specify who she was referring to. "I was watching an old episode of your show, and the TV filled with blinding white light, except for him. He turned to me then, as if he could see me through the screen, and said he was happy for us. He said he was at peace."

Carlos nodded. “I had the same dream. Except he told me I was much more handsome than him.”

Avery’s mouth twisted as she tried to suppress a smile before she turned serious once more. “Thank you for being here with me,” she whispered. “In Manila, and…in this life.”

He gave her a wink. “’Til death. And beyond.”

ACKNOWLEDGMENTS

I would need to fill another book to adequately thank all the people who have helped me with this one. I'm so grateful to my agent, Samantha Fabien, for her knowledge, support, and unwavering enthusiasm, and to my editor, Rachel Gilmer, who worked tirelessly on *She Waits Where Shadows Gather*. Rachel not only advocated for the book and patiently answered all my questions but also refined my novel into a version I truly love.

I'm grateful to Ruwan Tilakaratna for helping me fact-check my medical knowledge and making fun of me when I was wrong. Any errors that remain in this book are mine and mine alone.

I've been blessed with the kindest, most supportive writing friends on earth, and I'm so grateful you're all in my life. To the Query Wenches: Erin Rand, G.W. Prouse, L.J. Thomas, Olivia Woods, Tami Olsen, Johanna Randle, Lily Mehallick, Hester Steel, Erin Leo, Carlin Thomas, Cate Pearce, Ruby Martinez—thank you for your eyes, advice, jokes, and pet/baby pictures. I'm in awe of the talent and gorgeous stories I've seen from you, and I hope to continue learning from you for many more years to come. I'd also like to thank Dr. Jolie Toomajan, Timaeus Bloom, Chelsea Pumpkins, and Elton Skelter for allowing me to ramble, hyperfixate, and make terrible jokes without judging me (too much).

I also want to thank my beta readers and critique partners: D.S. Ritter, D.O. Moore, C. Thomas Lafollette, C.D. Tavenor, Christopher O'Halloran, Brett Mitchell Kent, Jim Doran, M.V. Viltch, Jessica Peter, and T.J. Price. I'm sure I would have given up on this story without your valuable feedback and encouragement.

I would never have started writing without the support and tutelage of Jenna Kalinsky, who eased me into the literary world like a patient midwife, and after that I would never have continued writing without my husband, William, and our children, Jacob and Grace, who always gave me quiet time to work.

Thank you to my mom, Arsenia ("Zen"), who read every line of my book to make sure the language and descriptions were accurate, even though she's incredibly busy and hates the horror genre. I'm grateful to both her and my dad, George, who left behind their dreams in Manila so we could pursue ours here. I can never think of your sacrifices and early hardships without a deep sense of gratitude for your courage and resilience. To my sisters, Liz and Aimee, thank you for allowing me to reach this point in my life by not murdering me in childhood.

This book is in loving memory of both of my Amas: Rosa Jao, whose early house was the inspiration for the one in this book (I know our memories diverge here, Aimee), and Eugenia Lingad Tan, who we recently lost but will always remember.

Finally, I am most grateful to God for helping a life's dream come true.

ABOUT THE AUTHOR

Michelle Tang writes speculative fiction from Canada, where she immigrated as a child. Her short stories have been published by Cemetery Gates, Escape Pod, and Flame Tree Publishing, among others, and her debut novella, *DuMort*, was released in 2025 by Ghost Orchid Press. When Michelle isn't writing, you can find her playing video games, napping, or lurking on social media.

Website: MichelleTangWrites.ca
Instagram: @MichelleTangWrites
Bluesky: @michelletang.bsky.social